"If you expect me to call you Sergeant Cooper,"

Liza said, "you're going to be disappointed."

"I've had plenty of experience being disappointed by you." Riley saw her stiffen, saw her eyes cloud over, and felt a moment of guilt. Was this why he'd wanted to see her—to accuse her? To insult her? To hurt her if he could? "I want to talk about your son, Liza. He seems to have a real problem working for me."

"Interesting. *He* says you pick on him."

She said it calmly, coolly, and it annoyed the hell out of him. "Just forget it. I'll talk to the major who's in charge and tell him to assign T.J. to someone else." He swung around to leave, but abruptly stopped when he felt her hand, small and warm, on his shoulder. For a moment he couldn't think, couldn't move. All he could do was remember the thousands of other times when she had touched him.

She looked so sweet, so sweet and innocent—when he knew damned well that she was neither.

Dear Reader,

The New Year is starting off splendidly here at Silhouette Intimate Moments. Take our American Hero, for instance. Riley Cooper, in Marilyn Pappano's *No Retreat,* is a soldier with a soft side. When his first love walks back into his life, troublemaking son in tow, it's surrender time for this tough guy.

Laurey Bright, long a favorite with readers of the Silhouette Special Edition line, makes her first Intimate Moments novel a winner. In *Summers Past* you'll find passion, betrayal and one all-important question: Who *is* little Carley's father? Allyson Ryan's *Secrets of Magnolia House* takes a few spooky detours along the road to romance; I think you'll enjoy the ride. *Two for the Road* is the first of Mary Anne Wilson's new "Sister, Sister" duo; look for *Two Against the World,* coming soon. Joanna Marks lights up the night with *Heat of the Moment,* and Justine Davis checks in with *Race Against Time,* a tale full of secrets, crackerjack suspense and irresistible desire. In short—I don't think you'll want to miss a single one of this month's books.

As the year goes on, look for books by more of your favorite authors. Kathleen Eagle, Doreen Roberts, Paula Detmer Riggs and Marilyn Pappano are only a few of the great writers who'll be coming your way in Silhouette Intimate Moments. And then there's our Tenth Anniversary celebration in May! Be sure to join us for all the fun.

Leslie Wainger
Senior Editor and Editorial Coordinator

AMERICAN HERO

NO RETREAT

Marilyn Pappano

Silhouette®

INTIMATE MOMENTS®

Published by Silhouette Books New York

America's Publisher of Contemporary Romance

SILHOUETTE BOOKS
300 East 42nd St., New York, N.Y. 10017

NO RETREAT

Copyright © 1993 by Marilyn Pappano

All rights reserved. Except for use in any review,
the reproduction or utilization of this work in
whole or in part in any form by any electronic,
mechanical or other means, now known or
hereafter invented, including xerography,
photocopying and recording, or in any information
storage or retrieval system, is forbidden without
the permission of the publisher, Silhouette Books,
300 E. 42nd St., New York, N.Y. 10017

ISBN: 0-373-07469-7

First Silhouette Books printing January 1993

Books by Marilyn Pappano

Silhouette Intimate Moments

Within Reach #182
The Lights of Home #214
Guilt by Association #233
Cody Daniels' Return #258
Room at the Inn #268
Something of Heaven #294
Somebody's Baby #310
Not Without Honor #338
Safe Haven #363
A Dangerous Man #381
Probable Cause #405
Operation Homefront #424
Somebody's Lady #437
No Retreat #469

Silhouette Books

Silhouette Christmas Stories 1989
"The Greatest Gift"
Silhouette Summer Sizzlers 1991
"Loving Abby"

MARILYN PAPPANO

has been writing for as long as she can remember, just for the fun of it, but a few years ago she decided to take her lifelong hobby seriously. She was encouraging a friend to write a romance novel and ended up writing one herself. It was accepted, and she plans to continue as an author for a long time. When she's not involved in writing, she enjoys camping, quilting, sewing and, most of all, reading. Not surprisingly, her favorite books are romance novels.

Her husband is in the Navy, and in the course of her marriage, she has lived all over the U.S. Currently, she lives in North Carolina with her husband and son.

To the Military Police Company,
551st Signal Battalion,
U.S. Army Signal Center
and Fort Gordon, Georgia.
With respect for the difficult
job you do—and do so well.

Thanks to
Sgt. Jean McCracken
Sgt. Andy Lyons
and
SFC Donald Danner

And a special thanks
to Sgt. Mac McCracken
and K-9 Duc
for showing how it's done.

Chapter 1

Staff Sergeant Riley Cooper stood motionless in the open doorway. Behind him the flashing blue lights of a military police car lit the dark night, and the radio transmissions and voices of his fellow MPs chased away the quiet. They were questioning the two boys he'd caught a few minutes ago coming out of this office building, arms loaded with equipment. They were asking the same questions he'd asked. *What are your names? What are you doing here? Are you alone? Is anyone else in the building?*

Frightened at being confronted by police officers and intimidated by their authority, the boys had been cooperative. They had given their names, had admitted to breaking into the building and insisted they were alone. There was no one still inside.

It was Riley's job to find out if they were telling the truth.

He smiled a thin, mirthless smile. It was *his* job to go inside this big, dark building. To search the rooms. To hope— maybe to pray—that no one was there; at least, no one who was armed. No one who was intent on doing him harm.

It had been more than ten years since he'd walked into a similar building on a similar night at a similar Army post...and been carried out on a stretcher. That night the burglars hadn't been ten- or twelve-year-old boys, but grown men who had wanted desperately to avoid arrest. Men who hadn't cared what price he paid for their escape. Men who hadn't cared if they'd killed him.

Ten years. That was a long time, but even now his heart was beating a little faster. His palms were sweaty, his throat dry.

Beside him his partner shifted restlessly. He was anxious to go in and do the job, but he wouldn't move until Riley gave the command, and Riley wasn't quite ready for that. In another moment...after one more deep breath...

Pulling the two-way radio from his gun belt, he keyed the microphone. "MP Control, this is Gordon seven-zero."

"Gordon seven-zero, MP Control. Go ahead" came the response from the radio operator.

"I'm going in with K-9 Jasper to clear the building."

The dispatcher's response barely registered as Riley returned the radio to his belt, then turned on his flashlight. Following regulations, just inside the door he paused and loudly announced, "Military police. I'm putting a working dog in the building."

His voice echoed down the long hall, then faded. Except for Jasper's excited panting, there was no other sound. "Let's go, boy," he said, removing the leash from the dog's collar. "Where is he, Jasper? Go find him. Find him, boy."

The big German shepherd didn't hesitate, but started down the hall, pausing in this door, entering that room, trotting back out. Riley followed behind, offering a steady flow of encouragement. His flashlight was in his left hand, and in his right, clasped close to his thigh, was his pistol. In all likelihood the boys had told the truth and there was no one here. But just in case...

They were somewhere in the middle of the building when Jasper found the scent he was searching for. He turned into the nearest office and began barking excitedly, a low, threatening rumble of sound. His fingers tightening around the grips of the 9 mm pistol, Riley entered the room, spoke to Jasper to calm him, then crouched beside him, a safe distance from the battered gray desk near the wall.

The first thing his flashlight beam touched underneath the desk was a pair of expensive high-top basketball shoes. He moved it up slowly, over fashionably faded and baggy jeans and a wildly colored T-shirt, and finally reached a thin, pale face dominated by big dark eyes.

Another kid, he thought, his relief bringing with it a sudden easing of the tightness in his chest and a brief tremor to his hands, causing the flashlight beam to dance crazily. Like the others, the boy couldn't be more than twelve, and he was obviously scared half to death. It wouldn't be a big surprise if he was armed—kids his age and younger were arrested every day with weapons—but Riley's instincts said not this one, and he trusted his instincts.

"Come out from under the desk and lie facedown on the floor," he ordered.

The boy hesitated when Jasper barked; then he scooted out and rolled onto his stomach.

"Spread your arms away from your sides." Getting to his feet, he holstered his pistol, then commanded, "Watch him, Jasper. Watch him, boy."

The dog immediately sat down a few feet away, his attention never wavering from the boy. He wouldn't go any closer unless Riley gave him the command, or unless this skinny little kid tried something stupid, like escape. And he was shaking too badly, Riley noticed when he searched him, to get very far.

"What's your name?"

"T-T-Thomas James D-Davis."

"How many of your friends came in here with you?"

"T-two. Mike and—and Bryan."

Riley finished and straightened. As he did, the boy started to roll over. With a low growl Jasper got to his feet. "Don't move," Riley said sharply. "If you do, that dog will bite you. I'll tell you when you can get up."

"Am I under arrest?" the boy asked, his stammer under control but his voice still trembling, still threatening to break.

"You're in custody." It was a minor distinction—especially to the kid, he thought, who sounded as if he was going to burst into tears any moment now—but technically they didn't arrest children. They took them into custody and turned them over to their parents. If the kids were military dependents, their cases would be referred to the post sergeant major, who generally gave sentences of community service, along with restitution for any damages.

"My mom will kill me," the boy whispered despairingly.

Riley put Jasper back on the leash, then ordered Thomas to his feet. There was something familiar about the kid—maybe those big eyes. He was sure he'd seen the boy before. Hell, he had probably arrested him before, he thought cynically, in which case Thomas's mother would likely kill him, especially if they lived in Army housing. An incorrigible kid could get a family thrown out of quarters, and housing on the civilian market in town was sometimes more than an Army salary could cover.

He escorted the boy outside, turned him over to one of the waiting MPs and returned with Jasper to finish clearing the building. The rest of the rooms were empty and quiet. They made one last circuit to make sure the windows and doors were locked, then returned to the small stoop outside the back door.

"The center guards are on their way over," the patrol supervisor told him. "Wait here until they arrive, then come on over to the station and fill out your reports."

Riley nodded and watched him drive away, then brushed broken glass from the top step and, with more relief than he cared to show, sank down. The kids had gained entry into the building through this door, breaking out the window and reaching in to open the lock. They would have had a pretty good haul, too, if he hadn't decided to park in the lot out front and update his patrol work sheet. In the time it had taken him to call in, get Jasper out of the truck and bring him around back, they had already gathered several calculators, an electronic typewriter, a VCR, an expensive radio and tape deck and—their prize—a laptop computer.

The dog rubbed against him, and he reached over to scratch between Jasper's ears the way the dog liked, while lavishly praising the dog's performance. At his last post he had worked with a quiet dog who had needed no more than a pat on the head and the words "Good job" to feel satisfied. The first time he'd tried that with Jasper, the shepherd had looked at him as if his feelings were hurt—which they probably had been. Like most people, Jasper wanted lots of encouragement and lots of praise when he worked.

As he sat there with the dog, the last of his fear subsided. His heart was beating normally again, his palms were dry and that sick feeling deep inside was gone. After ten years he could remember every thought, every feeling, every sound and even the smells, right up to the moment he'd been shot...and after ten years he still couldn't recall entire days afterward. They had slipped from his mind.

He wasn't ashamed to admit that sometimes he was afraid. The fear gave him an edge. It made him more careful. Everything he did, every action he took—especially on the job—was stacked in his favor. No one was going to hurt him again.

No one.

Sighing softly, he tilted his head back and let his thoughts wander. They didn't go far—just a few miles beyond the confines of the post where he'd been stationed the past four months to the city of Augusta, where he'd spent his first twenty-two years. Where he had grown up and, he sometimes thought, grown old. Where he had learned more about life than he'd ever wanted to know.

Where someone else had hurt him.

He hadn't been eager to accept his orders to Fort Gordon, and he had done so with the intention of immediately putting in for a swap, a trade with some other MP who liked Georgia, someone who didn't have bad memories of this place. But it had been kind of nice to be home again, to see his parents and his brothers and sisters whenever he wanted.

And the memories . . . He had simply ignored them. He'd become an expert at that in his first years away—at pretending that nothing was wrong, that he'd never been in love, never been betrayed. He had avoided the familiar old places—the sandy beach at Clarks Hill Lake, the quiet country road out near Wrens, the ramshackle hamburger joint on the road to Edgefield, the shady private corner on the campus of Augusta College. He had refused to remember those last few months of his life in Augusta.

He had refused to remember *her.*

Just as he refused to think about her now. Old loves, old dreams and old disappointments were best kept where they belonged. In the past.

The center guards arrived, relieving him of duty. Trainees at one of Fort Gordon's schools, they would act as roving patrols until morning, when the building could be properly secured. As much as he disliked big, dark buildings, he would trade places with them, Riley thought as he returned to the Jeep Cherokee around front, if it meant avoiding the pile of paperwork he now had to take care of. If getting shot was his least favorite part of the job, the paperwork was second.

It was a short drive to the MP station, a few miles down the Avenue of the States, then Rice Road. He knew the MPs transporting the kids had already arrived, and the duty investigator for Military Police Investigations, the Army counterpart of a police department's detective division, had also been notified. While MPI interviewed each of the boys, Riley would fill out his military police report and investigator's statement. By the time he finished the forms and got back out on patrol, it would be two in the morning. His shift would be nearly half over.

The station was a small, plain white building, probably as old as Fort Gordon itself. There were half a dozen parking spaces in front for patrol vehicles, along with another half dozen along the side for visitors. Riley backed the Cherokee into one of the front spaces, shut off the engine, then looked back at Jasper. "Don't make a racket while I'm inside," he warned.

The dog's one objectionable trait was a dislike of being left alone for any length of time in the Jeep. He expressed his dissatisfaction first in low, resounding barks that eventually gave way to mournful, pitiful whines. At the moment, though, he looked back at his handler with innocence, as if he couldn't possibly be guilty of such behavior.

Inside the station, two of the three boys waited in the small lobby. One sat beside his father, a sleepy-looking man whose appearance marked him as a soldier. The other, Thomas Davis, sat alone at the end of the row of seats. Riley knew he would find the third one, along with his parents, being interviewed in the squad room. The MPI investigator on duty tonight was good with juveniles, maybe because they found a woman easier to face. But if these kids thought she could be any easier on them because of that, they were wrong. Like the other women assigned to the MP Company, including the desk sergeant who greeted him as he passed the counter where she sat, the investigator was tough.

Riley entered the small room that opened off the lobby. The boy, his father and the investigator were seated at the first of two tables. He got the forms he needed from the cabinet, then took a seat at the back table and began working. He tuned out the sound of their voices—the investigator's calm and even, the boy's tearful, his father's angry— and concentrated instead on writing up an account of the incident.

By the time he was done, MPI had finished with the first boy, dismissed him and called the second one in. Riley laid the statement aside and started on the first of three 3975s, one report for each of the subjects. He filled in the same information on each form—the type and location of the offense, the list of MPs who had backed him on the call and a detailed list of the recovered property. The center section of each form—identifying information on the subjects—was left blank. When the MPI investigator had finished with her interviews, Riley would copy that information from her report.

The second interview was still going on when Riley finished. Since he had to hang around a while, he decided he might as well get something to drink. There was hot coffee in the next room, rich and fragrant—the desk sergeant and the radio operators took pride in brewing the best—but tonight he would take his caffeine in a cold soda instead.

After leaving the room through the rear door, he took a circuitous route past the desk sergeant and the radio operator into the back hall, then around to the soda machine in the central hallway. There he pulled some change from his pocket and dropped it into the machine, then made his selection. As the can fell to the shelf below, the front door opened, and for a moment he could hear distant but clear whining from the parking lot. Jasper, he thought, chagrined. No amount of work, training, ordering or pleading could break the dog of that one bad habit.

The MP who had come through the door was grinning when he passed him. "Hey, Sergeant Cooper, your dog's outside crying," he teased.

Riley scowled at him. Insulting a handler's dog was tantamount to putting down a mother's child. Even if the dog was ugly, even if he had funny ears, even if—like Jasper—he did whine pathetically, the last thing a handler wanted was for someone else to point out those flaws.

But the retort he was about to offer died unspoken, and his scowl slowly faded. Standing there in the lobby, looking down at Thomas Davis, was the remaining parent. Her hair, long and brown and carelessly combed, fell forward to hide her face, but it was clear from the low, heated tones of her voice and the taunt, angry lines of her body that she was upset.

When the boy burst into tears his mother stopped speaking. She looked up, sighed heavily, then brushed her hair back from her face.

Once more Riley felt sick deep inside. He forced himself to look away and tried to convince himself that it was just a mistake—it was late; the lighting in here wasn't the greatest; she'd been in his thoughts, however briefly, earlier tonight. But when he looked back he knew it was no mistake. The sweet innocence, the full mouth, the cheerleader-perfect nose—time hadn't changed any of those. And her eyes... Lord, those big brown eyes! No wonder Thomas's had seemed familiar. Because his mother's had haunted Riley for months—for years—after he'd lost her.

After she'd left him.

He should have made the connection when the kid had told him his name. Thomas Davis, son of Keith and Liza Davis. The man he had alternately envied and despised for the past fourteen years, and the woman he had loved for a few sweet months... and hated ever since. The woman he had hoped he would never see again as long as he lived. The woman he would never forgive.

Why was she here instead of Davis? he wondered. Where was her wealthy, socially acceptable husband, the man her parents had adored, the man Riley had endured frequent and unfavorable comparisons to? Why had he sent his wife out after midnight on a Saturday night to collect their wayward son? Maybe he was too busy counting his money, or too important to put in an appearance in a place so obviously beneath him.

She pressed her fingers to her eyes, rubbing wearily, and for a moment his bitterness slipped. God help him, she was still lovely. Even with her hair in disarray, without makeup, in the middle of an unpleasantly disturbed night, she was still one of the prettiest women he'd ever known.

And why shouldn't she be? Davis could easily afford whatever it took to keep his wife beautiful and young looking. With his money, what did she have to worry about? There must be servants to take care of the house, a nanny to take care of the kid, and a wide variety of others to deal with whatever other problems she might encounter.

There would even be lawyers to take care of this. With his parents' and grandparents' influence at work, young Thomas would never spend one minute in community service. He would never pay one penny of restitution. He would never feel one moment of remorse. Why should he? He was a Davis.

Riley stood motionless for a long moment. He needed to get away from here, as far away as he could, but he couldn't move. His feet wouldn't carry him back the way he'd come, and there was no way he could even consider going through the lobby and past Liza. No way he was going to let her know he was here. No way he was going to deal with her tonight.

But the decision was taken out of his hands when another MP, one of the dog handlers he supervised, came through the door. "Geez, Riley, can't you do something about your dog?" he asked as he approached. "His bad habits are rubbing off on mine. I swear, she's starting to sound more like Jasper every day."

If Liza had heard the earlier MP call him Cooper, it hadn't registered, but hearing Morris call him by his first name did. She glanced in his direction, then went utterly still. Even from this distance he could see recognition dawn in her eyes, followed quickly by shock, then shame. Embarrassment. Why not? he thought bitterly. She had always been ashamed of him before—ashamed to introduce him to her family, embarrassed to be seen with him by her friends. Some things never changed.

He had two options now: to walk away as if she were a stranger, or to confront her, to force her to acknowledge him. Since he suspected she would prefer the former, he deliberately chose the latter.

Her gaze never wavered as he closed the distance between them, not until he stopped only a few feet away. She looked away, back again, then settled her gaze somewhere on his chest. "Hello, Riley," she greeted him softly.

"Liza." He drew her name into two long, distinct syllables that were colored with more than a touch of hostility.

"I—" She exhaled softly. "I didn't know if you were still in Augusta. I hadn't heard you had joined the Army."

She spoke softly so that no one—the desk sergeant and the radio operator behind the counter, or her son seated nearby—could hear. For the same reason, so did Riley. "How could you know? You're the one who walked out without saying goodbye. You're the one who refused to see me or return my calls. You're the one who broke off all contact."

Guilt joined all the other emotions he'd seen cross her face. She didn't deny or defend her actions, but neither did she try to explain them. Even though he knew better than to believe anything she might say, he would have thought more of her if she had at least tried.

Her cheeks warm and her expression pained, she ignored what he'd said and awkwardly asked, "How have you been?"

He remained silent, his gaze locked intently on her face until finally she looked up at him. Then he spoke in a quiet, hard voice. "We're not old friends, Liza. Don't waste my time pretending we ever were." Then he stepped around her, crossed the lobby and paused in front of the desk sergeant. "Call me when MPI's done," he said stiffly, "and I'll finish up my reports."

In the moment before he turned away he saw that the sergeant wanted to protest. She needed the reports as soon as they were completed, and having to call him back off patrol would delay that. But she was a friend. She knew he rarely asked for favors, so she let him go. He would have to remember to thank her later—when Liza wasn't standing five feet away.

The night air was cool and sweet. He stopped beside his Jeep and breathed deeply, emptying the stale air of the station from his lungs. Getting rid of the sight and sound and scent of Liza wouldn't be so easy, he knew as he climbed inside and fastened his seat belt. For months after he'd left Augusta he had dreamed of her every night. He had studied every slender young wom with long brown hair, knowing it wouldn't be Liza but hoping, anyway, and always, always being disappointed.

Disappointment was one emotion he'd come to associate with her. Nothing about their relationship had ever been satisfying—not the time they'd spent together or the way they had spent it. He had always wanted *more*. He had wanted to be as welcome in her home as her previous boyfriends had been. He had wanted to know her friends. He had wanted to share more than the few nights a week she reserved for him, nights when she met him somewhere in town because she didn't want her parents to know she was seeing him. Nights when they went places her friends weren't likely to go because she didn't want to have to explain him to them. Nights that always left him feeling cheated, yet grateful as hell that she'd given him any time at all.

Jasper gave a low bark, drawing Riley's attention. The shepherd had quieted as soon as he'd seen his handler walking across the parking lot. Now he was looking innocent again, as if hoping to blame all the noise on Jackie, the Belgian malenois in the Cherokee beside them.

"You're a big baby, Jasper," Riley remarked as he started the engine. "I'm getting tired of defending you to everyone else."

The dog stretched out in back, contentedly thumping his tail against the floor.

Riley glanced back at him, shook his head in exasperation, then pulled out of the parking lot. "Let's get back to work, boy."

That sounded good. Work. Stay busy. Keep his mind occupied. Then maybe he would forget about seeing Liza. Maybe he would forget the memories that had come back all too easily. Maybe he would forget how deeply she had hurt him.

Maybe.

But probably not.

The investigator finished the last of her notes and laid her pen down. "That's about it. You can take Thomas home, Mrs. Davis."

Liza stood and picked up the jacket she'd hung on the back of the chair, folding it neatly over her arm. After a moment's hesitation, she asked, "Could I speak to the officer who—who picked up T.J.?" She couldn't bring herself to say arrested, even though the word had been echoing in her mind for the past two hours, ever since the desk sergeant's phone call had awakened her from a sound sleep. Her son arrested! She had thought it a horror when she'd gone through Keith's first arrest, but tonight had been ten times worse. At least her husband had been an adult, fully aware of the consequences of his actions, driven by no one and nothing but his own needs. But T.J. was her baby, her little boy, whose life had been difficult enough in the past few years without adding this to it.

Then, as if T.J.'s problems hadn't been a big enough shock, seeing Riley and discovering that he had been the one who arrested her child... That had been more than she could deal with. When she'd made the decision to move back to Augusta with T.J., her pride had hoped she would never see Riley again. How could she face him after the way she had behaved, the things she had done? How could she ever explain why she had ended their relationship so abruptly, so unexpectedly, so cravenly?

But just as she had betrayed him so many years ago, her heart had betrayed her. Coming home had brought back all the old memories, the precious ones that she'd been forced to bury in order to make her marriage to Keith work. Coming home had made her remember what it was like to be happy and in love. She hadn't been in town even a week when she'd pulled out the Augusta phone book and thumbed through it to the *C*'s. Though there had been plenty of listings for Coopers, Riley hadn't been one of them, and she'd never known his parents' names or where they lived. She'd found nothing... until tonight.

"That's no problem," the investigator was saying, drawing Liza's attention back to her. "He should be around the station, but if he's gone back out in the field, the desk sergeant can have him stop by."

Nodding, she thanked the woman, then followed T.J. into the lobby. The investigator left through the back door, spoke to the desk sergeant, then joined them in the lobby. "Mrs. Davis, Sergeant Cooper is on his way in."

"Thank you." She thought about the way Riley had acted earlier, then cleared her throat. There was no need to create a scene here inside, especially in front of people Riley worked with. "I—I'll wait outside."

"Why do you want to talk to this guy, Mom?" T.J. asked as she ushered him out the door. "You already know what happened. Can't we just go home?"

Giving him a sharp look, she shrugged into her jacket, then pulled her keys from her pocket and pressed them into his hand. "Go wait in the car, T.J. We'll go home when I'm through."

Hanging his head, he went to the car and got in. He reclined the front seat so that all Liza could see of him was a thatch of dark brown hair. Maybe she'd been too harsh, she thought. He was clearly upset by what had happened, but upset wasn't enough. She wanted remorse. She wanted fear. She wanted solemn vows that it would never happen again. She wanted . . .

Sighing, she leaned against the low concrete wall that formed a small enclosure in front of the station. She wanted to wake up and discover that this was merely a bad dream. She wanted to find out that it was a mistake, that T.J. really hadn't broken into that building with his friends, that Riley really hadn't found him hiding inside, that her son really didn't have to go to juvenile court. She wanted to believe that he was still the sweet, innocent, naive little boy she had always believed him to be.

Dear God, what she really wanted to believe was that it would never happen again.

Had she raised an aspiring delinquent? She had always taught him the difference between right and wrong, good and bad. She had punished him for lying and encouraged him to be honest. She had tried to instill in him the values, beliefs and qualities that she held dear. She had been the best mother she could, even when Keith's problems had prevented him from being any sort of a father at all.

Maybe this had just been peer pressure. Maybe it was the stress of the divorce or the adjustments he'd had to make moving from Dallas to Augusta six months ago. Maybe he was looking for attention—though, heaven knows, since his birth he'd been the center of her universe.

Pushing up her sleeve, she checked her watch. It was two-thirty. She knew this meeting with Riley wouldn't last long—he wouldn't allow it to—and then she could take T.J. home. By three-fifteen they should be in bed. Since tomorrow was Sunday they could sleep late, and then they would have a long, serious talk. She wanted some answers. She needed some reassurance. She . . .

The headlights of the silver Cherokee sliced across the building as its driver pulled into the parking lot, then backed into a space. She watched as Riley got out, spoke to the dog waiting anxiously in the back, then started across the parking lot. She couldn't quite accept the Riley she had known as a policeman, much less as a military policeman, and certainly not as a canine officer. While he hadn't been bad, he *had* had a reputation for being wild, for harboring a certain disrespect for authority. But the proof was right there before her—in the uniform he wore, the gun belt around his waist, the dog whose barking picked up in intensity with each step Riley took.

He had changed in the past fourteen years, but hadn't everyone? She sometimes felt as if she had aged twenty years in the past five alone. Still, she would have known him anywhere. He was still lean and muscular, still handsome, with dark hair, dark eyes and dark looks, and still undeniably sexy. The first time she had ever seen him she had been drawn to him—to his looks, to his charm, to his body. After everything that had passed between them, she thought with a humorless smile, the attraction hadn't faded.

She waited until he was near the door before she stepped out of the shadows. This time she didn't speak, but simply

waited and let him look. She felt his hostility rising, felt his
anger as it gathered strength and bitterness and heat.

He gave her a look that could freeze her soul, then moved
to go around her. "I'm busy," he said with cool disdain.

Liza also moved a step to the side. "I told them I wanted
to talk to you. I asked if they would call you."

"What do you want?"

His frigid, resentful tone made her hurt inside. Even on
the rare occasions when they had argued in the months they
had dated, he had never used that tone of voice with her—
as if he despised her. As if he hated her. He had always been
sweet and funny, gentle and charming, teasing and loving . . . oh, so loving.

And now he hated her.

She felt a sudden bone-deep weariness. Maybe she should
simply do as T.J. had suggested and go home, crawl into bed
and refuse to come out for at least six months. Until T.J.'s
problems were past and Riley was out of her mind and she
could face life again.

But how could she face knowing that her sweet, innocent
son could break into a building and attempt to steal three
thousand dollars' worth of office equipment?

How could she ever face knowing that, even after fourteen years, Riley hated her?

Shivering from the night chill, she pulled her jacket
tighter, then shoved her hands into her pockets so he
couldn't see them clench into tight fists. She took a deep
breath and a step back and quietly said, "It's been a long
time."

"Not long enough."

Not for him, she silently agreed. Forever wouldn't have
been long enough for him. "You know T.J.—Thomas—is
my son."

"I figured that out," he said dryly. "Kind of ironic, isn't
it? Your parents were always convinced that I was a troublemaker who would eventually wind up in jail. Instead it's
your little darling who got arrested, and I'm the cop who
caught him."

"He's not a bad kid."

"Yeah, sure."

"He isn't," she repeated, silently willing him to believe her. "He was spending the night with his friend Bryan, and he got talked into doing this. But he's not bad, honestly. He never would have done it on his own." She paused, then, with less certainty and more vulnerability, asked, "What will happen to him?"

Riley's smile was ugly. "Why, nothing at all. You just have your husband contact the district attorney's office. Better yet, have your father-in-law do it. His name carries a lot more weight around here. I'm sure he's got the political clout to get the charges dropped or, at the very least, to see that your precious little Thomas isn't inconvenienced by all of this."

"I'm serious, Riley. What will happen?"

Giving an impatient sigh, he explained in a bored, none-too-happy-to-be-of-service voice. "Since he's a civilian, his case will be referred to juvenile court in Richmond County. The sentence for a first offense is usually community service and restitution." Then his tone turned steely. "But we both know the Davises won't let it go that far. Now, is there anything else you want?"

Maybe some recognition that, in spite of his earlier claim, they had once been friends—and so much more. Some hint that he hadn't totally forgotten everything good that had ever happened between them.

Sadly, Liza shook her head. "I'm sorry I bothered you, Riley." Without waiting for a response, she turned away and walked to her car. She was grateful to find the keys already in the ignition, because her hands were trembling too badly to manage that small task. Her movements jerky, she fastened her seat belt, started the engine and drove out of the parking lot. Somehow she resisted the urge to take one last look at him as she drove away.

They were approaching the guard shack at the main gate of the post when T.J. finally sat up and adjusted his seat belt. "What did you say to that cop?" he asked in a small, uneven voice.

She didn't look at him but kept her attention riveted to the road. "Nothing that you need to know," she replied stiffly.

"You're mad at me, aren't you?"

Finally, as she left the post and turned onto Gordon Highway, she glanced at her son. In the light from the occasional streetlamp all she could make out was the pale oval of his face. She couldn't see what he was feeling or thinking, and frankly she didn't care. "I get a phone call in the middle of the night from a police officer telling me that my son has been arrested inside the building where he and his friends had broken in to steal a few things, and you want to know if I'm angry. What do *you* think, T.J.?"

He was silent except for a few loud sniffles for the next five miles. Finally, when Liza turned onto the street where they lived, he spoke again. "I'm sorry, Mom. I really am."

She pulled into their driveway and shut off the engine, then gave him a long, cold look. "We'll discuss this tomorrow. Right now you're going to bed."

In her haste to leave after the call from the desk sergeant, she'd left plenty of lights burning. They traced the route she had taken from her bedroom to the stairs to the foyer to the porch. Now, with T.J. dragging along in front of her, she reversed that route, leaving darkness behind her. Pausing in her bedroom door, she watched her son continue down the hall to his own room.

"I left my pajamas at Bryan's house," he said from his own doorway.

"Find another pair."

"My toothbrush is over there, too."

"I'll get you one in the morning."

"I need—"

"Don't push me, T.J.," she warned. "I'm not in the mood. Get to bed *now.*"

His shoulders slumped even more, and Liza would have sworn that even from fifteen feet away she could see the glimmer of fresh tears in his eyes. They tugged at her heart, but she refused to go to him and wipe them away. Maybe if he felt absolutely miserable about his adventure tonight, he would be less likely to take part in anything similar again. *Please, God,* she silently whispered.

But she couldn't send him to bed with nothing. In spite of his behavior, he was still her son. "T.J.?"

He mumbled an unintelligible response.

"I love you."

"I love you, too, Mom," he whispered, then went into his room and very quietly closed the door.

She turned off the hall light and went into her own room. The lamp on the night table was burning, the covers were carelessly tossed back, and her nightgown lay on the floor, a froth of pale green silk against the darker green carpet. She picked up the gown and laid it on the rocker in the corner, then removed her jacket and dropped it there, too. Her shoes came off next, then her jeans. Finally, wearing nothing but her T-shirt and plain cotton panties, she turned off the lamp and made her way by moonlight across the room to the padded seat beneath the window.

T.J. and Riley. Along with her father and Keith, they were the most important men in her life, and they were all, in a sense, connected. Her father had pulled her away from Riley and pushed her toward Keith, who had given her T.J., who had brought her back to Riley.

Riley, who didn't want to share this earth, much less this town, with her.

Riley, who hated her. With good cause.

She had been offended by his suggestion that she ask her former father-in-law to make T.J.'s problems go away. She would never take advantage of the Davis name that way, and she would certainly never allow T.J. to think that he could get away with a crime simply because of who he was.

But she wasn't surprised that Riley expected just that of her. He believed she had married Keith for only two reasons—his name and his money—so using them to her son's advantage must seem logical to him.

The worst part was that he was right. She *had* married Keith because of his family and their money. Because their parents had pushed them into it. Because her parents had pressured her. Because her father had needed that connection to the wealthier Davis family to keep his own business running. She had married Keith for all the wrong reasons. And she had stayed with him for twelve years for all the wrong reasons. She had even, in her own way, loved him.

But not the way she had loved Riley.

Puppy love, her mother had called her feelings for Riley. Rebellion, her father had insisted. When she was Mrs. Keith Davis, he had counseled, she would forget that punk from the poor part of town.

Punk. Her father had always called Riley that, even though he'd known next to nothing about him. He'd met him only once, the first time they'd gone out—the only time Riley had picked her up at the house. Her father had taken one look at Riley in his faded, ripped jeans and black leather jacket, sitting astride his battered black motorcycle, and he had seen wickedness personified. Even though Riley had been as polite and respectful as Keith ever was, Garrett Johnson had been convinced that he was going to corrupt his innocent little girl, that he would use, then discard her. He had never changed his mind.

Funny. In the end *she* had been the one to use, then discard Riley. *She* had been the one who had behaved dishonorably.

In the cool dark privacy of her room, she felt the heat of shame warming her face. Even as a naive, weak and foolish nineteen-year-old, she had known what she was doing was wrong. In the two weeks between her last date with Riley and her wedding to Keith, she had cried herself to sleep every night. She had wanted to call Riley, to somehow make him understand why she couldn't see him anymore. She had considered pleading with him to take her away to someplace where her family could never find her, someplace where they could be together forever.

But her parents had warned her against seeing Riley at all. The Davises had supplied their own pressure, working together with her folks to fill every moment of her free time with wedding preparations, gown fittings, celebratory parties and house hunting. And Keith . . .

Leaning her head against the window, she smiled sadly. Keith had been more determined than anyone that she would go through with the wedding. She honestly believed that he had loved and wanted her, but there had also been a darker side to his insistence. He hadn't liked competing with Riley when, in his mind, he was so obviously superior. He wouldn't have tolerated losing the woman he wanted to marry to a man who'd grown up in a poor section of town, a man whose family had never been successful at anything but producing more mouths to feed, a man who came home each day dirty and sweaty and smelling of the mill where he worked.

But, all that aside, she had only herself to blame. She had been grown-up enough to attend college. Grown-up enough to make love with a man. Grown-up enough to marry another man. She should have been grown-up enough to stand up for herself. She should have been grown-up enough to tell her parents no. And, failing that, she should have been grown-up enough to face Riley, to tell him the truth.

But she hadn't been.

And now, she thought with a shiver, she might finally have to pay for that.

Chapter 2

If the morning's temperatures were anything to judge by, Sunday was going to be a warm day, Riley thought as he walked into the MP station. It was after seven o'clock, and he had returned both Jasper and the Cherokee to the kennels. His shift was over, and he had the rest of the day to spend as he pleased—mostly sleeping—but there was one thing he had to do first.

Inside, he located the reports on last night's break-in. He skipped his own and went straight to the MPI work sheet, scanning the interviews with Bryan and Mike before reading the information regarding Thomas—or T.J., as Liza had called him—Davis. At the top he found the boy's full name, his address and his phone number. He recognized the address as an older, middle-class neighborhood not far from Augusta Mall. It wasn't a bad neighborhood, he thought with a frown—it was a world better than the one where he'd grown up—but it was nowhere near what he'd expected for Keith Davis.

He read through T.J.'s account of the break-in. Neither he nor Bryan had laid the blame on Mike, but the third boy had admitted that it was his idea and that he had talked the others into it. Not that that excused what T.J. had done. Of course, being a Davis, the boy probably thought he didn't need an excuse. His parents would pay the damages, his grandfather would get the charges cleared, and T.J. would be free to do the same—or worse—again.

Yawning, Riley looked away from the reports for a moment. He had arrested Liza's son. That thought had been in his mind all night, but it still hadn't quite sunk in. After her marriage, he had never allowed himself to think about her having children, not when those children should have been *his*. But she and Keith had had a son, and *he* had arrested him. On occasion he had arrested people he'd known, but this was different. This was unreal.

Finally he began reading again and reached the last page of the report. What he saw there made him stiffen. "Parents were divorced two years ago," the investigator had written. "Father lives in Dallas; T.J. and mother relocated to Augusta six months ago."

Divorced. The word couldn't have been more eye-catching if it had been highlighted, underlined and circled with stars. Liza was divorced. Her perfect marriage to her perfect husband had fallen apart somewhere along the way. Someplace deep down inside Riley felt vindicated. Fourteen years ago she had chosen money over love, and what had it gotten her? A divorce and a troublemaking son to raise alone. Maybe there was some justice in the world, after all.

Almost immediately he felt ashamed of himself. He'd seen enough troubled kids in his job that he wouldn't wish one on his worst enemy—which, if Liza wasn't, she came damn close to being. But even she didn't deserve that kind of grief.

He returned the report to the desk sergeant, then went outside to his pickup. He'd been up a long time and had put in a full night's work, to say nothing of a full night's remembering. It was time to go home and fall into bed, to sleep the rest of the day away. But when he drove out of the

parking lot, it wasn't toward the MP Company, the barracks where most of the single MPs lived, but toward Gate
One and Gordon Highway. Toward Augusta.

Toward Liza.

He didn't bother pointing out to himself the foolishness
of this trip. He was physically tired and emotionally weary.
The last thing he needed was to see where she lived. Alone
except for T.J. Without Keith.

The very last thing he needed was to risk seeing her again.

But it was only a short drive from the fort, and after her
own late night it wasn't likely that she would be up and
about at seven-thirty. He would simply drive by the house
and then return to the company, where he would start forgetting her. He'd done it before. He could do it again.

But before she had been married.

Now she wasn't.

Not that it mattered to him, of course. Other than the intense satisfaction he found in the evidence of her poor
judgment, he couldn't have cared less about her marital
status.

The neighborhood where she lived was a little shabbier
than he'd remembered. It was the sort of place where Keith
Davis, who'd grown up in the older, exclusive section of
Augusta known as the Hill, might own rental property but
would never set foot himself. Riley was surprised that, divorced or not, he allowed Liza to live there with his son. He
was equally surprised that the Davises or the Johnsons
hadn't provided her with a nice little cottage—the quaint
local word for the beautiful homes it was used to de-
scribe—near their own homes.

The street number he had automatically committed to
memory belonged to a rather small two-story house that sat
back from the road. It was white, with a dull green roof,
black shutters and a broad porch. There was nothing
wrong with the place—after sixty years of working hard, strug-
gling to raise six kids and make ends meet, his parents
had still never had a home so nice—but for someone with Liza's
ambitions, someone who loved wealth and luxury, who

craved security and the finer things in life, it was plain. Simple. A whole lot of steps down from what she'd undoubtedly become accustomed to as Mrs. Keith Davis.

He turned around in the driveway of an empty house, then drove past Liza's once more. What kind of divorce settlement had she gotten from her husband? he wondered. And what had she spent the money on? The top-of-the-line European sedan that sat in the driveway? It was about two years old. Probably that, and whatever else her greedy little heart had desired.

Once, her heart had desired him—or so he had believed. Later he'd realized that she had simply been amusing herself with him while she waited for the big chance—for Keith's proposal. She'd played them both along, giving to Riley what she had denied Keith until she had exactly what she wanted: a big diamond ring, a church date and promises of more, so much more, to come.

He headed back toward the post, too tired to think anymore, too emotionally sore to remember anymore. He needed sleep, hours of it, before he could deal any further with the past. He needed a few more years' emotional distance before he could think about Liza.

He needed a new life.

Riley stood in front of the mirror, scowling as he fastened his narrow black tie into a neat knot. He always worked in his battle dress uniform, but today he was wearing his Class A uniform—a dark green coat and trousers, a pale green shirt, and tie—because today he had to appear in court.

In Richmond County Juvenile Court.

At T.J. Davis's hearing.

He had never believed it would go this far. He had been so convinced that T.J.'s grandparents would band together to protect their precious little grandchild that the subpoena to appear today had caught him totally off guard.

Ordinarily he didn't mind going to court. It was a routine part of every cop's life, whether civilian or military. He wasn't intimidated by the process. Although it did interfere with his work schedule, it was simply part of the job.

The case itself was routine, simple. He and Jasper had found T.J. hiding inside the building, and the boy had admitted to his part in the crime. The best lawyers Davis money could buy couldn't change those facts.

It was seeing Liza again that bothered him. Not a day, not even an hour, or so it seemed, had gone by in the past week and a half that he hadn't thought of her. He had even on one occasion found himself driving by her house again. No matter what he'd done—working, visiting his parents, going out on a date—she had always been there in the back of his mind. She had even haunted his sleep.

He slipped on his coat and buttoned it, then adjusted the rows of ribbons above the left pocket. On his way out he picked up his hat, putting it on as soon as he stepped outside.

He could take some consolation from the fact that this would be the last time he would have to see Liza, he told himself on the drive downtown. He would appear at the hearing, the judge would most likely assign T.J. to some type of community service, and the kid and his mother would be out of Riley's life. Permanently.

Forever and ever.

Please.

At the courthouse he waited in the witness room until he was called into the courtroom. Though he tried not to look in the direction of the defense table, he couldn't stop himself, and, of course, the first person he saw—the only one—was Liza, sitting in the first row of seats behind her son. Her hair was drawn back from her face, and she wore a soft gray suit and a softer, grayer expression. She looked frightened, he thought with a twinge of sympathy that he immediately tamped down. Frightened and worried and concerned—like any mother whose eleven-year-old son was in trouble.

Except that she wasn't any mother, and T.J. wasn't any son. They were privileged. Special.

He was sworn in by the bailiff, then instructed to take a seat on the witness stand.

"State your name and occupation," the prosecutor requested.

"Staff Sergeant Riley Cooper, U.S. Army, Military Police Corps."

"Where are you assigned, Sergeant Cooper?"

"Fort Gordon."

"What is your current position there?"

"I'm the noncommissioned officer in charge of all canine units."

"How long have you been a military police officer?"

"Thirteen years."

"Sergeant Cooper, would you tell the court what happened on the night of September nineteenth?"

Deliberately looking away from Liza, he recounted the events of that night—how he had parked in front of the building to do his paperwork and had heard the sound of glass breaking, how he and Jasper had investigated and had caught two boys coming out of the building with their arms full of office equipment, and how Jasper had located the defendant hiding beneath a desk inside.

While he spoke he looked once at the boy he was speaking about in such impersonal tones. T.J. sat beside his lawyer, a gray-haired, older man. He was wearing dark slacks and a white dress shirt, and his hair, the same thick, dark brown as his mother's, had that just-combed look. His face was pale, which made his eyes more noticeable. Big brown eyes. Innocent-looking eyes . . . even when they weren't.

Just like his mother's.

If things had turned out differently, T.J. would have been *his* son, he thought, uncomfortable with the idea. He wasn't sure what kind of father he would have been—like his own, he supposed—but he was sure of one thing: *his* son would never have ended up in court like this. He wouldn't have caved in to peer pressure. He would have been strong enough to tell his friends no, thanks, he wasn't interested.

The prosecutor thanked him and sat down. T.J.'s attorney had no questions for him. His job today wasn't so much to defend as to plead for leniency. There was no way he could deny that T.J. had illegally entered the building or that he had done so for the purpose of taking property that didn't belong to him. All he could do was point out that his client was a good kid who had never been in trouble before, a kid whose parents had divorced not long ago, whose mother had recently uprooted him from the only home he'd ever known and brought him to Augusta, a kid with strong family ties—he wouldn't forget that, Riley thought uncharitably—in the community.

The judge dismissed Riley, and he left the courtroom. As he passed Liza he felt her gaze on him, but he didn't so much as glance at her. He'd seen enough of her to last a lifetime. Now he wanted only to forget her.

His only goal was to leave the courthouse and be well on his way back to Fort Gordon before the judge dismissed court, but in the corridor outside he ran into bad luck in the form of a Richmond County deputy, a former MP Riley had worked with in Alabama. During their conversation he kept edging closer to the elevator, finally reaching it and pressing the button just as someone called his name.

The deputy looked at Liza, then at Riley, and grinned. "Pretty lady," he remarked softly. "See you around, Cooper."

Riley continued to face the elevator doors so that all he could see of her was a soft blur—the gray of her suit, the pink of her blouse, the brown of her hair. But even without looking he was all too aware of her presence, from the tingling in his nerves to the tightness in his chest to the sick, angry feeling in his stomach.

Lacing her fingers tightly together, Liza studied his profile. For all the life he showed, he might have been carved in ice, she thought, then immediately amended that to stone. Ice eventually melted and revealed whatever was underneath, but this wall he'd erected against her would never crack. It would never crumble to reveal the man she had once loved. She wondered briefly if that man even existed now. She would never know. He would never show her.

"You were right," she said at last. "The judge gave him community service and ordered restitution. T.J. will have to earn the money to replace the window and to pay for any other damage they did, and he's been assigned to a community-service project out of Fort Gordon, some new program that's just starting up."

Just as she finished, the elevator arrived with a *ding* and the doors slid open, but Riley didn't step inside. Instead he slowly turned until he was looking at her. Cold indifference had given way to disbelief, then dismay. Wasn't that what he had expected? she wondered in confusion. Hadn't that been the sentence he'd told *her* to expect?

"At Fort Gordon?" he echoed sharply.

She nodded as the elevator doors closed again and the car went on its way.

"You're sure?"

"That's what the judge said."

Muttering a curse, he punched the button again, this time with barely restrained force. "He should have been assigned to something in Richmond County," he said, his tone dark and angry.

Hesitantly she pointed out, "Fort Gordon *is* in Richmond County—at least, part of it is. And that *is* where he committed the crime. Riley, what's wrong?"

He laughed a cold, humorless laugh, then shook his head in disgust. "Along with a dozen other people on post, *I* supervise the community-service program out there. *I'll* be supervising your kid."

Without waiting for the elevator, he walked away, disappearing through the door marked Exit and leaving Liza alone in the corridor. That was just what her son needed, she thought grimly. To be placed under the control of a man who despised T.J.'s father and hated his mother. To have to work for a man who'd already made up his mind that T.J. was a rotten kid simply because he was *her* kid.

But surely Riley wouldn't take out his hostility toward her on an eleven-year-old boy. No matter how he hated her, he was a better man than that. And it certainly wouldn't hurt T.J. to be exposed to a better man. To someone other than his father, who was going to die before he was forty if he didn't manage to straighten himself out, or his grandfather Johnson, who believed that all you needed to be happy in this world was money and lots of it, or his grandfather Davis, who truly believed he was superior to everyone else simply because he was one of *those* Davises.

"Hi, Mom," T.J. said glumly when he and Mr. Owensby joined her outside the courtroom.

Hal Owensby was an old friend of her family, a golf buddy of her father's. When Liza had gotten the notice for T.J. to appear in court, Mr. Owensby had been the only person she had considered calling. His specialty was corporate law and not criminal, but in this case, she had figured, a lawyer was a lawyer. Even the best defense attorney in town couldn't have gotten T.J. out of this mess—not fairly, at least. And that was what she had wanted: a fair punishment for his crime.

Mr. Owensby offered her a slip of paper. "Here's T.J.'s share of the damages. Also, his community service will start this Saturday. Have him at the MP station on post at one o'clock." He smiled reassuringly. "This new program of theirs sounds interesting. It consists of juveniles, of course, and it's supervised by volunteers from various departments on post—the legal office, social work, mental health services—"

"The MPs," Liza added without thinking.

"Yes, the MPs, too, and some others."

"Oh, Mom, I'm not going to have to work for that cop, am I?" T.J. asked in dismay.

"I guess so. Sergeant Cooper's one of the volunteers." She tried to sound even and bland, but from Mr. Owensby's expression she didn't think she'd succeeded.

"Cooper. I seem to recall a young man by that name...."

When his sentence faded away she smiled tightly. "Yes." Yes, he had often heard Garrett Johnson complain about her relationship—how had her father always put it? Her *foolishness*—with Riley Cooper. "T.J., would you wait over there, please?"

She watched him wander a short distance down the hall, then looked back at the lawyer. "Neither my parents nor the Davises know about any of this yet," she said softly. "That I've met Riley again, that T.J. was arrested, or that Riley was the one who arrested him. Please, Mr. Owensby, don't say anything to my father. Let me tell him."

"He won't be happy."

She glanced at her son, then thought of Riley's clear aversion to her and smiled bitterly. "No one's happy. Why should Daddy be any different?"

"I could ask the judge to rethink his decision," Owensby offered. "I can tell him that there was a past...involvement between you and one of the supervisors of the work program that might make things uncomfortable for both you and the boy now."

What about Riley? she wondered. Did anyone care that he might also be uncomfortable? Did anyone care that he might be suffering the most discomfort of all? "No, thank you, Mr. Owensby. Riley and T.J. and I will have to work this out on our own."

"If there's anything more I can do..."

"Thank you." She accepted his hug, then called her son back.

"I don't feel like going to school, Mom," T.J. said as they got into the waiting elevator. "Can I just go home?"

"No. I have to go to work, and you have to go to school. You've only missed a few hours."

"But they'll want to know where I was. You aren't going to tell them, are you, Mom? If you tell them, it'll get out, and everyone will know, and...please don't make me go, Mom," he pleaded.

She wanted to slip her arm around him and tell him that it was all right, that they would both go home and hide from the world. But they couldn't do that. They couldn't pretend that their lives hadn't changed in the past ten days. "I'll only tell the principal. Since Mike and Bryan don't go to your school, the only way the kids will find out is if you tell them, and you know how to keep your mouth shut, don't you?" She almost smiled then for the first time all day because, even though no sound was coming out, his mouth was open wide in silent protest.

They left the courthouse and walked to their car in the back parking lot. Slumping in the passenger seat, T.J. mumbled, "I *hate* that cop."

"You don't *know* that cop," Liza said stiffly. "And he has a name—Sergeant Cooper. You'd better learn to use it."

"You called him Riley that night at the police station. Do you know him?"

She hadn't realized that T.J. had heard part of her very brief conversation with Riley that night, but obviously he had. Not only was he correct, but he'd spoken in the accusing tone of voice that he reserved for the rare occasions since the divorce when she'd shown interest in any man other than his father. "Yes," she finally admitted. "I knew him a long time ago."

"Was he your boyfriend before Dad?"

She refused to look at him as she drove out of the parking lot. Her entire relationship with Riley had been nothing but lies. Lies to her parents, to her friends, to Keith, to Riley—and even to herself. How sad that she'd never had the courage to stand up and say, "Yes, I'm dating this man. We're friends and lovers, and I'm very much in love with him."

But this wasn't the time, and T.J. definitely wasn't the person, for that kind of honesty. And so she glanced at him and smiled, and she lied. Again. "We were friends when I was in college."

"How could you be friends with a *cop?*"

When had he become so disdainful of police officers? she wondered. That was something she would have to put a stop to immediately. Regardless of his own problems, she wouldn't tolerate that kind of disrespect from her son. "Don't use that tone of voice, T.J. You're in enough trouble as it is."

"It's not so bad. I'll take the money from my savings account to pay—" When he saw his mother shake her head, he broke off. "You mean I have to earn it? I have to work for it?"

"Every penny."

"But I have ten times that much in the bank already!"

"Most of that money was given to you by your grandparents. You have to earn this yourself."

"That's stupid, Mom, when I already have enough to pay."

She brought the car to a stop at a red light, then turned a cold glare on him. "That's the way it is, T.J. End of discussion."

"It's not a discussion," he said in a nasty tone. "A discussion is where people listen to what each other says, but you don't listen at all. You've got your mind made up, and it doesn't matter what I say. You think you know everything, and—"

"*That's enough.*" She stopped just short of shouting, then looked back at the street, breathing deeply. She wouldn't get into a screaming match with him. They argued from time to time, like all families, but he never got hateful. Was this something new to go along with his recent criminal behavior? Was he going to change from the sweet, loving child who'd never given her any real problems into an obnoxious delinquent who gave her nothing but grief?

Not bloody likely, she silently swore. He would have one hell of a battle on his hands if he tried. She wouldn't give up her son easily.

T.J. remained silent until she turned into the parking lot of his school. "I'm not doing any stupid community service," he announced sullenly.

She wouldn't respond to that, Liza promised. Her mouth set in a thin line to keep the words inside, she parked the car, shut off the engine, picked up her purse and got out.

"Community service," he repeated with disgust, joining her on the sidewalk. "You know what that means? They make you pick up trash. You have to clean out the stables, and you get all dirty and smelly and covered with horse—"

She shot him a stern look, and he meekly shut up and led the way inside the school to the office.

Twenty minutes later she was on her way to work. She worked in patient administration at one of the local hospitals, a career she had been studying for when she'd met Riley. Her marriage to Keith hadn't slowed her down; she had graduated right on schedule. But it was only in recent years that she'd been able to actually work in her field. She had been pregnant with T.J. when she graduated, and she'd been chosen to stay home with him when he was little.

But by the time he'd entered third grade, she had had no choice but to work. Keith's life had started spiraling out of control, and all too often her less-than-adequate salary was all they had to pay the bills and buy food. After his first arrest on drug charges, his company had put him through a rehabilitation program. Liza had been naive enough to believe things would be all right, and for a few months they had been. But Keith's desire for drugs had turned out to be far stronger than his desire for anything else—a job, a wife, or a son. After his second arrest in six months, he had lost his job, and they'd been on the verge of losing their house.

Finally she had turned to his family for help. The Davises had paid off their remaining creditors and picked up the bill for their son's second stay in a rehab clinic. They had offered further help to Liza, but she had turned it down. She'd had enough money to do the one thing she had felt necessary.

She had divorced him.

How many times had she closed her eyes to his problems? she wondered wearily. How many times had she blamed his strange behavior on alcohol, his lethargy on working too hard? Riley would get a kick out of knowing that her first clue, her first real knowledge that something was seriously wrong, had come from money. The credit-card bills that Keith had so routinely paid off in full in the early years of their marriage had begun arriving marked Past Due. Second Notice. Some cards were canceled by the banks. When she had turned to the savings account to pay them—the account into which he had regularly deposited a large percentage of his paycheck for years—she had discovered that it had been closed. The stocks and bonds they'd bought had been sold, the certificates of deposit cashed in. He had withdrawn and spent thousands of dollars without her knowledge.

Within a matter of days she had discovered that there was no money in the checking account, either, and that the house payment hadn't been made for months. Then had come Keith's first arrest. Rehab. Another arrest. Divorce. An already bad dream had turned into a full-fledged nightmare.

She had felt badly about leaving him when he was in such serious trouble, but she'd been pushed into a corner, and she'd had T.J. to think of. The only way to go was out. She had almost left once before when she had discovered that Keith, three months after his first stay in the rehab clinic and swearing that he was off drugs for good, was hiding his stash in T.J.'s room, in their son's toys and among his clothes. His second arrest had been the final straw.

She pulled into her parking space at the hospital and simply sat there for a moment. She had walked away from Riley when things had threatened to get tough, when the pressure to help her family by marrying Keith had gotten too strong. She had stayed around longer with Keith, but eventually she had left him, too. Maybe she didn't have the capacity to deal with serious problems. Maybe she was, as Riley believed, greedy and selfish, concerned only with her own needs. Maybe she lacked courage and compassion and character.

But she wouldn't walk away from T.J. No matter what he did, no matter how bad things got, she wouldn't turn away from her son. She wouldn't let anyone or anything take him away.

He was her child.
He was the light—and the love—of her life.
He was all she had.

Saturday was a bright, warm day. The sky was an incredible shade of blue, and the clouds were so thick and soft that it seemed you could almost touch them. It was a lazy sort of day, with a hint that fall was on its way but summer wasn't quite gone. It was a perfect day for going to the lake or riding down country roads or picnicking in the park.

But Riley was working.

The kids for the work-service program were gathering in the parking lot out in front of the MP station. Some had been sent here to finish out their sentences—a few hundred hours of community service, parceled out three or four hours at a time, could take a long time—and others, like T.J., were just starting. Some were habitual offenders; others were first-timers. There were officers' kids and the children of enlisted members, along with a civilian or two. Some came from obviously comfortable families, and some came from families that were barely getting by.

But they all had a few things in common. They were all kids. They had all been sent here either through the courts or the command sergeant major's office. And they were all in trouble.

They were also all here to work. Including him.

He'd seen Liza drop T.J. off a few minutes ago. Or rather, he'd seen the expensive car glide up, stop long enough for T.J. to climb out, then glide away. That was why he'd been waiting inside the MP station—so he wouldn't have to see her. Now it was time to get started with the program. Now it was safe to go outside.

When the provost marshal had explained this experimental program and asked for volunteers, Riley hadn't hesitated. He liked kids, liked working with them. And he had believed in the theory that mature, responsible adults working with small groups of troubled kids—not just supervising but working alongside—could provide positive reinforcement and positive role models.

Then he had found out at the volunteers' meeting this afternoon that *his* small group was going to include T.J. Davis, and he'd known he had made a major mistake getting involved. The kid certainly didn't need positive reinforcement—he already thought he was something special. And a more appropriate role model for a Davis would be some Wall Street raider or corporate whiz kid, not a blue-collar, working-class cop.

The simple fact was that he didn't want to work with T.J. He didn't want to be constantly reminded of Liza. He didn't want to be nice to Keith Davis's kid.

He didn't want to remember that T.J. should have been *his* son.

How was that for a mature, responsible attitude? he thought with a cynical smile as he joined the other volunteers outside.

They were dividing into groups, each adult escorting his charges off to the side to get acquainted. Riley waited until there were only three kids remaining, then said, "You three are mine. Come in closer."

"Oh, great," T.J. mumbled. "Of course *we* get stuck with the *cop.*"

Riley ignored him and glanced at the list of names he'd been given. "Which one of you is Trevor?"

A slim, small-for-his-age redhead raised his hand.

"Then you're Jamal."

The third boy, stocky and somber, nodded.

"And this is T.J. I'm Riley Cooper." The volunteers had agreed that there would be no use of rank or title. An officer's kid might have an attitude problem with an enlisted supervisor, while an enlisted member's kid might feel intimidated at taking orders from an officer. But instinct told him that the only attitude problem he was going to face today was the lone civilian in the group, a boy who probably knew nothing about rank and cared even less.

He knew the facts of T.J.'s case, of course, and he had read the basics on the other two. Trevor was twelve, the middle of three sons being raised by a single father. This was his third offense, all three for shoplifting at the exchange. Jamal, eleven and the only child of two captains, had vandalized a car in the parking lot near his housing area. Two of his friends had taken part, but only Jamal had gotten caught. He still hadn't revealed the identities of his accomplices.

"Well?" T.J. said sarcastically. "When are we going to start? I want to get this over with."

Riley leaned against the low concrete wall and gave him a long, unwavering look. His T-shirt looked casual and sloppy, but it bore an expensive logo. The same was true of his jeans, but not his shoes. Though unbranded, they were white, relatively new, and looked every bit as expensive as Riley knew them to be. "Is this how you dress to work at home?" he asked, his tone conversational, his expression open, his dislike for the boy well hidden.

"I don't work at home," T.J. replied sullenly.

I bet you don't. Riley kept his sarcastic reply unsaid, but just barely. If he couldn't treat the kids in the program fairly—*all* of them—regardless of his personal feelings for them, then he had no right being involved at all. "Nice shoes."

T.J. simply scowled.

"Expensive, aren't they?"

"More than you can afford," the boy boasted.

In a sense that was true, Riley silently acknowledged. While his bank balance could easily cover such a luxury, something in him, something that remembered wearing hand-me-downs and going without, balked at the idea of spending more than a hundred dollars on a pair of tennis shoes. "They look almost new," he remarked.

"They are."

Casually he folded his arms across his chest. "Why are you here, T.J.?"

For the first time the boy's bravado slipped. He didn't want to tell the other two what he'd done to get assigned to this program. If he was ashamed of it, that was a good sign. If he was simply ashamed of getting caught, that wasn't.

"Why are you here today? To do what?"

T.J.'s reply came grudgingly. "To work."

"To work. And you came dressed like that."

One of the other boys snickered, and Riley gave him a stern look before turning his attention back to T.J., who was glaring at him with nothing less than pure hatred.

"Picking up trash for a while isn't going to ruin my clothes."

"No, it wouldn't. Unfortunately you're not going to be picking up trash." He gestured to the gray van parked nearby. "You're going to clean out the stables. Let's go, guys."

They were halfway to the van when he decided to acknowledge that T.J. wasn't following. He *liked* kids, he reminded himself when he turned around. He had occasionally done volunteer work with them, and he had always gotten along well with his friends' children. And, modesty aside, his nieces and nephews adored him.

But he didn't like smart-mouthed kids.

He didn't like troublemakers.

He didn't like *this* kid.

"Are you coming?"

"You're doing this on purpose, aren't you?" T.J. asked, his voice low and sharp and taut. "Because of my mom."

Stiffening, Riley moved a few steps closer. "This doesn't have anything to do with your mother. It has to do with you and the trouble you got yourself into and the trouble you're creating for yourself now. I didn't choose this assignment, and I didn't choose to have you on my team. Now, you can refuse to work, and we'll be back in court next week so the judge can select another punishment for you. But trust me, T.J., it goes downhill from here. Community service is the easiest it's going to get."

He paused for a moment, letting those words sink in, then quietly repeated, "Are you coming?"

Muttering something that sounded suspiciously like a curse, T.J. shoved past him and joined the other two boys at the van. Riley looked at his watch, then muttered his own silent curse.

It was going to be a long two hours.

Chapter 3

The stables were only a few miles from the building where Riley had caught T.J. and the others. He was out in this area at least twice a day when he was working, to pick up Jasper at the kennels just down the road and again to drop him off at the end of the shift.

He introduced the three boys to the stables manager, who handed out gloves and equipment and showed them where to start. Since it was such a pretty day, all the horses had been rented and were out on the trails that crisscrossed this part of the post. That made their job a little easier.

"This is gross," T.J. announced after only a few minutes.

Riley didn't respond. This was the dirtiest of all the community-service jobs, and on a warm day like today it was particularly nasty. To someone who had never been around horses, the odor inside the stables was foul, and dust, straw and worse stuck to their clothes and sweat-damp skin.

After another few minutes, T.J. protested, "My shoes are getting ruined."

"You can always take them off and work barefoot," Riley suggested.

The boy scowled at him.

The next time the kid started to whine, Riley laid his shovel aside and approached him. "Look, you're not the only one working here. You're not the only one who doesn't like the smell, or who's hot and sweaty, or who's getting covered with manure. Interesting that you're the only one who's complaining about it."

He had to tilt his head back to do it, but T.J. met his gaze. "I'm not coming back here again."

"Fine. Don't come back. But the judge will probably send you to the Youth Development Center. The kids there aren't pretending to be bad, T.J., they *are* bad. They're tough. After a little time there, cleaning out these stalls in ninety-degree weather will be your idea of heaven."

Without another word T.J. returned to work, and so did Riley. As he did, he noticed that the other two boys had watched their exchange, but had quickly and silently gone back to work. Were they always this quiet and uncomplaining? he wondered. Was this punishment still new enough to them that they were somewhat intimidated by it? Or did they figure he had enough trouble with T.J., that they didn't need to add to it?

How could Liza have had such a rotten kid? Immediately he answered his own question. Easily. She'd had him with Keith Davis.

He had known when he was dating Liza that she occasionally went out with Davis. Duty dates, she had called them. Elegant parties, country-club dances, social gatherings—the sort of places where *he* would have stood out like a sore thumb. At first he had hated those occasions, but soon he had realized that she was much more attentive, much more affectionate to him after a date with Keith. After one of those dull, boring evenings had ended with no more than a chaste kiss—or so she had always sworn—she had usually slipped away to be with Riley, to make out in the beginning, to make love at the end.

For years he had wondered if she'd been truthful about her feelings for Keith and her behavior with him. After all, a woman just didn't suddenly marry a man she'd dated only on occasion and only to please her parents. At least he knew that in the beginning she hadn't lied about not making love with Davis—there had been no hiding her virginity that quiet night at the lake—but before that, just how chaste had those kisses been? And afterward all he'd had were her promises. Promises from a woman who had lied to him. Used him. Betrayed him.

Words of honor from a woman who'd had none.

He still remembered the day he'd found out she was marrying Davis. He had known something was wrong when she had stood him up two nights in a row. Uneasiness had turned to worry when she had refused his phone calls, when he'd heard her one time—the last time—in the background instructing her sister in what to tell him.

Then he had come home from work one evening, home to the small house where he'd grown up, the house he'd still shared with his parents, two brothers and three sisters. There had been times when he'd felt foolish, twenty-two and still living at home. It had meant he had no place to take a date—to take Liza. It had meant no quiet hours together, watching television or listening to music or just playing house. It had meant making love on a deserted beach at Clarks Hill Lake or in the back seat of her cramped little car.

But Liza had understood, or so she'd said. His parents had needed whatever help he and his two-years-younger sister, Robbie, could give them.

That particular night he had come home, sick with worry over Liza, and Robbie had been waiting for him outside, a ragged piece of newspaper in her hand. When she had offered it to him, he'd seen that it had been torn from the Lifestyles section, wadded, smoothed out, folded and re-folded. He had looked at it blankly, then read the announcement all the way through without understanding a word.

Almost in tears, Robbie had grasped his arm, squeezing it tightly, and whispered, "I'm sorry, Riley."

Then he had read it again, and that time he had understood. "Mr. and Mrs. Garrett Johnson announce the engagement and upcoming marriage of their daughter Liza Renee to Thomas Keith Davis, son of Mr. and Mrs. Alexander Davis." He had read on, interesting little tidbits about Liza's attendance at Augusta College, about how Davis had graduated from there and was currently employed in his father's business. It had ended with the date of the wedding—Saturday, June third, little more than a week away—and the church where it would be held.

He had left the house again, climbing back on his motorcycle without a word, and had returned hours later, drunk and gut-wrenchingly sick, to pass out in his bed. It had been a pattern that he'd fallen into all too easily, working all day with a miserable hangover, only to spend his evenings getting drunk again. He hadn't spent so much as one minute without feeling the effects of too much alcohol one way or another.

Until the day of Liza's wedding, when he had waited in the parking lot across the street from the church. He had been sober then, cold sober. For the first time since finding out that she was marrying Keith, he had wanted to be clear-headed. He had wanted to feel the pain. He had wanted to forever remember her coming out of the church, heartachingly beautiful in a lovely white gown, with her husband at her side.

Her husband.

That night he'd gone on the worst binge of all, and Sunday he had been as sick as a dog. Monday he had enlisted in the Army.

Pushing the memories away and returning to the present required effort, but Riley managed. He took a deep breath, straightened his shoulders and focused his gaze, only to find that he was staring into a pair of startlingly familiar brown eyes. Expressive eyes. Sullen eyes. And T.J. was staring back.

He flushed almost guiltily and made a show of working again. What did the kid know about Riley's connection to Liza? he wondered. He must know something; he'd hinted earlier that Riley had singled him out for special treatment—for worse treatment—because of her. Surely he didn't know that they had dated. She had hidden their relationship from her family and friends; she certainly wouldn't have told her son about it years later. Still, he seemed particularly eager to dislike Riley, something that seemed to go beyond resenting the cop who had caught him.

There was a honk outside, and through the open doors Riley could see the gray van. A glance at his watch confirmed that it was time to leave. Before he could speak to the boys, T.J. dropped his shovel where he stood, yanked his gloves off and tossed them on a nearby shelf and headed out the door. Trevor and Jamal stood nearby, waiting for Riley's response.

"T.J." He had to speak loudly, because the kid was already halfway to the van.

His steps slowed, then stopped, and reluctantly he turned around.

"Come back here and put your equipment away."

For a moment Riley thought T.J. was going to refuse. And what would he do if that was the case? he wondered wryly. He couldn't *make* the boy obey. He couldn't use physical force. All he could do was threaten—no credit for the work done today, added hours in the stables instead of the easier and more pleasant trash pickup, yard or maintenance work. He couldn't even use what was often the most effective threat of all—I'll tell your parents you've been uncooperative—because the kid's father was a thousand miles away, and his mother... Well, he would rather not tell Liza anything. He would rather not see her ever again.

But after a long, tense standoff, T.J. picked up the shovel and the gloves and put them back where he'd gotten them. Off to one side Riley heard a small sigh of relief—from Jamal, he thought—and silently he echoed it. But he didn't fool himself. Before T.J.'s three hundred hours of community service were completed, they were going to have some problems. Someday he was going to give the kid an order, and T.J. wasn't going to give in. What would he do then?

Riley climbed back into the front seat of the van, and the boys settled in back. Jamal and Trevor shared the middle seat, exchanging typical adolescent small talk, and T.J. sat in the back, his face turned away, shutting them all out, scowling even with no one to scowl at. With his attitude, it wouldn't take him long to alienate the other kids in the program, Riley thought, and for one brief moment he felt a twinge of sympathy for the kid. Maybe being a Davis wasn't so easy. Certainly leaving his home, his friends and his school in Dallas and coming here hadn't been easy for him. Plus, his parents' divorce must have been tough.

And he seemed determined to make life even tougher.

But that wasn't Riley's concern. He only had to tolerate T.J. for a few hours each week. Away from the program he was Liza's responsibility. Liza's problem.

Her problem, Liza thought as she got out of the car and joined the other parents waiting in the parking lot, was that no matter how hard she tried, she simply couldn't get Riley out of her mind. Every day at the strangest moments he crept in, memories from the past providing a curious mix with more recent images. Whether she was in a meeting at work, on her knees in the garden or trying to put something together for dinner, her mind was all too willing to turn to him.

Knowing that he was part of the community-service project had made things even more difficult for her today. She had hoped to catch a glimpse of him when she'd dropped T.J. off earlier, but there had been no sign of him. He was probably avoiding her, she admitted, and that saddened her. Once they had been so special to each other. Now he couldn't stand to look at her.

And she had no one but herself to blame.

The kids and their supervisors began returning to the station, and she watched them curiously. For the most part the kids all looked average, normal. There was a little sullenness, a little bitterness in some faces, but there was nothing to suggest that they were all in legal trouble.

Of course, the same could be said of T.J. How many times had her parents and Keith's seen him since his arrest without guessing that anything was wrong? Soon she would have to tell them. His grandfathers had already wondered why he couldn't play golf with them at the Augusta National this afternoon, and Liza's mother would want to know why he was skipping their traditional Sunday after-church dinner tomorrow.

She had told herself that she'd kept silent so far because her parents' and her ex-in-laws' immediate response would be exactly what Riley had suggested: they would want to use their influence to get T.J. off the hook. This way, by the time she told them it would be too late for them to interfere. He had already had his hearing and received his sentence.

But in reality, she admitted as she sat on a picnic table, she was afraid. Afraid that they might question her fitness as a mother. Afraid that they might secretly wonder what was wrong with her that the males closest to her had such problems. Afraid that they might suspect she had somehow been responsible for Keith's drug addiction, and that now she was somehow responsible for T.J.'s lawlessness.

And she was ashamed. Breaking into buildings, stealing things, getting arrested—those were things that happened to other people's children. Not hers.

From her seat she watched a van pull into the parking lot behind the MP station, coming to a stop only a few feet away. Her attention was torn between Riley in the front seat and T.J., looking small and lost and all alone, in the back. Her son, for the moment, won out.

The other boys were talking as if they were old friends, and they didn't break off until one of them spotted his father waiting. T.J. shuffled along behind them, his head down, that grim, moping look she was coming to know too well on his face. Why wasn't he talking, too? Why was he so down?

"Hey, kiddo," she greeted him when he would have passed her by. He came to a stop beside the table but didn't look at her. "How was your afternoon?"

"Awful. Can we go home now?"

"In a moment." She looked around and spotted Riley talking to the van driver. Like everyone else, he was dressed in old clothes—worn jeans and a faded red T-shirt. Unlike everyone else, he looked wonderful, even hot, sweaty and dirty. Just like old times....

While she watched, he turned and came around toward them. Was he actually going to speak to her? she wondered.

He didn't even stop, but simply spoke as he passed. "Tomorrow, T.J. Two to five."

The answer to her question was painful and sharp. No. He wasn't going to speak to *her* at all.

She twisted around to watch him. He stopped beside the redheaded boy who had shared the van with them, offered his hand to the boy's father and talked with them for a moment. Next he caught up with the black boy and his mother and repeated the brief exchange. She smiled bleakly. He had time for everyone but her.

"Let's go, Mom," T.J. insisted. "I want to take a shower and clean this stuff off my shoes. Grandma will have a fit if she sees them like this. You know how long it took me to talk her into getting them for me for my birthday."

Liza looked absently at his shoes. Yes, it had taken T.J. quite some time to convince her mother to buy them...and it had taken *her* even longer to get over her annoyance at the purchase. Even when their financial situation had been more than healthy, she had never been extravagant in her spending. Now that she was supporting the two of them herself, she certainly didn't have the money to waste on fancy shoes that would be outgrown and forgotten in a few months.

Sliding off the table, she searched the parking lot once more for Riley and found him with a small group—the supervisors, she assumed. Most of them were men, but there were two women, one gray haired and grandmotherly sweet, the other younger, slender and pretty. She was standing beside Riley, and his arm was resting on her shoulder—not around her shoulders, Liza thought consolingly, but simply on her right shoulder.

They looked like friends.

Good friends, judging from the way he was smiling down at her.

And probably more.

"Let's go," she said, steering T.J. toward the car. They had to pass the group to get there, and she steadfastly ignored them. She tried to ignore the dark, ugly tightness in her chest, but that was harder. She wasn't used to jealousy, and God knew she certainly didn't have the right to be jealous of any woman in Riley's life. *She* was the one who had left. *She* was the one who had married someone else. He deserved whatever happiness he found.

But it still hurt to see him with that woman, smiling at her, touching her, when he wouldn't even look at *her*.

In the car she started the engine and turned the air conditioner on, then wrinkled her nose. "You smell a wee bit strong, kiddo."

"I told you, that stuff's on my shoes. It's probably on my clothes, too. And it's all *his* fault," he said with a jerk in Riley's direction.

"What stuff are we talking about?"

"Horse—" He broke off, then substituted another word. "Manure. He made us clean out the stables."

Liza turned off the air conditioner and pressed the buttons that rolled down the windows. "How did it go?"

It was a long time before he answered. "He made fun of my clothes and my shoes, and he picked on me."

Remembering her momentary concern at the courthouse that Riley might take out his dislike of her on her son, she cautiously asked, "Made fun of you in what way?"

He repeated the conversation regarding his clothes, and she smiled faintly, more relieved than she cared to admit. "But he was right, wasn't he? You certainly weren't dressed for that kind of work."

"He doesn't like me, Mom. He's out to get me."

"And of course you did nothing to antagonize him, did you?" His guilty blush gave him away, and she sighed softly. "T.J., don't go looking for more trouble. You don't have to like Riley or anyone else involved in this program. But you do have to respect them. You have to respect their authority."

"He made me clean up after a bunch of dumb horses," he said, carefully enunciating each word.

"And were you the only one?"

He was reluctant to answer but finally did. "No. They all worked—even him. But he watched *me*. He got onto *me*."

Liza pulled into the driveway, then turned to look at him. "I want to make something clear, T.J. If you're not being treated the same as the other kids, naturally I want to know. But don't come complaining to me just because you don't like the work or because you have an attitude problem. Don't act as if Riley's the bad guy and you're the poor little innocent who's done nothing wrong. If you do, I'm going to have to meet with him to find out the whole story, and if I find out that you're not cooperating or you're being obnoxious with him, you're going to be in even more trouble than you already are. Do you understand?"

Instead of glumly replying as she expected, T.J. burst out angrily, "You're supposed to be on my side, not his! Just because that stupid cop used to be a friend of yours, you automatically assume that I'm the one who's misbehaving! And he doesn't even like you anymore! He went to talk to Trevor's dad and Jamal's mom, but he pretended like you weren't even there, because he didn't want to have to talk to you, even when you waited just to see him!"

He jumped out of the car, slammed the door and stomped off behind the house. There was a hammock there, tied between two eighty-foot pines. Liza knew that was where she would find him if she went looking.

But she didn't. She got out of the car and slowly climbed the six steps to the porch. There were two rockers there, gleaming and almost new, housewarming gifts from her parents when she'd moved back. She sat in one and drew her feet onto the seat, hugging her knees to her chest.

Had her loitering on the picnic table been so obvious, or had T.J. merely made a lucky guess? She *had* waited to see Riley, to find out if he would acknowledge her, even if for no other reason than to comment on T.J.'s first day. Heavens, even just a look would have been something.

But he hadn't given her even that, because T.J. was right: Riley didn't like her anymore. He would rather pretend she didn't exist than speak to her.

Maybe she should do them all a favor and stay away from the post. A brief explanation and an appeal to her sister's generous nature, and Gretchen would drop T.J. off for future work dates and pick him up. He could do his entire three hundred hours of service without Riley ever having to see Liza again, even accidentally. That would improve his frame of mind, and eventually maybe he could forget that T.J. was her son. Maybe he could learn to see him as just another child.

But could she do that? Could she stand knowing he was just a few miles away and never seeing him? Could she pass up such perfect opportunities four times every weekend?

Yes.

If it was best for T.J.

If it was best for Riley.

Even if it could never be best for her.

Riley was on his way to his truck early Sunday afternoon when Robbie called his name. Slowing his steps, he muttered a soft curse. He loved his sister dearly—she'd been his best friend for more years than he could recall—but he had hoped to escape today's family dinner without getting cornered by her. His parents and the rest of the kids, he could fool. He could pretend that nothing was on his mind, nothing had gone wrong in the past few weeks.

But Robbie... He had never been able to fool her. She had known he was involved with Liza when they'd had no more

than a few dates; she had figured out that he was in love
with Liza before he'd admitted it to himself. She had known,
too, how deeply losing her had hurt him. Those nights when
he had come home almost too drunk to stand, it had been
Robbie who had gotten him to bed. It had been Robbie who
had held his head when he'd been in the bathroom on his
knees, so sick that he'd wished he would die. It had been
Robbie who had assured him that he would survive, even if
he didn't want to.

Now it was Robbie crossing the yard, determined to talk
before she let him go.

"What's up?" he asked, turning to greet her with a smile
that he certainly didn't feel.

"Funny. I was going to ask you the same thing."

"There's nothing new with me," he lied. "All I do is
work."

"Sure," she said skeptically. "There's nothing new.
That's why you were so preoccupied all through dinner.
That's why you didn't hear half of what was said inside.
That's why you've been avoiding me. Because there's noth-
ing new."

He simply shrugged and said, "I've got to be at work by
two."

"You have plenty of time."

Her arms were folded, her stance aggressive, her expression determined. Riley knew the look. He had faced it often enough in the past, and he had always been defeated by
it. He leaned back against his truck, feeling the sun-warmed
metal through his shirt, and quietly surrendered. "I ran into
Liza Davis two weeks ago."

That was all it took—a mention of a fourteen-year-old
memory, a woman Robbie had never met—and his sister
knew exactly who he was talking about. "Is she living in
Augusta again?"

He delayed answering. "Again? How do you know she
had moved away?"

"I remember seeing in the paper that she and her . . . that they had moved to Texas. He had some hotshot job there, and they—they had a little boy."

"You knew that, and you never mentioned it."

She refused to feel guilty. "I remembered what you were like when she got married. I didn't think you needed to hear every little bit of news about her and her husband."

Liza having a baby. That was a major "little bit of news," Riley thought. But Robbie was right. Hearing about it back then would have damn near destroyed him.

"How did you happen to run into her?"

"I arrested her 'little boy' out on post. She came to the MP station to pick him up."

"Is she still pretty?"

Her image began to form almost instantly, but he blocked it by staring hard at the ground. "Yes."

"Is she still married?"

"No."

"Do you still . . . ? Is she still special?"

For a moment his breath caught in his chest; then he exhaled heavily. "I hate her, Robbie."

She laid her hand on his arm, the same way she had all those years ago when she'd shown him Liza's engagement announcement. "You've never really gotten over her, have you?" she asked sympathetically.

He gave her a sharp look. "Of course I have. For God's sake, it was fourteen years ago."

"And after fourteen years you hate her. Not dislike, not resent, not think of without fondness, but hate. Riley, to feel something that strong after so long . . ."

He shook off her hand. "I won't deny that I was in love with her back then, and I won't deny that it hurt like hell when she married Davis. But there's nothing left. I don't want to see her. I don't want to talk to her or touch her or spend time with her." Deep down inside he felt a twinge of guilt. Because deep down inside he feared that that was exactly what he *did* want? Scowling at the idea, he muttered, "I just want to forget I ever knew her."

"What about her son? What is he like?"

"He's a troublemaker, a bratty little punk." When his sister broke into a smile, Riley stopped and considered his words. *Punk.* Liza's father had called him that the one and only time they'd ever met. *My daughter's not going out with some punk like you.* At the time the word had amused him. The message—that he wasn't good enough, that Liza deserved better—hadn't.

He tried again. "He's an obnoxious, spoiled, rude, snotty kid. He's assigned to our community-service project on post. After spending two hours with him yesterday, I can tell you that one of us isn't going to last long."

"Were you hard on him?"

"No. I may not like him, but no one else is going to know that."

"Why don't you like him?"

With an exaggeratedly patient sigh, he repeated, "He's obnoxious, spoiled—"

"And he's the son that Liza had with another man."

He stood still for a moment, then pushed himself away from the truck, circled around to the driver's side and climbed inside. Robbie didn't budge from her spot at the end of the sidewalk. After starting the engine he looked at her, then spoke through the open window. "You're suggesting that I resent T.J. because Liza dumped me for his father, that I'm blaming him for what she did."

Robbie merely shrugged.

Was that possible? he wondered. That he didn't dislike the kid for himself but because of his parents?

No. He disliked T.J. because he was arrogant, hateful and loudmouthed. Because he had no respect for the law or for other people's property. Because he thought he was better than everyone else because his family had money and social standing. The fact that he was Liza and Keith Davis's son was immaterial.

"This time you're wrong, little sister," he remarked. "One has nothing to do with the other."

"I hope not." She took a step back. "Get to work. I'll see you around sometime."

With a wave he backed out of the narrow driveway and headed toward the post. When he arrived at the station, there were a dozen kids milling around. He spotted Jamal and Trevor right away, and by the time he had gotten their work assignment, T.J. had joined them. Quickly Riley searched the parking lot. When he realized with an unwelcome jolt that he was looking for Liza, he forced his attention back to the boys.

"We're going to do some landscaping along Chamberlain Avenue," he announced. He looked the three over, noticing with some satisfaction that today T.J. was dressed more like the other two in old jeans and worn sneakers. "Since it's so close, we'll walk from here. The tools and supplies have already been delivered."

They formed a ragged group—Trevor and Jamal in front, Riley a few steps behind and T.J. trailing along at the rear. Riley wished he would join the other boys, that he would make some effort to join in their conversation. These long hours working were going to get awfully lonely for him if he deliberately shut out his partners.

He slowed down until T.J. was, however reluctantly, at his side. "Did you get your shoes cleaned last night?"

"Yeah."

They walked a little farther in silence. What did you say to an eleven-year-old kid when your dislike for him was exceeded only by his dislike for you? Riley wondered. It wasn't easy, especially when the only questions on his mind—Why did your parents get divorced? Does your mother ever see your father? Does she go out with other men?—were totally inappropriate.

"What do you think of Augusta?" That seemed a safe enough, simple enough question.

T.J.'s frown turned dark. "It's a dumb town. I don't like it, and I want to go back to Dallas."

"Augusta's not so bad. At least you're close to your grandparents." Riley called to the others to wait, then they crossed the street together. Immediately Jamal and Trevor set off ahead again.

"I'd rather be close to my dad." T.J. gave Riley a sly, calculating look. "My dad lives in a great big house with a pool that has a waterfall. He's got a real good job—he's the youngest vice president his company ever had—and he makes a whole lot of money. He says I can come visit him whenever I want and he'll take me wherever I want to go. We used to go to Mexico a lot and to the Cowboys games and to this dude ranch. He says I can fly down to see him every month, even if it's just for a weekend."

Now the frown was on Riley's face instead of T.J.'s. "That's nice," he said, cloaking his hostility. And it was no more than he had expected from the great Keith Davis. He'd had everything he'd ever wanted from birth. He had succeeded at everything he'd ever tried—unlike Riley, who was good at being a son, a cop and a dog handler, but not much else.

But there was one thing Davis had tried and failed at. Marriage. Unless the failure had been Liza's, instead. After all, she had married him for his money. Would she ever have voluntarily chosen to give up the big house with its pool, the prestige and the trips, for an average little nothing-fancy house here in Augusta?

No. Which meant Davis must have been the one to initiate the divorce. Maybe he had tired of her greediness. Maybe he'd wanted a woman who cared about *him* and not about what he could give her.

Divorcing Liza. Now that was an odd thought. If *he* had been her husband, if *he* had lived with her and slept with her and fought and made up with her, he could guarantee that divorce would have been the last thing on his mind.

He gave the boys their instructions, and they set to work. Shrubs in two- and three-gallon containers had been set out earlier in the spots where each was to be planted. Trevor and T.J. got that job, while Jamal went to work planting flats of pansies at the base of a newly erected sign for the nearby hospital.

Today Riley did more supervising than working. The tasks were simple enough, although on occasion he had to take over a shovel where the ground was rocky. After an hour he switched the kids around, sending Trevor to plant flowers and bringing Jamal over to dig. He noticed T.J. giving him a less-than-friendly look at being kept on the shovel for two hours straight, but he didn't respond. He was hoping that, by pairing him up with each of the other boys, the kid would make some effort at friendship with them. So far, though, he had resisted their overtures, answering their questions in monosyllables or not at all, ending their attempts at conversation by pointedly turning away.

The supervisors were scheduled to meet later this evening to discuss their progress and their problems. No trouble with Jamal and Trevor, he would report, but T.J. is hostile, uncooperative and unfriendly. He would suggest that they assign him to someone else's group. Let him antagonize someone else's team.

T.J. would be happy to be away from him. Liza would probably be happy, too. She couldn't have been thrilled to learn that her son would be spending so much time with him. Jamal and Trevor wouldn't be sorry to see him go. They worked well together, and they would probably welcome someone more like them, someone who was more of a team player, to take T.J.'s place.

Placing the boy under someone else's supervision would be the best thing for all of them. It was common sense. Good management.

So why did it feel like quitting? Why did it feel like giving up?

No, he decided. He would report T.J.'s problems, but he wouldn't make any recommendations. He would give the kid a chance—a few weeks, maybe a month. Then if they had to transfer him, at least he would know it wasn't his fault. He would know he had tried.

Under the circumstances, that was the best he could do.

* * *

"I'm taking the kids out for pizza tomorrow afternoon. Can T.J. come?"

Liza was about to say yes to her sister's invitation when she remembered that T.J. had to work Saturday. She swallowed back her affirmative answer and shook her head instead. "We've already got plans."

"We'll be through in time for him to keep his golf date with Daddy and Mr. Davis," Gretchen cajoled. "And we're going to that place over by your house—you know, with the big mouse and the video games and everything? We would even let Aunt Liza come along, wouldn't we, Brittany?"

Her niece, four years old and beautiful, nodded vigorously, setting her long dark curls bouncing. "We like the mouse," she said in a soft, sweet voice.

"I'm sorry, Brittany, but T.J. can't come. Thanks, anyway, Gretchen."

Her sister set Brittany on the floor and shooed her off to play with her brothers and T.J. in the next room. She began stacking the dirty dishes from their dinner, and Liza stood to help, grateful to have gotten out of the invitation so easily.

Her relief was premature.

"I don't suppose T.J. is going to keep his golf date with Daddy tomorrow, either, is he?"

"No."

"Or go to their house after church Sunday for dinner?"

Liza busied herself with rinsing leftover nachos and hot dogs from the plates, handing each plate to her sister to load into the dishwasher. Finally she turned on the garbage disposal, watched it suck away the remains, then shut it off and looked at Gretchen. "No. Not for a long time."

"What's going on, Liza?"

She dried her hands, closed the kitchen door and faced her sister again. "Do you remember Riley Cooper?"

"Six foot something, long dark hair, eyes so brown they were black, and a body to die for?" Gretchen paused, then replied dryly, "He seems vaguely familiar. What about him?"

"He's in the Army now. He's an MP. He's..." She moistened her lips. "He's out at Fort Gordon."

"Oh."

That one tiny word made Liza feel uncomfortable. Fourteen years ago Gretchen had thought she was crazy to break up with Riley and marry Keith simply because it was what her parents had wanted. She had tried to change Liza's mind, had tried to dissuade her from letting her parents and Keith's turn her marriage into a business deal. After Liza had forced her to tell Riley on the phone that she didn't want to see him again, that she didn't want him bothering her again, Gretchen had refused to act as her maid of honor at the wedding. She wouldn't even have attended if their parents hadn't made her, and her first comment when Liza had told her that she was divorcing Keith had been succinct. *Good.*

"Does he still have a body to die for?"

Liza closed her eyes, briefly remembering the way he'd looked last Saturday in those worn jeans and that tight T-shirt. Then she looked at her sister and grinned wryly. "Would you believe me if I said I didn't notice?"

"You're divorced, sweetheart, not dead." Gretchen took a cheesecake from the refrigerator and set it on the table, then sat down while Liza gathered plates and silverware. "So... has he forgiven you?"

Handing her a knife, Liza slid into the seat beside her sister and watched as she cut two very narrow wedges from the cake. The action made her smile. Those two tiny pieces, she knew from experience, were just the start. Depending on how serious the conversation was—and this one threatened to be very serious—they could put away an entire cake before they resolved anything.

"You say that as if you expect him to hold a grudge," she commented, tasting the creamy cheesecake. Unlike desserts in her house, which came in boxes from grocery stores and bakeries, Gretchen's were always freshly baked. Liza had baked a lot herself when things were all right with Keith, when her only occupation was full-time wife and mother. Now she didn't have the time or, after a full's day work, the energy. Now store-bought desserts were good enough.

"Let's just say I would be surprised if he didn't. That boy might not have had much of anything else, but he had *pride.*" Gretchen sobered. "Besides, he was in love with you, and you just dumped him."

"He never said—"

"Oh, come on. Why else would he have let you treat him the way you did? And don't say sex, because, honey, he could have gotten just as good, just as easily, from some- one else. You sneaked around to see him, meeting him in town and lying to Mama and Daddy every time you were out with him. If he hadn't been in love with you, he would have gotten rid of you and found some woman who appreciated what she had in him."

"I don't want to get into that, okay? I know you think my marrying Keith was a mistake, and in the end you were right. I never should have done it, but I don't regret it, because at least I have T.J."

"You could have had children with Riley, too."

"Children, yes, but not *that* child."

Acceding to her on that point, Gretchen cut two more slices of cake. "So Riley Cooper is a military cop and is liv- ing in Augusta again. How did you find that out?"

Liza stared down at the table, her appetite momentarily forgotten as she remembered that Saturday night. The phone call had come at around twelve-thirty, awakening her from a peaceful sleep. That late, with T.J. away, she had panicked before she even found the phone in the darkness. As she'd listened to the desk sergeant, the panic had given way to nausea, shock and disbelief. Not her son. Not her *baby.*

"Liza?" Gretchen prompted.

Without looking at her sister, she recounted every- thing—the phone call, meeting Riley at the station, the interview with the investigator, the hearing downtown. When she finished, they sat quietly for a long time.

"Daddy's going to hit the ceiling when he finds out," Gretchen remarked softly. "And Mr. Davis . . . Lord, Liza, I'd hate to be in your shoes. Why didn't you tell them right away? Why didn't you ask for their help?"

"What kind of help could they have given?"

"Daddy knows just about everybody in town, and anyone he doesn't know, Mr. Davis does. They could have gotten T.J. off."

"I didn't want him to get off. I didn't want some lawyer or judge or politician pulling strings for him. I didn't want him to think that what he did was okay."

"No, I guess not." Gretchen cut the cake one more time. "You have to tell them, you know. T.J. can't keep turning down those Saturday golf games and Sunday dinners without some explanation."

"I know," Liza admitted woefully. "It wouldn't even be so bad if he had gotten caught by anyone in the world other than Riley. You know Daddy hasn't forgotten him—heavens, even Mr. Owensby remembered his name."

And she really wasn't sure which would upset Garrett Johnson more, she glumly admitted to herself.

The fact that T.J. had been arrested?

Or that it was Riley who had done it?

Chapter 4

Riley waited in front of the MP station, watching the parents picking up their kids. It was five o'clock on Saturday afternoon, the third Saturday T.J. had taken part in the program. Three of the four weeks Riley had decided to give him before turning him over to someone else were almost gone, and today had been no better—worse, in fact—than the previous weekends. T.J. had grumbled and whined. He had complained about every task Riley had given him, no matter how small, and he had alienated the other two boys—for good this time, Riley suspected—when he'd accused them of doing less than their share of the work.

Now he sat on the picnic table, tugging at the loose sole of one sneaker, waiting for his mother to pick him up. And that was why Riley was waiting, too. Next weekend was T.J.'s last chance—at least, with him, Jamal and Trevor—and Riley intended to make the most of it. He would appreciate any help Liza could give him.

At least, that was what he told himself. That was his official reason for waiting here when he could have gone home five minutes ago. But was he really so dedicated, so concerned about one obnoxious, smart-mouthed brat? he wondered cynically.

Or was he merely missing the brat's mother?

He hated to admit that that was a possibility. Two weeks ago he had told his sister that he didn't want to see Liza again, and he hadn't seen her since then, hadn't even caught a glimpse of her. Last weekend she had dropped T.J. off, then rushed away, and she had picked him up without getting out of her car. It had been the same when she dropped him off this afternoon.

And so he waited. This time he would see her. He would talk to her. He would look into her sweet brown eyes, listen to her soft Georgia voice, and he would—

He mouthed a silent curse. In spite of his earlier doubts, he must have a hell of a lot of dedication to put himself through this for a kid who hated the sight of him. And he would pay for it later, when she disturbed his sleep. When he was alone and she was all he could think about. When he found himself remembering the good things and, God help him, the good times they had shared.

Before he could change his mind and escape, her car pulled into the parking lot. T.J. stood up from the table and started toward it, stopping when Riley called his name. "Tell your mother I want to talk to her."

"Tell her yourself," he muttered, but a moment after he climbed into the car Liza shut off the engine and got out, looking at him over the roof of the car. Sunglasses hid her eyes, but Riley didn't need to see them to know that she was annoyed. It was in the narrow line of her mouth and the rigid set of her jaw.

He waited for her to approach him. He didn't want T.J. to overhear any part of their conversation. Aware of the other volunteers nearby, he greeted her quietly. "Mrs. Davis."

The hard edge to his voice brought her a few steps closer. "Formality?" she asked softly, removing her sunglasses. "If you expect me to call you Sergeant Cooper, you're going to be disappointed."

"I've had plenty of experience being disappointed by you." He saw her stiffen, saw her eyes cloud over, and felt a moment of guilt. Was this really why he'd wanted to see her—to accuse her? To insult her? To hurt her if he could?

Taking a deep breath, he went straight to the point. "I want to talk about T.J. He seems to have a real problem working for me."

"Interesting. *He* says you pick on him."

She said it calmly, coolly, and it annoyed the hell out of him. He stared at her for a moment, then curtly said, "This was a mistake. Just forget it. I'll talk to the major who's in charge and tell him to assign T.J. to someone else." He swung around to leave, but abruptly stopped when he felt her hand, small and warm, on his shoulder. For a moment he couldn't think, couldn't move. All he could do was remember the thousands of other times she had touched him, every one of them somehow intimate, whether they were alone on a moonlit beach or in the middle of a crowded, sun-bright park.

Then she withdrew her hand and pointed out, "I didn't say I believed him, Riley."

Slowly he turned to face her again. She looked so sweet standing there, so sweet and innocent when he knew damned well that she was neither. Once before she had fooled him completely. Had used him callously. For one agonizingly long moment, looking at her, he thought she could probably do it again if she got bored enough. If she didn't find someone more appealing to play her games with. If he was foolish enough to let her get close again.

Meeting her softness with his own hardness, he scowled at her. "Does he have trouble at school?"

She shook her head. "He makes good grades, has several close friends and gets satisfactory marks in conduct."

"What about at home?"

"I won't deny he's been angry since this happened. But most of the time nothing's changed." Pushing her hands into her pockets, she leaned against the low wall. "He resents coming here. He usually spends Saturday afternoons with his grandfathers and Sundays with my family. He can't do that anymore because of this.''

One of the lawyers from the staff judge advocate's office who was also volunteering passed by. Riley waited until he was gone before he asked his next question. It came out low, stiff, accusing. ''What did you tell T.J. about me?''

A blush warmed her face. It should have looked silly on a thirty-three-year-old woman, but Riley thought it made her look more appealing. Less distant. More touchable.

''Just that I knew you a long time ago,'' she said, her voice a bit unsteady. ''That we were friends.''

''Friends?'' he echoed sarcastically. Of all the things between them back then, friendship hadn't been one of them. Lust, desire and need—those were the things that had brought them together, had held them together. Those... and love. *His* love.

Liza ignored his sarcasm and thoughtfully considered the problem. ''Maybe that's part of it,'' she said softly.

Before she could go on, the woman she'd noticed that first day came up, linking her arm through Riley's. ''Is this a private conversation, or can anyone join in?''

She was smiling and sunny and even prettier close up than from a distance. Liza disliked her on sight.

''This is T.J.'s mother,'' Riley said.

T.J.'s mother. True though they were, those impersonal words hurt. Once he had called her sweetheart and honey, and when they had made love, he had always called her baby. Now he couldn't even bring himself to say her name. She was simply T.J.'s mother.

''I'm Colette Saunders. From social work.''

''Liza Davis.'' The woman didn't offer her hand—she would have had to let go of Riley to do so—so Liza kept hers in her pockets, where they slowly curled into tight fists.

''We were just talking about T.J.,'' Riley said.

He was awfully quick to assure the gorgeous blonde that this was strictly business, Liza thought with a frown. Was she the jealous type? It didn't matter if she was. Liza was jealous enough for both of them.

"T.J.... Oh, yeah. He's a good-looking kid. But he seems to have a lot of anger, especially toward Riley. That's not really so unusual—a lot of people who do something wrong resent the cop who catches them—but it does make these afternoon sessions unpleasant for everyone."

For the first time since the woman had joined them, Riley turned his attention back to Liza. She could feel his gaze on her, even though she couldn't meet it. "What were you saying when Colette came up? That part of the problem is...?"

"I don't remember." Of course she did, but she would be damned if she would stand there in front of this possessive little blonde and say she thought T.J. was, on his father's behalf, jealous of Riley. That since the divorce he had always resented any man Liza had seemed the least bit interested in. That he was determined to hate any man who might conceivably take his father's place in her life.

"You and T.J.'s father are divorced, aren't you?"

Slowly she looked at Colette. "Yes, we are."

"What does he have to say about his son's trouble?"

She sighed. She hadn't talked to Keith in nearly eight months, when she had told him that as soon as the lease was up on her apartment, she and T.J. were going home to Augusta. He had accused her of running out on him—again. He had always known, he had said, that she couldn't be counted on, that she was too selfish to care about anyone but herself. When he had started to blame her for his own situation, she had walked out. She hadn't seen or spoken to him since.

Aware that Colette and especially Riley were waiting for her answer, she cleared her throat. "Keith doesn't know. I—I thought it best not to tell him."

"T.J. is his son, Mrs. Davis. Don't you think he has a right to know that his son is in serious trouble?"

The patronizing tone of the social worker's voice irritated Liza. She wanted to answer sharply, without censoring herself, "T.J.'s father is a cocaine addict. He's thirty-eight years old but looks closer to fifty. He can't keep a job. His parents support him. He's sick all the time, either from using drugs or from trying not to use them. He can't deal with his own problems, much less his son's."

But she couldn't say that here.

Not like that.

Not in front of Riley.

"Trust me, Ms. Saunders," she said with exaggerated patience. "If there were any way that telling T.J.'s father would help, I would do it."

"T.J. talks about him quite a bit. According to Riley, he boasts about him—about his money, his house, his career and the things they do together." She paused. "Does he see him often?"

"No."

"Is that his father's choice... or yours?"

Liza stared down at the ground. "Right now it's by mutual agreement. I hope... I hope it changes soon."

The social worker's voice softened. "Does he have any contact with his father at all?"

"He talks to him on the phone every few weeks." The calls were placed from his grandparents' house. Alexander or his wife, Margaret, made the calls, talking to Keith first to find out if he was in any condition to speak to his son. When he wasn't, the Davises offered T.J. the standard excuse—your father can't talk today; he's not feeling well. And T.J. accepted it as he always had. He had never asked what was wrong with his father that he was sick so often.

Liza was hiding something, Riley thought, watching as she traced a random pattern on the ground with the toe of her shoe. Her actions were guilty—her sudden restlessness, her inability to meet their gazes, the stiffness in her body and the resentment in her voice. But why? What secrets was she keeping?

Was it her failure to hang on to the rich husband she had finally trapped that embarrassed her? Anger over Colette's implication that Keith could help T.J. in ways she couldn't? Or maybe discomfort discussing this in front of *him?* He certainly wasn't a disinterested observer.

"I'll give T.J. another week," he said quietly. "If he's not making more of an effort, then he'll have to be assigned to someone else." And that might create even more problems, he silently acknowledged. Even though T.J. was the source of the trouble, he could easily view reassignment as rejection, as evidence that he wasn't wanted.

Liza nodded solemnly, then walked away. Riley watched her go. Even when she was hidden inside the car, even as she drove out of the parking lot and out of sight, he still watched.

"She seems like a nice woman."

"Appearances can be deceiving." He gently pulled away from Colette and put a few feet of distance between them. "What are you doing still hanging around? I thought you had a date with your colonel tonight."

"I'd cancel it if you offered a better deal."

He gave her a disbelieving look. "You would dump a colonel for a lowly sergeant?"

"I would dump *anyone* for you." Giving him her most appealing smile, she came closer. "Come on, Riley, what do you say? It's been a long time."

It *had* been a long time. He had met her his first week at Fort Gordon. They'd gone out a few times, had gone to bed a few times more, and then she had gone back to the officer she was dating, and he... He'd gone back to being alone. He had spent nearly half his life alone, unable to have Liza because of Davis and unable to want any other woman because of Liza. She had never given him any peace.

And nothing had changed. Here he was with a truly beautiful woman offering him her time and her body and anything else he might want, and all he could think about was Liza.

"It's rude to break a date because someone better came along," he teased, but underlying the lightness was a layer of painful understanding. Hadn't Liza broken his heart because someone better—someone richer—had come along? "Go have a good time with your colonel."

"Sure I can't change your mind?"

"I'm sure."

"I won't stop trying."

He ignored her warning. "See you tomorrow, Colette."

He drove to the company, showered, then stretched out on the bed. It was only a few minutes after six, and a long, empty, boring evening stretched out before him. Ordinarily he didn't mind being bored, but these days that meant thinking about Liza. About the long Saturday evenings they had spent together at the movies, or dancing at one of Augusta's numerous clubs, or off someplace quiet, kissing, touching, arousing each other until they were both aching with unfulfilled need. She had been so innocent, and so eager to give up that innocence. She had wanted to know his body better than her own and had touched him everywhere with such gentleness, such pleasure.

He hoped Keith had appreciated all the lessons he had taught her.

Rolling onto his side, he took his wallet from the nightstand where he'd left it. There wasn't much in it—his military ID card, his Georgia and military driver's licenses, pictures of his nieces and nephews, two ten-dollar bills and one small, wrinkled piece of paper. Some men kept letters from old loves, and others saved photographs, but he had never had either of those. All he had from Liza was this paper, back-and-white proof of her betrayal.

"Mr. and Mrs. Garrett Johnson announce the engagement and upcoming marriage of their daughter Liza Renee to Thomas Keith Davis, son of Mr. and Mrs. Alexander Davis."

He rarely looked at the newspaper announcement, and he never read beyond that first line. But he kept it to make certain he never forgot.

To make certain that he never forgave?

He tucked the scrap of paper back into place, then lay down again. What would she do tonight? Spend a quiet evening at home with her son? Visit her sister, whom she'd always been close to, or her family? Maybe go out on a date?

That last thought made him stiffen uncomfortably, even though he knew there must be men in her life. She'd been divorced for two years. She was a young woman. A pretty woman. Not beautiful like Colette, who was blond, sexy and a little bit flashy, but serenely, elegantly pretty. She needed companionship and friendship and... He had to force himself to finish the sentence. And sex.

Sex. Sex with Liza had been incredible, even the first time, when there had been almost as much pain as pleasure, when he had kissed away her tears, when he had been too damned close to tears himself because he had hurt her. Sex had been his first clue that there was something more than lust between them. He had been with other women—not a lot, but enough to know that what they had shared was special, that it involved not merely their bodies but their hearts. Their souls.

At least, *his* heart. *His* soul.

He wished the relationship had ended differently. He wished she had never married Keith.

Failing that, he wished he had never met her.

Most of all, he wished he had never loved her.

At three-thirty Sunday afternoon Riley called a break and opened the small cooler he'd brought along. He would have preferred to give the kids water, especially in this heat, but the small bottles of fruit juice had been more convenient to pack. He tossed one each to Trevor and Jamal, who were sprawled under a tree, then carried the other two to T.J., sitting on a tree stump a few yards away.

T.J. looked at the bottle he offered, then shook his head. "I'm not thirsty."

"Drink it, anyway. It'll replace the fluid you're sweating out." After the kid took the juice, Riley lowered himself to the ground nearby and opened his own bottle, draining half of it in one gulp. "You've been awfully quiet today."

"Wasn't that what you wanted?"

"No, it wasn't. I wanted you to quit complaining all the time. I wanted you to at least make an effort to become friends with Trevor and Jamal. I wanted you to quit taking it out on us because you got in trouble.''

"They're already friends with each other," T.J. said listlessly. "They go to the same school. They know the same people."

"And you have the same interests—school, Nintendo, sports, music."

"My mom finally told my grandparents last night that I'd been arrested."

The announcement was totally unexpected, and it made Riley stiffen. If one of the other kids had said it, he wouldn't have thought twice about responding to it, about asking how it had gone. But he hadn't been lovers with any of the other kids' mothers. He hadn't been judged worthless and unfit by any of the other kids' grandfathers.

But T.J. didn't seem to expect or need a response. "Everybody met at my aunt Gretchen's house. They sent me upstairs with her kids. I wasn't supposed to be able to hear them yelling up there. Grandpa Davis said Mom was irresponsible, and my grandmother said I'd be better off living with Dad." He drank, then twisted the lid back in place and turned the bottle in his hands. "My other grandfather said that you were nothing but trouble, that you always had been and always would be."

"Your grandfather never did like me much," Riley said quietly. Apparently that hadn't changed. Even though fourteen years had passed, even though Garrett Johnson had won and Liza had dumped him for Keith, the old man still disapproved of him.

T.J. gave him a dry look. "My grandfather never liked you *at all,*" he said, the corners of his mouth starting to lift in a grin. Then, as if he had suddenly remembered who he was talking to, the grin died unfinished.

Too bad, Riley thought. For a moment there the kid had reminded him of Liza when she'd been nineteen and a little immature, loving and playful and mischievous as hell.

T.J. uncapped his bottle and drank again, then used the toe of his sneaker to dig at an exposed tree root. "They made my mom cry," he whispered.

The image of Liza in tears was one Riley recalled all too well. He'd made her cry twice—the night he had taken her virginity, and later when they had argued over some silly matter. He had cut the evening short and taken her back to the empty parking lot where she'd left her car. There, when she had removed the helmet he had always made her wear, he'd seen the tears on her cheeks. He had driven away without a word, but before he had gone more than a hundred feet, he'd gone back. He had held her close, comforting her, covering her face with kisses, and before either of them had realized it, they were making hurried, hungry love in the back seat of her car.

His face uncomfortably warm, he finished the last of his juice. He glanced at his watch and was about to announce an end to the break when T.J. spoke again.

"She wouldn't send me to live with my dad, would she?"

Riley got to his feet and brushed his jeans off while he considered the question. Liza voluntarily giving up custody of her only child? Even with everything negative he knew about her, with everything negative he felt for her, he couldn't imagine her doing that. That was unmotherly. It was unnatural. It was unthinkable. "Not unless you really wanted to go," he finally replied. "And not unless she was positive you'd be better off there than here."

"I like my dad," T.J. said quietly. After a long moment he added, "But I don't want to live with him." He finished his juice, tossed the bottle with the others next to the cooler, then joined Jamal and Trevor.

Things were definitely looking a little better, Riley thought as he joined them in their work. And they brightened even more an hour and a half later when he and the kids returned to the MP station and he saw Liza sitting alone on the picnic table. Some part of him, some foolishly tender and forgetful part, wanted to join her, just to let her know that T.J. was doing better. Just to see if *she* was doing better.

But he remained where he was, looking at her so hard that she seemed to feel it. She raised her head, her gaze locking with his. From this distance he couldn't see if her eyes were red from last night's tears. He couldn't see their soft, hazy brown tint...but he almost believed he could. He almost believed that he could touch her, that he could forget about trust and betrayal and loss, that he could erase fourteen years of loneliness, that she could heal fourteen years of pain. He almost believed....

Slowly her gaze shifted to his left. He felt its loss immediately, the same way he'd missed her hand on his shoulder yesterday. He knew she was watching someone approach, knew before the person reached his side that it was Colette. Yesterday he had paid no attention to the social worker's teasing promise that she wouldn't give up on him. Now he wished he had. He wished he had told her to forget their affair and him, to keep the colonel she was happy with and to forget about the sergeant who had never been happy with anyone.

Except Liza.

She looked at him again, and this time he thought he saw a hint of sadness on her face. Discomfort at seeing him with Colette. Acceptance of how drastically things had changed between them.

Then T.J. called her, and she slid to the ground and walked away. Even with Colette beside him, waiting to claim his attention, even with all the other parents and kids and volunteers nearby, he felt alone.

One more thing that had never changed, he thought bleakly.

Without Liza, he'd always felt so damned alone.

The past week had been a miserable one, Liza thought as she slipped off her heels. The Davises weren't speaking to her, her father wouldn't *stop* speaking to her, and she'd even gotten a barely coherent call from Keith, wanting to know why his parents were telling him to get better and come home so he could take control of their grandson. To top it all off, the computer system in her department at the hospital had undergone a complete upgrading, and she had been forced to give up her Saturday off to learn the new programs.

But now she was home, and in another minute she would be out of her work clothes. She would dress casually—but not *too* casually, she thought with an indulgent smile as she hung up her skirt, stepped out of her slip and stripped off her hose. When she had informed Riley this afternoon that she would be late picking T.J. up because of work, he had offered to drop him off. He was coming here. To her house. Where she could see him without all those other people around.

This was T.J.'s fourth weekend in the work-service program. What had Riley decided to do with him? she wondered as she removed a cotton skirt and the matching top from the closet. Would he continue working with him, or would he pass him along to someone else?

She hoped T.J. had been given another chance. He needed a strong male figure in his life, one who wouldn't pressure him to think and act a certain way, one who asked for nothing from him but hard work, common courtesy and respect.

And she needed Riley in her life, too. Seeing him every weekend, even just these brief glimpses, gave her something to look forward to. It made her remember better times. It made her believe that maybe she could find those good times again, maybe not with Riley, but with someone.

It gave her hope.

She went downstairs, noticing for the first time the flashing light on the answering machine on the hall table. She was hesitant to press the playback button, afraid she would hear her father's voice. Finally she pushed the button and waited, her hands on her hips.

Worse than her father, it was Keith's father on the tape. "I've got a call in to Judge Carmichael to see about getting

T.J.'s sentence dropped or at least reduced. Carmichael owes me a few favors, so there shouldn't be any problem. I'll let you know what I find out."

The machine beeped when the message was finished. She erased it, then dialed the Davises' number. By the time Alexander was on the line, Liza was shaking. She spoke carefully, each word distinct and clear. "Don't interfere with my son, Alexander. Do you understand?"

Her former father-in-law seemed not to hear her anger, but she knew better than that. He knew she was angry. He simply didn't care. "Liza, you're being ridiculous. What T.J. did wasn't so bad. It was just a little prank. The Army got their property back, and the boys are paying for the broken window. Where's the harm?"

"I mean it, Alexander. T.J. committed a crime, he was given a sentence, and he's going to serve it. He's going to work every minute of every hour, and he'll earn every penny of every dollar he owes them. If you interfere, if you ask one of your cronies to pull a few strings to get him off, I promise you I'll give you more grief than Keith ever dreamed of."

"Are you threatening me, Liza?" His jovial, patronizing tone had given way to steely anger. "Now you listen here, girl—"

Her hands trembling, she hung up the phone. Almost immediately it rang again. On the third ring the answering machine would pick it up. She didn't wait. She turned and walked out the door, settling in one of the rockers, safely out of earshot.

She was still shivering when a battered blue truck pulled into her driveway. Riley. The pleasure of seeing him made her forget for a moment the displeasure of that phone call.

T.J. jumped out of the truck. "Hey, Mom," he greeted her. "Can I go to Jody's before dinner?"

Leaving the chair to stand at the top of the steps, she nodded. "Come home when the streetlights come on."

"Thanks for the ride," he called to Riley as he raced across the yard.

Riley wasn't going to get out, she thought with a twinge of disappointment. He wasn't going to speak to her. He had dropped T.J. off, as he'd offered, and he was going to leave again.

But after a moment he shut off the engine and opened the door with a squeak. He came around the truck, across the yellowing grass and stopped at the bottom of the steps. He looked so handsome. So dear. Just like in her memories, only better.

She cleared her throat, but her voice still came out hoarse. "Thanks for bringing T.J. home."

He nodded. After a moment he pushed his hands into his hip pockets and looked away from her. She watched him survey the porch, the wide flower beds that kept her sane and the winding stone path she and T.J. had built this summer.

"I've decided to keep him," Riley said abruptly.

It took Liza a moment to understand what he meant. When she figured it out, she offered him a too-grateful smile. "Thank you. I know he probably would have been okay with one of the others, but..." But there was something special about knowing that T.J. was spending all those hours with Riley. There was something special about knowing Riley was willing to even consider spending all those hours with her son.

"Your phone's ringing."

She tilted her head to one side and heard the faint trill. "I'm out here avoiding it," she admitted. "The machine will pick it up."

"Problems?"

Slowly she sat on the top step. "Keith's father thinks he's going to ask Judge Carmichael, who's one of his old buddies, to clean up T.J.'s mess so that he doesn't have to finish out his community service."

Just as slowly as she had done, Riley took a seat on the bottom step. "He thinks?" he echoed. "Who's going to stop him?"

"I am."

He looked as if he might smile, and she waited expectantly, but he didn't. "When were you ever any good at saying no to anyone? Not with me. Not with your father." He paused. "Not with your husband."

Shifting uneasily, she returned to the subject. "I told Alexander not to interfere, then I hung up on him. That's why he's calling. *No one* hangs up on Alexander Davis."

"If you think he's going to listen to you, you're kidding yourself," he said bluntly. "He'll do whatever he wants, and you'd better not get in his way."

"Can he do that?" she asked uncertainly. "Can he go against my wishes on this?"

"He is—was—your father-in-law. You know better than I do what he can do."

"But you're a cop. You know the law."

He stood, his back to her for a moment. Then he faced her again, coming a little closer. "I know the law doesn't mean much when you have money, power and status on your side." He shrugged expressively. "But you're the kid's mother. Maybe that will count for something."

Liza got to her feet as he started toward his truck. "Riley?"

He stopped and waited.

"I was wondering. . . . Why did you join the Army?"

He went around the truck and opened the door. Resting his arm on it, he shrugged again. "Because of you, Liza." For the first time in years, he smiled at her, but it was sad and tinged with bitterness. "Because of you."

Riley went through the drive-through lane of the hamburger restaurant on post, picked up his order at the window and drove across the street to park in the exchange lot. He could have gone inside the restaurant and eaten more comfortably, but Jasper, standing in back with his head pressing against the wire mesh, wouldn't have liked that.

The dog watched, panting heavily, as Riley removed the food from the bag. When he took the time to spread out a napkin for his French fries, Jasper barked, a hollow-sounding demand for speed. Giving him a dry look, Riley unwrapped one of the hamburgers, tore it in pieces and passed them through the mesh.

The shepherd finished his burger in a few bites, then returned to the screen, watching greedily as Riley unwrapped and divided a second sandwich. This time he settled down and ate more slowly. Any food that wasn't on the kennel diet was a special treat for Jasper, and he knew two hamburgers were Riley's limit, so he savored the second.

Riley turned to his own dinner. It was Wednesday—hump day, the local radio stations called it. The middle of the week. It was a long time until Saturday.

Weekends had never been anything special—at least, not since he'd joined the Army. He had worked his share of them, had partied through more than his share. They had never carried any special significance. He had never anticipated them.

Until recently.

It wasn't just because he saw Liza then. He liked being with the kids. He'd gotten to know them pretty well in the past month. Trevor was a clown, always ready with a joke— usually a bad one—and always cheerful. Jamal was more serious, intent on doing well in school and living up to the high expectations his parents had for him. And T.J.—well, T.J. was trying. There were still times when he complained too much, when he preferred to work alone rather than share a job and a laugh with the others. But he was making an effort, and Trevor and Jamal seemed to recognize that. They were willing to give him another chance or two to fit in.

But, of course, seeing Liza for those few short minutes was the high point of the day. He had come to count on those glimpses to get him through the rest of the week without her.

And that worried him.

Traffic was light in the parking lot. It was nearly nine o'clock, closing time for the PX. Being a Wednesday, business at the Network Club, the noncommissioned officers' club on Nineteenth Street, would also be light. On weekends that was where he and Jasper spent a good deal of their shifts, breaking up fights, picking up drunks and dispersing unruly crowds. So far on this midweek shift he'd had only three traffic stops and one burglar-alarm call. The remaining hours weren't likely to be any more exciting. He would have plenty of time to think about Liza.

And to worry about himself.

You've never really gotten over her, have you? Robbie had asked that day at their parents' house, and he'd taken offense. Of course he had. It had been a long time ago. She had been his first love, and first loves weren't meant to last. He had stopped loving her the day he'd watched her walk out of the church in her wedding gown, her new husband at her side. Everything he had felt for her these long years was negative—anger, bitterness, resentment, hatred.

Or so he'd told himself.

Now he knew Robbie had been more accurate than he'd wanted to admit even to himself. He hadn't stopped loving Liza on her wedding day. He hadn't stopped caring about her that quickly, that easily.

In some ways he still cared.

He would never trust her again. He didn't like her values or her ideas of what was important—money and prestige—and what wasn't—love, commitment, caring. She wasn't the kind of woman he wanted to get involved with, the kind of woman he could imagine himself marrying and settling down with. There was still a part of him that would rather never see her again, that would like to face a future where, thirty years from now, hearing the name Liza wouldn't even stir a memory, much less make the muscles in his stomach clench and the bands around his heart tighten.

But the past had such a hold on him that, regardless of whether he wanted it, he *was* involved with her. And hearing her name not only made his muscles clench and his chest tighten, it set off a wave of longing so fierce that it hurt. He wanted to know once more how it felt to love a woman the way he had loved Liza. He wanted to trade the simple enjoyment of sex with women like Colette for the sweetly painful pleasure of making love with Liza.

He wanted to fill the empty place she had left in his life when she'd deserted him.

He could try other women, he thought, gathering the wrappers from their dinner. An instant later, though, he denied that option. He *had* tried other women. When he had completed basic training at Fort Jackson fourteen years ago, he had found plenty of willing, even eager, women, and he had used them carelessly, selfishly, in a desperate attempt to get Liza out of his system. It hadn't worked then, and it wouldn't work now. Hadn't Colette been trying long enough to get him back into bed? But even before Liza had put in an appearance, he'd had little desire for the blonde. Lately that had diminished to none. Zero. Zilch. And that was true of all the other women he came in contact with.

Except Liza.

Just thinking about her could make him hard. Looking at her created a bittersweet ache that wouldn't stop. Touching her, even though he hadn't done it in fourteen years, could make him plead.

So what could he do about it?

Quitting the volunteer program wasn't an option. That wouldn't be fair to the kids, and it wouldn't make a difference. He would still know that she was back in Augusta. He would still know that she was living in that little white house off Wrightsboro Road. He would still know that she was lovely and sweet and incredibly desirable.

Trying to ignore her or to keep his distance wasn't working, either. He was going quietly insane remembering her, thinking about her, hating her, distrusting her, but wanting her, God help him, more than he could bear. Wanting to be with her. Wanting to touch her. Wanting to love her.

That left only one choice, and he didn't want to even consider it. He didn't want to think about salvaging their old relationship or building a new one. He didn't want to study the risks of getting trapped in her spell again, of falling in love with her again. He didn't want to calculate the odds against surviving another affair with her. He didn't want to examine the depth of the pain and torment the nineteen-year-old girl had caused him or to determine how much more damage the thirty-three-year-old woman she had become could do.

He wanted to close his eyes to the risks, the odds, the distrust and the pain. If he was going to do this—to see her, to spend time with her, to start again with her—he had to do it blindly. That was the only way he could ever find the courage. That was the only way he could ever forget the betrayal.

"Gordon seven-zero, MP Control."

He heard the radio operator's voice, but he didn't move. He was too stiff, too clammy, too damned near paralyzed with fear at the prospect of starting over with Liza, to reach for the microphone.

"Gordon seven-zero, this is MP Control."

In back, Jasper stood, then gave a low bark. With a sickly smile for the dog, Riley picked up the microphone and gave his call sign, location and status. "This is Gordon seven-zero. Parking lot, main PX. Negative."

The radio operator came back with a call. "Gordon seven-zero, ten-one-five building 34501 at Brainard and Kilbourne. Open back door."

"Two-one," Riley replied, then replaced the microphone, started the engine and backed out of the space. A possible break-in at an office building, empty for the night. He and Jasper would have to go inside to clear the building. In the dark.

For ten years that had been his worst nightmare. Even as recently as six weeks ago, when he had caught T.J. and his friends, going into a dark, supposedly empty building where an intruder might or might not be hiding had been his biggest fear. But not anymore. One sweet, pretty, treacherous woman had changed that.

Finally, he thought bleakly, something *had* changed.

Chapter 5

Liza rocked lazily back and forth, listening to the evening sounds of the neighborhood. The teenager down the street had his stereo blasting again, but it was rock music, her favorite, so she didn't mind. Next door, her neighbor's dog was barking at everything that passed his way—an insect, a leaf, a shadow, the wind. From farther away came the sounds of a football game in progress. Occasionally she could make out T.J.'s voice and his friend Jody's. The other voices all sounded the same.

She let the rocker come to a slow stop and propped her feet on the railing. The occasional breeze this evening made her shiver, reminding her that fall had indeed arrived. Autumn in Georgia was her favorite time of the year, when the days were bright and sunny and comfortable, when the leaves began changing color before falling into crackly heaps that covered the yard, when the nights were cool enough for her to sleep with the windows open and listen to the birds' songs.

She had missed this season in Dallas. Not that they didn't have it there, too. The weather got cooler, the days grew shorter and the trees lost their leaves there, as well. But it just wasn't the same, not when the city went on for miles and miles, and not when the sweet, crisp, woodsy scent was all but lost in the haze of pollution.

Maybe she and T.J. could take a weekend trip to the Blue Ridge Mountains when the leaves were at their peak. It was one of her favorite places, but her son had never seen it. They could leave early some Saturday morning and come home...

Not while he was working every Saturday and Sunday. Of course, she could ask if he could miss one weekend—surely they would allow that—but it somehow didn't seem right to ask for time off from his punishment so he could go and play in the mountains.

Maybe next year, she thought with a sigh.

Tilting her head back, she closed her eyes. Considering how awful last weekend had been, the week hadn't gone too badly. After some harsh words from her mother, her father had stopped calling and nagging her every day. Alexander had agreed, ever so reluctantly, to trust her judgment in what was best for T.J. Everything had gone smoothly at work, with no headaches from the new computer system, the patients or her co-workers.

And tomorrow was Saturday.

The sound of a car door penetrated her thoughts, but she didn't open her eyes. She and T.J. rarely had company here. None of his grandparents had approved of this house when she had chosen it. They had wanted something a little closer to them, meaning something a little more suitable for the daughter and grandson of Garrett Johnson and Alexander Davis, but she had insisted that this place was fine. It wasn't far from her job, the middle school T.J. attended was a good one, and she could comfortably afford the rent on her own salary with no help from them. As a result, her mother and Gretchen were the only relatives who ever visited.

"Hey."

The quiet greeting made her eyes open wide, and bit by bit she raised her head. Standing there at the bottom of the

steps was the last person in the world she would have expected to find at her house. Unless it was business, of
course, something to do with T.J.'s case or with the work
program. For more reasons than one, she fervently hoped
that wasn't his reason for being here now, even though she
knew it must be.

He looked uncomfortable—shifting from side to side, his
gaze unsteady, his hands in his jacket pockets—and she felt
uncomfortable, because it was so obvious that he didn't
want to be here. He didn't want anything to do with her, and
she couldn't blame him. If she couldn't forgive herself for
the way she had treated him so long ago, how could she ever
expect him to forgive her?

"Would you like to sit down?" she offered.

He climbed the steps, but instead of brushing past her to
reach the other rocker, he leaned against the railing.
"Where's T.J.?"

"Playing ball down the street." Her smile was tight and
more than a little disappointed. "Do you need to see him?"

"No. This isn't about work."

Then what was it about? she wondered. It wasn't business, and, judging from his expression, it certainly wasn't
pleasure.

"Did you get things settled with his grandfather?"

She sighed softly. The Davises weren't her idea of a good
subject to discuss with Riley, but he could have picked some
that would have been a lot worse—such as why she had left
him the way she had, or her marriage to Keith, or, even
worse, their divorce. He could give her plenty of grief with
a few well-phrased questions about the divorce.

"For the time being," she replied. "I know Alexander
means well. T.J.'s probably the only grandchild he'll ever
have, and he wants to make everything easy for him. He
doesn't realize how that can harm a child."

"I take it your ex hasn't remarried." At her blank look,
he explained, "You said T.J. will probably be the only
grandchild."

She shifted uncomfortably. "I don't think Keith has time for marriage now. Definitely not for another child."

"Is that why T.J. never sees him?" Riley kept his attention focused on her face and not on her feet beside him. Definitely not on her long lovely legs close enough for him to touch. Long, lovely silken legs that more than once he had felt wrapped tightly around his hips, pulling him closer, deeper....

His expression became stonier, the set of his jaw more stubborn. Now wasn't the time to remember that. Maybe later, when he was alone, but not now. Not when she was sitting here staring off into the yard. Not when she was talking about her ex-husband, about the man whose money she had wanted far more than she'd ever wanted Riley.

"T.J. doesn't see Keith because we live a thousand miles away. Because Keith has...other things going on right now."

"More important things than his son?"

She didn't take any time to think about it, but answered quietly, simply, "Yes."

He wanted to ask her what things. What could possibly be more important to a man than his child? But he knew from the closed expression on her face that asking would accomplish nothing but adding more strain to this meeting. "Do you miss Dallas?" he asked instead.

"No." She smiled faintly. It made her lovelier than ever.

"Do you miss any of the places the Army's sent you?"

"No. Just some of the people there. And the dogs." He missed each of his dogs—Wolf and Rex and Ginny, who in a foul mood had been as likely to bite him as a suspect. Wolf had been the gentlest, Ginny the most vicious, but Jasper was his favorite.

"Where have you lived?"

"South Carolina, Alabama, New Jersey, Texas."

He noticed that the last piqued her interest. Maybe the irony amused her—that he had left Georgia to get away from her and wound up living in the same state as she had. It certainly didn't amuse him. His time there, shortly after his recovery from the shooting, had been difficult enough.

He wasn't sure he could have endured it if he'd known that she was living only a few hundred miles away.

"Where in Texas?"

"Lackland Air Force Base. Near San Antonio. That's where I went to dog handlers' school." He had considered putting in a request for the special school for several months, but getting shot had decided the issue for him. His courage had been shaken. If he was going to continue as an MP, he had needed a partner, one he could trust implicitly. He'd gotten that in his dogs.

"That's right—you work with dogs." Liza smiled again, this time the warm, bright smile that had never failed to touch him, to make him believe that everything would work out. It touched him this time, too. It hurt him.

"T.J. was impressed by how well your dog obeys commands," she went on. "He had a dog in Dallas, a gorgeous Irish setter that he tried forever to teach a few simple commands to—you know, sit, heel, that sort of thing. But he never had any luck with her."

"Does he still have her?" Dogs were one of his few areas of expertise. Maybe he could help the kid train his setter and build up a little more trust in the process. And if by chance it increased Liza's regard for him...

Her eyes became shadowy, and her pleasure disappeared. "No," she all but whispered. "Keith sold her right after T.J. and I moved out. We had an apartment, so we couldn't take her with us, and she was supposed to stay at the house so T.J. could see her when he visited, but...Keith got rid of her." Suddenly she looked at him. "T.J. thinks she ran away. He doesn't know...."

"What are you hiding, Liza?" She lowered her gaze to avoid him, so he crouched in front of her, where she had to look at him. "Every time Davis comes up in the conversation, you get evasive. What secrets are you keeping?"

Wouldn't it be nice, she thought wistfully, to tell him everything? To confide it all in a man who, because of his job, would understand better than anyone else what the past few years had been like? It would certainly lift a load from her shoulders. She didn't like keeping secrets, as he called it, and for three years she'd been keeping them from T.J. and everyone else except her family.

And the tale of Keith's fall from glory would certainly help Riley's self-esteem, if it needed a boost. He could have the pleasure of knowing just how wrong her parents had been, how terribly wrong *she* had been. He could know that the perfect life she was supposed to have had with Keith— the perfect life that no one, not even she herself, had believed Riley could ever give her—had never quite come together.

But something kept her quiet. Loyalty to Keith? Maybe. After all, he *was* her son's father. Family reputation? More likely. There were too many people, Riley probably included, who would like to dig up such dirt on the Davis family. And fair or not, Keith's problems reflected on his son and on her. T.J. had done nothing to deserve that. *She* didn't deserve that.

But most likely of all it was shame that stopped her from answering. She was ashamed that she couldn't understand Keith's weakness, that she couldn't forgive his deceit. The truth about T.J.'s dog was that Keith had sold her to get money to buy drugs. She'd been a purebred setter with a valuable pedigree, and he had gotten enough money for her to cover an expensive few days' supply of cocaine. That was just one of the many things Liza couldn't forgive.

And she was ashamed because her biggest concern at this moment wasn't Keith and his problems, or T.J. and how those problems might affect him. It was Riley. What would he think if he knew the truth? He was a cop, for heaven's sake. He arrested people like Keith. He sent them to jail. Would he want to spend time with her if he knew the truth? Would he want to spend time with T.J.?

"Correct me if I'm wrong," she began quietly, meeting his gaze, "but I don't think there's anything unusual about not wanting to discuss my ex-husband, especially with you."

He stood and leaned once more against the railing. Liza let her feet fall to the floor and set the rocker in motion. The rocking came to a sudden stop, though, with his next question.

"Why did he divorce you?"

Trying to ignore the tight little pain centered in her chest, she answered with an airiness she was far from feeling. "Thank you for automatically assuming that the divorce was his idea, that he had no further use for me."

"My assumption is based on the knowledge of the lengths to which you went to become Mrs. Keith Davis. I can't imagine you willingly giving up the money, the security and the prestige."

Maybe she *should* tell him everything, she thought, leaving the chair and walking to the end of the porch. Maybe she should show him just how wrong he was, how unfairly he had judged her.

But he had a right to believe that she was greedy and selfish. He was entitled to think the worst of her.

She touched the hummingbird feeder that hung from a hook above, and a drop of sticky red syrup fell on her finger. She hadn't seen any hummingbirds in almost a month. She should take the feeder down, clean it and put it away until spring. Maybe this weekend.

Then she turned and walked back to the center of the porch. She stopped directly in front of Riley, closer, she knew, than he wanted her to be. "You're right," she said flatly. "I didn't willingly give up anything. Keith found something better, something that he wanted far more than he'd ever wanted me. He took everything... but I got T.J. I got his only son. I got Alexander's only grandson."

She waited a moment to let the implications of that sink in—that as long as she had T.J., Alexander would see that she was more than comfortable—then she moved back. "Go away, Riley," she said, suddenly tired and achingly bleak. "Go away and leave me alone."

He didn't believe her.

Last night Liza had confirmed what Riley had suspected all along—that Davis had tired of her greed, that he had found another woman, one who cared for *him* and not his bank balance or his social standing, that the divorce had been his doing—but he didn't believe her.

Maybe it was the part she'd thrown in about T.J., talking about him as if he were simply a weapon to be used against his father or a means to ensure her own support. Her love for her son was one of the few things Riley was certain of. She had custody of him because she could never give him up. She could never live without him.

And as far as support went, judging from the house and the neighborhood where they lived, they couldn't be receiving much help from either Davis or his parents. He knew Liza too well. If she had any money, she would show it off. She would buy one of those expensive riverfront condos downtown. She would dress in something other than faded jeans and well-worn shorts. She would wear the jewels that had always held such fascination for her. She would flaunt her wealth for everyone to see.

She wouldn't settle for a simple little house in a simple little neighborhood.

What had really happened to her marriage? Had Davis been the one to end it? Had he thrown his wife and his son out of his house, out of his life? Or had it been Liza's decision to leave?

Had she ever come to love her husband, to care about him? Had she been hurt when she found out about the new woman in his life? Or had she simply accepted her failure and resigned herself to trying again? Was that why she had come back to Augusta—so her family could help her locate another gullible fool with more money than pride?

He wanted to believe that she had come back here because it was her home. Because her family lived here. Because T.J.'s father had more important things in his life than his son, and because his son needed grandparents, aunts, uncles and cousins to make up for his absent father.

But he also wanted to believe that she hadn't meant to be so cruel fourteen years ago. He wanted to believe that he had meant something to her, that she hadn't simply used him for her own selfish amusement. He wanted to believe that she was sorry she had hurt him.

And he couldn't believe any of it. All her actions then had been deliberate and calculated. Why should they be any different now?

"Why are you so grouchy today?"

He shifted his gaze a few feet to the right, where T.J. was standing. The boy's face was damp with sweat and streaked with dirt. They had a tough job today. The last of the Second-World-War-era buildings scheduled for demolition had been torn down, and his kids, along with several groups of teenagers, had been assigned to clean up the rubble. They had been working hard for nearly four hours. Soon it would be quitting time.

Soon he would see Liza again.

He wanted to scowl at the boy for making him think of her yet again, for making him think of her every time he saw T.J.'s dark eyes or his shy smile or his teasing grin. But it wasn't T.J.'s fault that he resembled his mother. It wasn't his fault that Riley couldn't get her out of his thoughts. It damn sure wasn't the boy's fault that those thoughts revolved around lust. Desire. Need.

"Who says I'm grouchy?" he asked, narrowing his eyes against the western sun so he could see more clearly.

"We took a poll. No one else was willing to get near you. You've been sitting over here looking like you're mad at the world."

He was frowning, Riley realized, and he forced the muscles in his face to relax. Years ago he had worn a permanent frown because it had kept the hurt under control. It had also kept people away from him; he had finished basic training as friendless as when he'd started. Over the years the pain had gradually faded into a curious numbness, returning at odd moments with a fierceness that had made him ache, then burying itself even deeper inside him.

"So you were the only one who wasn't afraid I'd bite his head off."

T.J. gave him a steady, solemn look that made Riley smile. In spite of the kid's parents, in spite of the attitude that still surfaced occasionally, Riley had finally discovered that he was a kid Riley could like. He was a decent kid with some problems: a broken family, a father who didn't have time for him, grandfathers who thought they ruled the world—at least, their small corner of it—and a mother whose love, loyalty and compassion could be measured in dollars and cents. A mother who...

A mother who loved him, Riley admitted. A mother who was trying to do her best for him. A mother who fought with her parents and in-laws to keep them from buying T.J.'s way out of trouble, to keep them from sending him the message that it was okay to screw up, to behave recklessly, to break the law, because he was a Davis.

"It's almost five," T.J. announced. "Can we take a break?"

"Sure. Tell the others, will you?"

T.J. did, then returned and sat beside Riley on a set of concrete steps that led nowhere. The building they had provided a stoop for was long gone.

"You like football?" Riley asked, gesturing to his Dallas Cowboys T-shirt.

"Yeah. My dad used to have season tickets, and we went to all the home games. But a couple of years ago he sort of lost interest, so we quit going." He studied the dirt on his hands, wiped them on his shirt, then quietly added, "He lost interest in a lot of things."

A couple of years ago. Keith and Liza had been divorced for two years. Was that about the time he'd met this other woman? Riley wondered. And what had happened with her? Liza had told him last night that Keith hadn't married again, that he didn't have time for another marriage now. Why not? What was going on in Davis's life that he had no time for relationships?

"You must miss him." Riley kept his voice even, showing no more and no less interest than he would if he were talking to any of the other kids in the program.

"Yeah."

"At least you get to see a lot of your grandfathers." As if that could make up for never seeing his father, he thought silently.

"Yeah. Before this happened—" T.J. gestured to the people around them "—I used to spend every Saturday afternoon with my grandfathers." His expression turned wry. "Playing golf at the National."

Golf. Of course that would be Alexander Davis's game, and Garrett Johnson's, too. And of course they played at the prestigious, exclusive Augusta National course. The closest *he'd* ever come to the National in twenty-two years of living here was driving past it on Washington Road. When he had been eleven years old, they never would have let him through the gate. He hadn't even lived in the same world as the people who'd had privileges there. As Liza's former father-in-law.

Her father.

Her son.

And he thought he actually stood a chance of getting back together with her, even for just a while?

Aware that T.J. was waiting for a response, he offered him a halfhearted smile. "So you like golf."

"I didn't say that. I said I played every Saturday."

"But you would rather be doing something else."

"*Anything* else—even this. But... well, Grandpa Davis used to play every weekend with my dad, before he and Mom moved away. And Grandpa Johnson never had a son to play with, so..." He finished with a shrug.

So he gave up his Saturday afternoons to please two old men who hadn't once considered *his* feelings. Riley was impressed. As the van pulled up to take them back to the station, he stood and rested his hand briefly on the boy's shoulder. "You're not as tough as you like to pretend, are you?" he asked softly.

Instead of being embarrassed or defensive, T.J. simply gave him a measuring look that was too wise for an eleven-year-old. "Neither are you," he replied, his voice equally soft. Then he grinned, becoming a child again, and raced off to join Trevor and Jamal at the van.

No, he wasn't, Riley admitted, following at a slower pace. Being a cop for so many years had taught him a good act, but maybe that was all it was. Because he wasn't tough when it came to troubled little boys, and he wasn't at all tough in dealing with their lovely mothers.

And he owed this one's lovely mother an apology. His questions and his attitude about her divorce had been out of line, although, under the circumstances, he thought he was entitled to at least a brief explanation of what had gone wrong between her and Davis.

And she had given it. Davis had found someone new, someone better, someone he wanted more. Riley knew the admission must have hurt her; he couldn't forget the bleakness in her eyes when she'd told him to go away. He knew what it was like to be dumped for someone else, to be compared to someone else and always found lacking. If Liza had broken off their affair because she had lost interest, because she simply didn't want to see him again, he would have been hurt, of course, but he could have dealt with it far more easily. But knowing that she had left him for someone else, for another man who could give her more than *he* ever could ... That had been unbearable.

He supposed the divorce must have been the same for Liza. If her marriage had simply failed, the way marriages so often did, she wouldn't have been hurt or embarrassed. But the marriage hadn't failed; she had. She hadn't measured up against Keith's new love. She hadn't been able to compete.

What kind of woman would a man choose over Liza? He couldn't imagine such a creature, and he had searched fourteen years for her. He had tried for fourteen years to forget Liza, to stop caring for her, to stop wanting her.

And for fourteen years he had failed.

She was waiting in her car when they reached the station. Riley intended to go over with T.J., apologize and ... Well, he wasn't sure what else. But before he'd gone more than a few feet, Colette called his name. "How's it going?"

He watched T.J. continue across the parking lot, then turned back to the social worker. "Okay."

"No problems with T.J.?"

"No."

"How about Jamal?"

"No problems with any of them." A quick glance showed that T.J. had reached the car and was opening the door.

"I don't suppose he's shown any interest in talking about his partners in crime."

"No. Jamal talks about the pressures his parents have put on him and the goals they've set for him, but he doesn't talk about his friends. He's not going to rat on them."

Colette shifted around in front of him. Now he could see her and, over her shoulder, Liza's car as it drove away. Disappointed, he settled his gaze on the blonde. "Is that all?"

"She's not your type, Riley."

He hid his annoyance behind a deliberately bland look. "Why do you say that?"

"Because you're like me. We come from the same background. We've both had to work like hell for whatever we got. You had to go into the Army just to get some job training, and I went into debt for ten years to pay for my education. We'll never have a lot, but we'll get by, and for people who grew up like we did, that's success." She gestured in the direction Liza had disappeared. "She's had everything given to her on a silver platter. She went to an expensive private school, went to college merely to find a husband, and, until her divorce, her only work was playing the perfect society wife."

She was guessing—Riley knew she didn't have access to that type of information about Liza—but she was damned accurate. Liza *had* gone to a private school, and she *had* begun seeing Davis in college. And it was a fair bet that she hadn't put her education to use until Davis had left her and she'd been forced to support herself and T.J. Until then her only occupation had been being Mrs. Keith Davis.

But Colette's description, in spite of its accuracy, left him feeling uneasy. It was unfair. There was no place in the picture she had painted for a loving mother. No place for sweetness, for innocence or fierceness or gentleness. No place for the girl he had once loved or for the woman who now haunted him.

"I've known Liza a long time," he said quietly.

Colette smiled, a sad and wistful kind of smile. "I've known men like her. Men who promised anything, took everything and gave back nothing. Men who felt it was their God-given right, because of who they were, to use a woman like me, because I wasn't important. I wasn't one of them, so I didn't matter."

He wanted to defend Liza, to insist that she wasn't like that. But she was exactly like that. She had sworn that she loved him, had made love with him. But when something better had come along in the form of Keith Davis, she had walked away from him without a moment's hesitation. Without a second thought. Without a single regret.

"She can hurt you, Riley."

"Not if I'm careful." Not if he remembered that she didn't deserve his trust. Not if he kept a tight rein on his emotions. Not if he prevented her from touching every part of his life.

Not if he refused to love her.

Sharing without trusting. Using without loving. Having sex instead of making love. He suppressed a wince of shame. That sounded suspiciously like the men Colette had just described, like Liza's selfish and self-centered male counterparts. Taking everything and giving nothing.

But that was exactly what he wanted to do, what he intended to do. To take anything, everything, she would give him and offer her nothing in return.

To leave her with nothing when it ended.

To walk away from her without regret.

This time, he thought with a bleakly silent prayer, he intended to survive her.

* * *

"Why are you taking me home?" T.J. asked as they climbed into Riley's truck early Sunday evening. "Mom doesn't do anything important on Sundays. She could have come after me."

"I want to talk to your mother." And after yesterday's conversation with Colette, Riley preferred to do it away from the post.

"I didn't do anything wrong," T.J. said with a sudden frown.

Riley gave him a long look. "Did I say it was about you?"

For a moment the boy looked surprised, as if he couldn't imagine the two of them having anything to discuss that didn't include him. Then his frown returned. "Do you like my mom?"

Riley pretended to concentrate on the traffic ahead of him. "She's nice enough."

"I mean do you *like* her? You know..." He paused, but not long enough for an answer. "Because if you do, you might as well forget it. She said after we moved out of my dad's house that she was never getting married again. And besides, if she did want to get married again, she would probably go back to my dad. She didn't want to get divorced, and she would go back if he asked."

He could tell the kid that marriage to Liza was the last thing in the world he wanted, although time with her, and definitely sex with her, ranked pretty high on his list. But that was no one's business but his own—certainly not an eleven-year-old's—and so all he said was, "I want to talk to her, T.J. Nothing else."

Satisfied, the boy fell silent. Riley wondered as he drove how much of what T.J. had said was true. Had marriage to Keith soured Liza on marriage in general? Or would she return to Dallas and her ex-husband if he asked her to? What would it cost Davis to get her back? Would she be so happy to resume her position as his wife that she wouldn't ask for anything? Or would she make him pay for choosing someone else, even temporarily, over her?

When they reached the house, there was no sign of Liza, although her car was parked in the driveway. Her expensive, two-year-old car. Davis hadn't taken everything, he thought cynically as he followed T.J. to the porch. He'd left her with a car that cost more than Riley made in two years.

The front door was open, the screen unlatched. T.J. hurried inside, leaving Riley to catch the screen door. "Mom, I'm home!" he shouted before making a beeline for the kitchen at the end of the hall.

"No kidding" came the dry response from the room on the left.

Riley let the door close, then stepped into the broad entryway. Liza was rising from the sofa, a polite but wary smile fixed in place. She was wearing an emerald green dress with a low V neck, her hair was sleekly, chicly styled, and around her neck was a heavy diamond pendant. She looked lovely. Elegant. Untouchable. Had she dressed this way deliberately, to remind him of the differences between them, of the distance that should remain between them?

He didn't think so. If she had wanted to remind him to keep his distance, she never would have chosen that pendant. He hadn't seen it in years, but he had never forgotten it. He had never forgotten making love to her while she was wearing nothing but that diamond. He had never forgotten the sight of that stone nestled between her breasts or the feel of it pressing against his skin when he'd covered her body with his. He had never forgotten how it felt to want her, to have her, to bury himself deep inside her. No matter how hard he tried, God help him, he would never forget.

And he would never forgive, either.

"I'm going down to Jody's," T.J. yelled as he passed through the hall.

"Be back by six-thirty," Liza replied as the screen door slammed. She stiffened at the sound, then quiet returned to the house. Disquiet, because now Riley was here.

She wondered why he had come. Did he want to nag her for more information about her marriage? Did he want to

hear again how Keith had stopped caring about her and
T.J.? Did he want—

"I'm sorry."

She stared at him, at the dark, angry look in his eyes.
Angry eyes, so at odds with the words he'd just spoken. The
first time she'd met him, in spite of his wild reputation, she
had known she would be safe with him because he'd had the
gentlest eyes. And she had been safe. He had treated her
better than she'd ever deserved. But she had repaid his
kindness with cruelty, his gentleness with deceit, and he was
never going to forgive her for it.

Deep down inside she wanted to run away and cry—for
Riley, for herself, for what they had lost and could never get
back. But instead of fleeing she cleared her throat and
moved a little closer. "Sorry for what?"

"Friday night."

She couldn't deny that his brief visit had left her hurting,
but she didn't want to hear an apology, not when she'd done
so much worse to him and hadn't found the courage to even
try to apologize. "It's all right," she said uncomfortably.
After a moment she returned to the sofa and offered a silent invitation to Riley. He hesitated, then sat in the nearest
chair.

"Do you still love him?" he asked, then cynically re-
phrased his question. "Did you ever love him?"

Tilting her head back, she gazed at the ceiling for a moment, then directed a wry smile his way. "Don't you have
any easy questions?"

He didn't smile back. He didn't yield at all. He just sat
there, his expression stony and hostile, his eyes dark and
unforgiving. Maybe there were some questions he had to
have answers to before they could go on to anything else,
Liza thought, resigning herself to an uncomfortable few
minutes. He was entitled to those answers. After all, he was
the man she had promised to love forever only days before
she had married Keith.

"I cared a great deal about Keith," she said slowly. "I
guess in a way I did love him." In the way that she loved her

friends or her cousins, she silently clarified. Not in the way she had loved Riley. She had never loved anyone the way she had loved Riley.

"What's the old saying? It's as easy to fall in love with a rich man as it is with a poor one?"

She smiled again, sadly this time. "No," she disagreed in a whisper. "It isn't."

"But you managed."

Nothing she could say would change his mind, so she said just that. Nothing.

After a moment Riley spoke again, this time without cynicism or sarcasm, without accusations. "Would you go back to him if he asked?"

"No."

She wasn't sure which had surprised him most, her answer or the speed with which she'd given it, but he looked skeptical. "No? You wouldn't give up your job and this little house and go back to being Mrs. Davis again?"

"No," she repeated. Go back to that nightmarish life? To studying Keith's every move, searching for some sign that he was using drugs again? To accounting for every penny he spent, hiding her purse from him so he couldn't take her money or her checkbook or her car keys and disappear? To visiting him, sick and shaky and vulnerable as hell, in the rehab center? To dreading every ring of the phone when he was gone, fearing that it would be Keith to say that he had been arrested again, or, worse, the police reporting that he'd been found dead from an overdose or had become one more victim of the violence surrounding the drug trade? "I'd rather live in hell," she murmured. Hell had to be an improvement over that kind of life.

When she looked at him she saw that he was uncomfortable and embarrassed. Getting to his feet, he mumbled another apology and something about leaving, about not coming back. She stood, too, and moved quickly, catching him at the door, reaching out but not touching him. "Please don't go, Riley," she said in a rush. "I know this isn't easy, but please . . ."

He looked down at her then. The anger was gone from his eyes, replaced by a mix of emotions too complicated to sort through. "I didn't come here to question you." His voice was harsh and cold, the anger directed more toward himself, she suspected, than her.

"You have a lot of questions." Including the big ones. Like why. Why had she ended their affair so cruelly? Why hadn't she told him herself that she didn't want to see him, instead of making Gretchen do it? Why hadn't she told him herself that she was marrying Keith instead of letting him find out some other way? Why had she treated him so badly?

"It was a long time ago."

She smiled tautly. "Not long enough."

"Sometimes I hate you."

Such soft-spoken words to create such pain. She shuddered inside with it, but outwardly she merely smiled again. "I don't blame you. But please, Riley, don't go. We can talk...." But not about the past. She couldn't remember the times they'd spent together, the times they'd made love, the laughter and the tenderness and the joy, when he had just told her that he hated her.

Riley stared through the screen at the empty yard. She was so close that he could feel her heat. He could smell her fragrance. He remembered exactly where the scent was strongest—behind each ear, between her breasts, on the pulse that throbbed in each wrist. She was so close that if he took two steps, maybe three, he would be against her, their bodies intimately touching. He would get hard, and she would know....

He muttered a silent curse. He didn't want to hurt her, but that was exactly what he'd done Friday night and again this evening. He didn't want to do it again, but he seemed unable to control himself around her. Each time he looked at her he remembered how deeply he had loved her and how desperately he had missed her. He had so many questions, so much anger, such deep resentment . . . and such relentless desire.

If he had any decency, he would leave now and never come back. He would forget about seeing her. About wanting her. About needing her. He would forget her and go on with his life.

But forgetting wasn't that easy. If it were, he would have done it years ago. He would have found someone else to love, and he would be raising a houseful of his own kids instead of playing on weekends with other people's. No, he was afraid that the only way to forget her was to die, and he wasn't that desperate.

Not yet, at least.

"Riley?"

She touched him, just his arm, and he sucked in his breath. There was no justice in the world when a beautiful woman like Colette couldn't arouse even the slightest bit of desire in him, while the simplest touch from Liza could bring him to his knees. No justice at all.

He took a couple of steps back so that her hand fell away, then gave her an unsteady look. "You have to do me one favor," he said, his voice equally unsteady.

"What?"

"Take that diamond off. This isn't the time to be remembering. . . ."

Blushing, she wrapped her fingers around the stone, hiding it from sight. "Go on in and sit down," she invited, a hint of a plea in her voice. "I'll be right back."

He watched her climb the stairs, then disappear down the hall. Now was his chance to leave, to escape relatively intact. But when he moved, he didn't head out the door. Instead he returned to the living room. He sat down, this time on the sofa.

Maybe he had no decency.

Maybe he would hurt her again.

Maybe *she* would hurt *him* again.

But he was going to spend at least the next few minutes of this cool Sunday evening with the woman who had made the past fourteen years of his life sheer hell. The woman who had made the few months before that pure heaven.

The woman, he thought bleakly, who could make the next few months go either way.

Chapter 6

When she came back downstairs a few minutes later the dress had been traded for jeans and a sweatshirt, the sleek hairstyle pulled back into a ponytail. Her heels were gone, her feet were bare and there was no sign of that damned pendant. She looked warmer now. Much more approachable. Much more touchable.

Too touchable.

He wished he had left while she was upstairs. He wished he had never come. He wished—God, how he wished—he could forget everything bad and remember only the good. Relive the good.

"Is T.J. behaving better?" she asked as she settled in the chair where he had sat earlier.

He watched her draw her feet into the chair, tucking them beneath her. In those clothes, with her hair up like that, she looked ten years younger—no, fourteen years younger, he amended. She looked like the Liza he had known so well...and not known at all. She looked like the girl he had loved. The girl he had lost.

Mentally he warned himself to pay attention to the conversation. Talk he could handle. Memories he couldn't. "He's okay. He's getting along better with the other kids, and he doesn't complain nearly as much."

"You have a lot of kids in trouble out there, don't you?"

She sounded concerned, not just for her son, but for all the children she didn't know, too. As he answered, Riley wondered if the concern was genuine. "There are about twenty-five kids on community service right now. Except for T.J. and one other, they're all military dependents. For the most part they're not any worse than civilian kids you see in town. They have the same stresses and pressures, plus a few added ones—frequent moves, deployments, family separations. Money's tight in most families, especially the enlisted ones. Some career soldiers, those who are real gung ho, have unreasonable expectations of their kids. We also have a lot of single parents in the Army, so a lot of kids are left pretty much on their own."

She was smiling faintly when he finished. Unsure of what she found amusing—certainly nothing he'd said—he asked uneasily, "Why are you smiling?"

"You sound so... authoritative. So serious. Not like the Riley I used to know."

He didn't tell her that he was, without a doubt, the same man she'd known back then, the same man she had betrayed. He had simply grown up, very quickly and very harshly, in the space of less than two weeks. He didn't say anything at all.

"Why did you become a cop?"

There was no easy answer to that. He had been smart enough, his entrance test scores high enough, that he could have chosen any number of specialties. But police work had appealed to him, maybe because it was difficult to find a job as a tank driver, a missile crew member or an artilleryman in the civilian world, while jobs in law enforcement were plentiful. Also, at the time, he had never intended to make the Army a career. All he'd been looking for was an escape from Augusta, from Liza and her new husband.

"It seemed interesting," he finally said. "It was training that could help me in the civilian market when my enlistment was up."

"But you reenlisted."

He shrugged. Four years hadn't been enough time away. He had learned that on a visit home to his family. Returning to Augusta would have been too painful, and he hadn't been willing to try someplace new on his own, so he had stayed in the Army. He had stuck with the routine, the people and the life-style he'd become familiar with, and before he'd realized it, he had been well on his way to twenty years of service.

"So you've been in..." She paused, apparently not certain when he had left town. Of course not. She'd been too busy playing the newlywed to care what had happened to him.

"Fourteen years." He deliberately added, "I joined up two days after you got married."

Her cheeks turned pink, and she quickly looked away from him. A blush on a thirty-three-year-old woman could be charming, but this one wasn't. There was pain behind this one—pain, guilt and shame. She *should* feel guilty and ashamed, he thought, hardening his defenses against her.

"Riley..."

He silenced her with a quick look as footsteps crossed the porch. A moment later the screen door banged and T.J. came into the room, stopping beside his mother. Although he must have seen Riley's truck in the driveway, the boy looked surprised to find him sitting there. "Why are you still here?"

Liza gave his arm a warning tug. "You know how to speak to a guest in our home, T.J."

"I just didn't expect him to still be here. It's been a long time. Is he staying for supper?"

She released her son's arm and looked at Riley. He saw the invitation in her eyes before she offered it. "Would you like to join us? We're just having pasta salad and ham. Nothing fancy, but it beats fast food."

"No, thanks." Talking to Liza was one thing. Sitting down to eat supper with her and her son was another, one he wasn't ready for. Feeling T.J.'s gaze on him, he stood up from the sofa before looking at the boy.

The kid had made it clear earlier that the only man he wanted in his mother's life was his father. Now he was judging Riley, trying to determine if he presented any sort of a threat. Apparently not, he decided, because abruptly he shrugged. "You can stay. Mom's a pretty good cook."

Riley almost smiled. Even her eleven-year-old kid didn't consider him worth worrying about. Even T.J. knew that he wasn't the type of man his mother would choose. How many times did he have to learn that lesson? How many times did he have to come face-to-face with the fact that he could never be what Liza wanted before the message sank in?

"Thanks," he said, hearing the stiffness in his voice and knowing the others were also aware of it. "But I've got to be going."

Liza followed him to the door, then out onto the porch. She waited until he was at the bottom of the steps to speak. "Good night, Riley," she said softly.

Good night. Not goodbye.

Maybe he would never learn, he thought as he backed out of her driveway. Maybe he'd spent too many years wanting her too badly to accept that he could never have her. Maybe he would just have to get hurt all over again.

But as long as she let him come around, as long as she said things like, *Please, Riley, don't go,* as long as she said goodnight and not goodbye . . .

He would be here.

It was a warm Saturday afternoon, and Liza was doing her favorite chore of the entire week—working in the yard. She had dropped T.J. off at the MP station, then come home and changed into a ragged pair of sweatpants and a T-shirt. She had carelessly put her hair up in a ponytail, and now she was kneeling beside a bed of fading periwinkles. She loved yard work, tending the flowers, mulching the beds, mowing the grass. Even weeding held its own pleasure.

This was something she hadn't been allowed to do in Dallas. In their neighborhood of big houses and bigger lawns, everyone had used yard services, and Keith had refused to be different. *His* wife wasn't going to put on grungy clothes and go outside and work like the hired help. Rather than argue the point, Liza had satisfied her gardening urges by filling the house with plants and flowers and even, in a sunny corner of the kitchen, tomatoes and herbs.

Now she had her own yard, and nobody to tell her that she couldn't work in it.

She was bent over, gently tapping seeds from the open pods on the periwinkles into a plastic butter dish, when she first heard the motorcycle. She smiled faintly, thinking of Riley.

She had loved his motorcycle. She had felt free, wild and reckless, although Riley had never been a wild or reckless driver. He had always insisted that she wear a helmet, and he'd driven so cautiously that even her father couldn't have complained. Still, she had fond memories of that machine, of the places it had taken them.

As the engine revved behind her, she emptied another half-dozen seeds into the cup, then slowly set it down on the pine bark and turned around. Just as slowly she smiled.

In those few seconds she could have turned back the clock fourteen years. It was a different cycle, sleeker, although still midnight black. The helmet was different, too, newer and less battered, but also black. But the jacket was the same: scuffed, worn leather. The jeans, faded and fraying, the heavy black boots, even the way he sat, bracing the bike between his thighs...

He cut off the engine and slowly removed his helmet. For an instant she expected to see thick, black hair tumble into place over his collar. He'd always had such beautiful hair, long, shaggy and soft. But she wasn't disappointed that it was gone. He was even more handsome with the Army short trim.

"What are you doing?" he asked, balancing the helmet on the cycle's tank.

"Gathering seeds."

"Isn't it easier to just buy new plants next spring?"

"Yes. But these plants came from seeds my mother gave me. She got them from plants grown from seeds by my grandmother. It's tradition." She stood, automatically brushing off her knees, then pushed a strand of loose hair back. Since leaving Dallas, she had delighted in wearing grungy gardening clothes, but today she wished she looked a little neater. A little cleaner. A little prettier. A little more appealing to the man she found so damned appealing.

"Why aren't you working?" she asked.

"I've had the last few weekends off from my regular job because of the work-service program, but tonight I have to work the midnight shift, so someone's filling in for me with the kids."

She moved a few steps closer. "Do you usually work weekends when you're not volunteering with the kids?"

"We rotate. Saturday nights are always busy, so we try to have three or four canine units working then. Tonight they need Jasper."

"Jasper? Odd name for a dog."

He almost smiled. She would have sworn it. "Don't make fun of my dog. He's my best friend."

"Lucky dog," she murmured beneath her breath.

They remained silent for a moment, each watching the other. Liza could think of dozens of things to say . . . if she could only find the courage. Like how happy she was to see him. How glad she was that they had met again. How sorry she was for the way she'd treated him. How much she had missed him over the years, even when she had refused to think of him, even when she had deliberately shut him out of her mind for months at a time because that was the only way she could make her life with Keith bearable.

It was Riley who broke the silence. "Want to go for a ride?"

Her smile came slowly, but it filled her entire face. She could feel it. A ride. With Riley. On his cycle. She couldn't think of a single thing in the world she would like better. "Okay. Let me get my keys."

"Get a jacket, too," he called as she climbed the steps.

Her keys were on the hall table, but she didn't stop there. She went to her room and quickly changed into jeans and a clean shirt. After grabbing a jacket from the downstairs closet and her keys, she locked the door and hurried down the steps.

She slowed, though, as she approached him. Riding the cycle meant sitting close to him. It meant holding on to him—not that she objected, of course, but maybe *he* would. Maybe he hadn't realized . . .

Of course he had, she chided herself. He'd given plenty of women rides on his bike. He knew what he was getting into.

Riley unstrapped the extra helmet from the back and offered it to her. The first time they had gone through this ritual, he remembered, she had complained that the helmet was too tight, that it would muss her hair, that it muffled the sounds and made talking difficult. They weren't going to be talking much at fifty-five miles an hour, anyway, he'd told her, and she had to wear it if she wanted to go with him. She had meekly put it on and had never complained about it again.

He watched as she pulled it on now, fastening the strap beneath her chin, then lowering the transparent face shield. On bright days like this he preferred the tinted shield—for protection from the sun, he had always insisted. Because, like dark glasses, it gave him an aura of mystery, Liza had always disagreed.

He put on his own helmet, then started the engine and waited for her to climb on. She was a little hesitant to touch him, though no more hesitant than he was to be touched, but after a moment she braced her hand on his shoulder, swung her leg over and settled into place on the rear portion of the seat.

When he had left the company half an hour ago, he'd had no real plans, just a vague desire to see Liza and an even vaguer desire to stir up some memories. What better way to do both than by taking her for a ride? he had decided on the way over.

And what better place to do both, he thought when he realized where he was heading, than the place where they had spent their last evening together?

He hadn't traveled this road in fourteen years, and things had changed. It took longer to leave the city behind. What had been two lanes then was five now. Trees had been chopped down and fields paved over for housing subdivisions. But with each mile the countryside looked more the way he remembered. When they crossed the dam on the Savannah River, everything was familiar—the lake spreading off to the left, the river on the right, the bright afternoon, the coolness of the wind offset by the warmth of the sun, and Liza. Liza behind him, her arms around his waist, her hands clasped loosely over his belt buckle. *That* felt so damned familiar.

He turned onto a narrow side road, slowing to only a few miles an hour to negotiate the downhill curves. The angle forced her forward until they were as close as two people could possibly get. He knew it had to be uncomfortable for her, but she didn't make any sudden movements that might upset their balance. She waited until he had parked beside an empty picnic table, then she released him, slid back and climbed off.

Leaving the helmets on the table, they both looked around. This was the right place—there was no way he would ever forget it—but little looked the same. What had been a boat ramp then was now a sandy beach. Where the land had once sloped down to the water's edge, gently in some places, in jagged, erosion-carved fingers in others, now there was a retaining wall on all sides. Bathrooms and tables had been added. Except for the small beach, railings made access to the water difficult.

They hadn't had any problems reaching the water when they'd come here before. He had parked his motorcycle beneath one of these trees and jumped the few feet to the beach below. He had always lifted Liza down, usually setting her down beside him, sometimes sinking to the sand with her, unable to wait any longer. A few times they had made love right there, wearing more clothes than they had managed to discard. Other times, like the first—and the last—they had chosen a sandy spot a few hundred yards away along the curve of the small cove. There they had made love in the shadows of a downed tree that had hidden them safely from sight.

He glanced across the cove. The water level was higher now than it had been that year, but in about the right spot a weathered old branch extended above the surface. He smiled grimly. Their tree was underwater.

Liza walked to the railing, leaned back against it and watched him. He remained where he was, leaning against the picnic table, his hands braced on the rough concrete, his ankles crossed, and looked back.

"I never meant to hurt you, Riley."

He analyzed the words with a sense of detachment. An apology. Had he ever wanted that from her? Had he ever wanted to hear her say that she hadn't deliberately set out to hurt him? *Yes.* He had wanted that and more, but not now. Not this afternoon. Not here. "I didn't know Davises were capable of making apologies."

What he had intended as a mild comment, a simple statement of fact, had come out with sharp edges and accusing undertones that made her flinch just a little before she answered. "I'm not a Davis, not by birth."

"No, you became one by choice."

She shook her head, and her hair, its thick strands slipping free from the restraining band, shimmered in the sunlight. "It wasn't my choice," she murmured. "I *am* sorry, Riley."

The first remark intrigued him, and so, perversely, he ignored it, focusing instead on the second. "What am I sup-

posed to say? It's all right? I understand? I forgive you?"
With a gesture of disgust he turned away. "'I'm sorry' can't
make up for what you did. It can't make everything all
right." It certainly couldn't erase fourteen years of pain, of
bitterness and sorrow.

"Why did you bring me here, Riley?"

He stared across the lake so he couldn't see her, but he
heard the sadness in her voice. It created a raw ache inside
him, one that made him long to touch her, to hold her, even
if only for a moment.

"Why here, of all places?" she asked. "Did you want me
to remember all the times we made love here? Did you want
to remind me that this was where we spent our last evening
together?" She paused only for a moment, then continued,
her voice thick and quavery. "My God, do you think I could
ever forget?"

Slowly he approached her. He knew it was a bad idea,
knew this entire afternoon had been a bad idea, but he
couldn't stop himself. He was drawn to her, the way he had
always been drawn to her. To the source of his happiness. To
the source of his pain. "Did Davis mind? Did he care that
you weren't a virgin? Did it bother him that while you were
planning to marry him, you were coming out here to—"

He was close now, and his voice, already a growl, dropped
to a low, nasty murmur to finish the question. Tense and
edgy, Liza focused on his last words and ignored the ob-
scenity that preceded them—*with me in the sand?* Odd how
one word could change the meaning so drastically. *She*
would have said make love. Making love with Riley on the
beach had been romantic and special and tender. But his
word... His word turned it into something dirty and cheap,
something shameful.

He was waiting for an answer, his menacing presence demanding one. She gave it with a taut little smile. "Why
should it have mattered to Keith that you and I had been
lovers?"

"Because it mattered to me," he said fiercely. "That was
the one thing you couldn't take away from me. You de-

stroyed everything else, but you can't ever deny that *I* was first."

"I would never try to deny it." Her voice was a mere whisper, but he was so close there was no doubt he heard it. "Riley—" Breaking off, she raised her hand, but he stopped her with one piercing look from his dark, angry eyes. He didn't want her to touch him.

That knowledge hurt. Fourteen years ago he had craved physical contact with her, simple contact such as holding hands or sliding his arm around her shoulders or resting his hand on her thigh in a movie theater. In private he had taught her more intimate forms of contact, how to accept his kisses with his tongue in her mouth, how to touch him and make him hard, how to cradle his hardness gently in her palm, how to stroke him and make him groan with pleasure.

Now he didn't want her to touch him at all.

With a painful tightness in her chest, Liza watched as he lifted his hand and reached behind her to remove the band that still held a portion of her hair. She didn't look to see what he did with it. She couldn't tear her gaze from his face.

At least, not until he spoke. "Whose choice was it, Liza?"

Hastily she refocused her attention on the span of his T-shirt visible through his open jacket. The cotton was soft, faded and stretched taut. It left little to the imagination, but then, she didn't need to imagine. She'd seen Riley without a shirt many times.

She had seem him without any clothing at all.

He tugged at her hair, exerting a steady pressure that forced her to tilt her head back to avoid pain. Once more, reluctantly, her eyes locked with his. Dark eyes. Gorgeous eyes. Unforgiving eyes.

"You said becoming a Davis wasn't your choice," he reminded her. "So why? Why did you marry him if you didn't want him?"

She gave him the answer she knew he expected. The answer that would convince him he was right to hate her. The answer that would destroy any chance she might have had for a future with him.

She told him the truth.

"Money. I married Keith for his family's money."

Abruptly Riley dropped his hold on her hair, spun around and walked off. He paused beside the picnic table to pick up his helmet, then climbed onto the cycle.

"Don't you want to hear the rest?" Liza asked as she started toward him.

He replied with the scowl that had become all too familiar. "It doesn't matter."

"It matters to me." She picked up the remaining helmet, but, like him, she didn't put it on. She simply held on to it tightly with both hands. "After everything I gave up, everything I lost—"

"What did you give up, Liza?" he demanded. "What sacrifices did you have to make to marry Keith? You got everything you ever wanted. All the money your greedy little heart desired, an even higher social standing than your own family could provide, security, prestige, *everything*. So just exactly what the hell was it that you lost?"

"You."

Her voice was as soft as his was sharp, as sad as his was angry. For an instant it drew him up short, stemming his words, blocking his anger... but only for an instant. Then a look of cold fury settled over his features. A look of disgust. A look of hatred.

He didn't believe her.

He couldn't believe her.

Liza gripped the helmet tighter, until her fingers ached and her nails turned white. She wanted to sink down on the bench behind her and weep, but instead she tugged the helmet into place, balanced carefully and climbed onto the cycle without touching Riley at all. Instead of wrapping her arms around him, as she had on the drive up, this time she settled her hands at his waist, one on each side. Even that, she thought with a heavy dose of self-pity, was more contact than he wanted with her.

The trip home seemed to take forever, although she knew it was less than thirty minutes. In her driveway she got off, removed the helmet and faced him. "Why won't you listen to me?" she asked, her voice pitched loud because of the idling engine. "Why won't you give me a chance to explain?"

It was like talking to a statue, she thought despairingly. He sat there motionless, protected by the shield that hid his face and the engine that drowned out her words.

With a hopeless sigh she handed the helmet to him, then turned and walked away. She was at the door, fiddling with the key in the lock, when he shut off the engine. For a moment the absence of sound was deafening, then her ears adjusted and she heard the normal neighborhood Saturday sounds—kids playing, dogs barking, music, lawn mowers and, from two houses down, the steady tap of a hammer.

"I'm listening."

His voice came from nearby—behind her on the steps, she thought, but she didn't turn to see. First she needed to still the trembling in her hands. She needed to blink away the tears that stung her eyes.

Finally she faced him. "You're not listening, Riley," she disagreed. "You're passing judgment. I've had to live with what I did for the last fourteen years. I don't need your guilt, too."

"*I've* lived with what you did," he corrected her. "*You've* lived in style with Davis."

"Nothing I say, nothing you see or hear or feel, is going to change your mind about me, is it? So why are you here? Why do you keep coming around?"

He answered with more honesty, she suspected, than he would have liked. "Because I can't stay away."

The words stunned her. Her first response was a rush of pleasure that, in spite of all the years and all the sorrow, he still felt the same pull, the same attraction, that she did. But almost immediately sadness replaced pleasure. He didn't want to feel that pull. He didn't want to be attracted to her. He didn't want anything at all to do with her.

"I'm sorry," she said quietly, wearily. "I wish I could change things. I wish I could make everything all right. But I can't. All I can do is tell you why I married Keith." Tears filling her eyes once again, she smiled. "But I can't make you believe it."

Riley watched her move to one of the rockers. After a moment he sat in the other, but he didn't rock. He sat perfectly still, barely even breathing, and waited.

With a heavy sigh, she began. "My parents never did like you. They made no secret of that. But it really wasn't even you they disliked, just what you represented. The motorcycle, the black leather jacket, the long hair. You came from a different part of town. A different background. A different class."

He shifted a little. An interesting way of saying he had been not only poor, but without a distinguished Southern name to make up for it. Plenty of illustrious Southerners had lost their fortunes in the past hundred and thirty years, but they still had the family name, the family history, so they were still respectable. Acceptable. The Coopers had never had a fortune to lose, and the name had never stood for anything. They had never been more than tenant farmers in the old days and lower-class, blue-collar laborers in this century.

"Mama and Daddy were very close to the Davises. Nothing could have pleased them more than strengthening those ties through marriage. They were always pushing Keith and me together, engineering dates, pointing out what a nice couple we made. I went out with him from time to time, whenever I couldn't avoid it. He was nice. I liked him. But I didn't want to marry him."

But in a very short time she had gone from not wanting to marry Davis to standing beside him on the church steps in a long white gown with a trailing bouquet of peach-colored roses. A convenient change of heart, Riley thought skeptically.

"The last time I went out with you was a Saturday. The next day we went to church, as we always did, and had dinner at my grandmother's. When we got home, Daddy called me into his office for a private talk. I wasn't eager to go, since all our private chats, and most of the public ones, too, revolved around how unsuitable you were for me. But this one was different.

"This time he had some sobering news. His business, the company that had been in our family for eighty years, the company that had prospered in hard times and even profited during the Great Depression, was on the verge of bankruptcy. His father had retired only three years earlier, passing on control of the company to my father, his only son, and Daddy's management skills hadn't been up to the test. Business had slipped. He'd lost several lucrative contracts. He'd gotten himself so deeply in debt that he could never climb out without help." She paused, her gaze distant, then added, "Without my help."

Then she focused on him again. "Alexander Davis knew about Daddy's problems. He had business interests everywhere, and he had promised to give Daddy more than enough contracts to save the company. There was just one catch, and that was what Daddy wanted to discuss with me. He wanted me to marry Keith. It was a business proposition, pure and simple. If I cooperated, Alexander would help out my father and the company would be saved. Daddy's reputation would remain intact, and my family's future would be assured." She paused again, and her voice softened. "All I had to do was quit seeing you and marry Keith."

"You've got to be kidding." Riley made no attempt to disguise his disbelief. "You want me to believe you married Keith for your father? So he wouldn't have to admit what a failure he was in business?"

"If Daddy had lost the company, he would have lost everything. My mother had never worked a day in her life, and Gretchen and I cost money. We had never brought any in. My father's pride and self-respect were on the line."

"He was too proud to admit failure, but not too proud to sell his daughter to the highest bidder? You were lucky Davis wanted you for his handsome, twenty-four-year-old son and not himself."

Liza couldn't have looked more surprised, or more hurt, if he'd struck her. It made Riley feel about six inches tall.

"Why do you find this so hard to believe?" she asked, clasping her hands tightly together in her lap. "You got a part-time job when you were sixteen years old so you could help your parents. You lived at home for five years after you graduated from high school, five years after you started working full-time, after you wanted a place of your own, because that way you could give more of your salary to them. You made decent money, but you rarely kept any of it for yourself, because they needed it more."

"That's hardly the same as marrying someone I didn't love. At least it was *my* money I was giving them, money I *earned*. It wasn't a payoff for sleeping with some rich kid."

"Thank you, Riley," she said quietly, rising from the chair and walking to the door, where she paused. "It isn't enough that I've spent the last fourteen years feeling guilty as hell for what I did, is it? Now you've got to make me feel like a whore, too."

"Liza..." He whispered her name, but it was too soft for her to hear as the door closed behind her.

He'd been wrong a moment ago. She *could* look more hurt.

Muttering a curse, he squeezed his eyes shut, trying to erase that wounded look from his memory. Swearing again, he got to his feet to leave, but instead of going down the steps, he faced the door. He knew she hadn't locked it, because he would have heard it click. All he had to do was open it, go inside and...

And do what?

Apologizing—again—would be a good start. Asking her forgiveness wouldn't do much for her pain, but it would help ease his own. Explaining to her why he was behaving like such an ass might help them both.

Hesitantly he wrapped his fingers around the knob and twisted. The door swung open without a sound. He stepped inside and closed it behind him, then stood motionless for a moment, listening to the sounds of the house.

A soft sniffle came from down the hall, and he headed in that direction. He found himself in the kitchen, a bright room with lots of windows. Liza stood in front of one, her head bowed, her arms folded across her chest. She looked so sad. So defeated.

Without thinking, he crossed the room to her and wrapped his arms around her from behind. She gave a start. Surprised that he hadn't left after doing his damage? Startled that he was actually touching her? Then she settled all too easily against him, as if fourteen years hadn't passed since he'd last held her.

As if she didn't hate him for what he'd said.

As if this was where she belonged.

God help him, maybe it was.

For a moment he simply held her, giving her warmth, absorbing the tremors that slowly left her body, remembering all the dozens of other times he had held her. And for the first time in years, even though he still owed her an apology, even though he still felt like a bastard for hurting her, he felt satisfied. At peace.

He felt as if he had come home.

"I'm sorry, Liza," he murmured, his words filtering through her hair where his cheek rested. "I didn't mean what I said. I just—I just wanted to hurt you because you hurt me so damn badly."

She didn't say anything, although he felt her breath catch. A moment later he felt something else, something that even in the best of times had held the power to break him, something that now could force him to his knees: a teardrop, hot and fat, that landed on the back of his wrist, then slid away.

"Oh, Liza," he groaned, turning her around. "Don't cry. Please don't cry."

"I'm not," she lied, wiping her eyes with both hands.

With his foot he pushed a chair back from the small dining table, then guided her into it. Taking a paper napkin from the holder on the table, he knelt in front of her and awkwardly dried her cheeks. "Please don't do this. I can't handle tears."

She pulled the napkin from his fingers and blew her nose, then laughed and hiccuped at the same time. "I know. That's why—"

"Hey, Liza, whose motorcycle—?" A tall, dark-haired woman came to a sudden halt just inside the door. "Oh. That answers that question." She came farther into the room, extending her hand. "Hello. I'm Gretchen. You probably don't remember me, but we met once a long time ago."

He did remember her. How could he forget, when she was the one who had told him on the phone that Liza never wanted to see him again, that she didn't want him bothering her anymore? *Bothering* her? *He* had thought he was loving her.

He stood, shook her hand and quickly released it. "I'm Riley," he said uneasily.

"Oh, I remember you. Boy, do I ever," she said with a smile. It faded when she looked at her sister. "I came at a bad time, didn't I?"

Liza wadded the napkin in her hand, then stood. "It wouldn't have hurt if you'd knocked before you came in."

"I did, a half-dozen times. I figured you were too busy to hear." Gretchen smiled again, a little slyly this time. "And I guess I was right. Listen, why don't I get lost for a while? I'll come back in a couple of hours."

"That's all right," Riley said quickly, too quickly. He looked at Liza, wondering if she could see his reluctance to go. He hadn't explained anything yet, hadn't resolved anything, but he couldn't stay. Seeing Gretchen, or any member of Liza's family, was more than he could deal with. "I'd better be going."

When Liza met his gaze, there was disappointment and resignation in her eyes. She offered him a small smile. "I wish you would stay."

"I can't." Because of her sister's intrusion. Because even the thought of her family made him feel unwelcome. Because the intimacy between them had been broken. Because he had enjoyed it, while it had lasted, too damned much.

"Nice seeing you again," Gretchen said as he passed her. "Sorry for the interruption."

He closed the kitchen door behind him and started toward the front door. When he was halfway there, Liza stopped him. "I'm sorry for the interruption, too."

That made it unanimous, he thought, although it shouldn't be. He should be grateful, not sorry, that her sister had barged in. If she hadn't, God only knew what he might have done. Holding Liza had felt so good that he might have touched her—*really* touched her. He might have kissed her. He might have told her that he'd never stopped wanting her, that he hated her only because he was afraid he still cared for her. Afraid he still needed her.

He was afraid he still . . .

Refusing to finish the thought, to let the words form, he smiled grimly. "It seems like every time we get together, one of us is apologizing."

She smiled a little, too. "I have a lot to apologize for."

Slowly he shook his head. "Why don't we just forget about it?"

Her eyes widened in dismay. Did she still want him to plead, the way he had intended to? he wondered with a touch of cynicism. Then he heard the echo of his question. *Why don't we just forget about it?* It sounded like a brush-off.

It sounded like goodbye.

"Everything?" she whispered. "Forget everything?"

He touched her hair lightly, briefly, just enough to satisfy the yearning inside him. "No. Just the bad stuff."

"Then I'll see you again?"

The note of hopefulness in her voice touched him deep inside, and even though it was utter lunacy he gave her the answer she wanted. "Tomorrow afternoon?" he asked.

"I would like that."

He should go now, but for a moment he hesitated. He wished he had the courage to kiss her—nothing intense, just a brush of his mouth against hers—but he would never be able to stop with that. "I'll see you tomorrow around two."

She didn't follow him out but remained beside the hall table, her eyes a little red from the tears she'd sworn she hadn't cried. She was the last thing he saw before he closed the door. All sweet. All soft and lovely.

For a while, long ago, she had been his to look at, to hold, to possess and to love.

For a while she would be his again. For a short while. A few weeks, a few months, a few years—no matter how long the time they had together, he acknowledged as he started his cycle, it wouldn't be enough.

Nothing less than a lifetime could ever be enough.

But he would be satisfied with whatever he got.

He had to be.

When Liza returned to the kitchen she found Gretchen at the table, a dish of ice cream in front of her. Her sister licked the spoon clean, then shrugged. "What can I say? I never thought you would be with a man, especially that man, or I wouldn't have come in."

"What *did* you think, Gretchen? That I'd taken up motorcycling in my spare time?"

Her sister slid the bowl to the center of the table and, with a coaxing smile, offered an extra spoon. After a moment Liza relented and sat across from her.

"I don't guess I thought anything," Gretchen replied. "For heaven's sake, Liza, you've been divorced more than two years, and you've never been out on a date. You hardly even look at other men. How was I to know I'd walk in here and find you on the floor with some gorgeous hunk from the past?"

"I wasn't on the floor," Liza pointed out sternly.

"*He* was—and on his knees, no less. My, my, the things you can do with a man on his knees." Gretchen concentrated on scooping a chunk of chocolate onto her spoon. "What are your intentions this time?"

The sudden change of direction surprised Liza. "My intentions?"

"Toward Riley. Are you going to use him until someone better comes along? Or until Daddy wears you down with his harping about finding someone *suitable?* Are you going to break his heart again?"

Liza took a small bite of ice cream. For sheer indulgence it was her favorite food, but today, thanks to her younger sister, it had no flavor. "You don't think much of me, do you?" she asked quietly.

Gretchen refused to meet her gaze. "You're my sister."

"But you don't trust me to treat Riley fairly this time."

Gretchen stalled, but she couldn't avoid answering. "Remember, Liza? I'm the one who had to tell him that it was over last time. I'm the one who had to break his heart for you because you were too cowardly to do it yourself. Do you know what it's like to cause a total stranger that kind of pain through no fault of your own?" She paused, but when her sister didn't answer, she went on. "He was the best thing that ever happened to you, and you treated him like an object, not a person. As if he weren't important. As if he didn't matter."

"That's not true—at least, not until the end, when I had no choice. And I've spent nearly half my life regretting it." Liza dropped her spoon into the bowl and slid it back to her sister. "That last year with Keith, after I found out about the drugs, was miserable. When he was home I was angry with him, and when he was gone I was afraid for him. I was afraid all the time, so afraid that I was sick with it. I used to lie awake at night, too stressed out to sleep, and think that my life was no more than I deserved after what I'd done to Riley. So he couldn't have helped save Daddy's business. So he never could have given me a big, fancy house or an expensive car or diamonds or luxury vacations. So he never could have given me anything that required money."

She sighed softly. "At least he never would have left me alone all those nights. He never would have been so selfish. He never would have taken the money meant to support his family and spent it on himself. He never would have been so weak. On those nights I used to pray that he was married and madly in love with his wife. I figured one of us deserved more happiness . . . and it certainly wasn't me."

After a long, heavy silence, Gretchen asked, "So what are you planning?"

"To take whatever he'll give." Liza shrugged. "To give whatever he'll take. Anything beyond that is up to Riley. I've done an awful lot that needs forgiveness, and he hasn't been in a very forgiving mood these last few weeks."

"He didn't look like a man holding a grudge when I walked in."

"He's trying," she replied, her smile wry. "It isn't easy for him, though. Part of him still hates me. Part of him will never trust me. Part of him never wants to see me again. And some part remembers how good it was between us."

"Maybe it can be that way again."

Liza thought of their conversation in the yard, easy and friendly, and of their ride to the lake. There had been some bad moments after that, but then had come those few, all-too-brief minutes in this room when Riley had held her so gently, so naturally, when she had felt so right, when she had believed that all the pain and heartache they had both suffered just might pay off.

Maybe Gretchen was right.

Maybe it *could* be that way again.

Chapter 7

Riley turned the Cherokee onto Brainard Avenue, switched the blue lights on, then followed the car ahead of him into an empty parking lot. He had been behind the car for four blocks, more than long enough to convince him that the driver was intoxicated. If he was right, this would be his third drunk-driving arrest of the night.

Contacting the radio operator, he gave his location, a description of the car, its license number, the number of occupants and the reason for stopping them. If the driver failed the field sobriety test and one of his friends was sober, the friend would be allowed to drive the others home. If none of them was sober, they would leave the car in this lot for the owner to retrieve later, after paying a substantial fine and, most likely, losing his on-post driving privileges for a year. It was a steep price to pay for a few drinks.

Jasper barked excitedly when Riley opened the door. He glanced back at the dog. Jasper frequently got out on traffic stops with him, especially when there was more than one occupant in the car. Knowing they were being watched by the big shepherd put a stop to any thoughts of escaping on foot. "Not this time," he said with a shake of his head. Not with backup only a few blocks away.

Giving him an all-too-human look of disappointment, Jasper settled down in back to wait.

Riley approached the car and asked for the driver's military identification card, license and registration as another MP drove up and parked behind the Jeep. He watched her give the Cherokee a wide berth as she came toward him. Jasper didn't mind if some of his fellow MPs came right up to the vehicle, and there were even one or two who could pet him through the wire mesh. But if some, including this one, got within five feet of the dog when he wasn't working, he got very angry and very vocal about it.

The driver failed the sobriety test, as Riley had expected, and his three passengers were in no better condition. They were trainees at one of the signal schools, out celebrating the fact that, having reached fifth-week status, they were no longer restricted to post. They wouldn't have much to celebrate when their senior drill instructor, who would be called out of bed at three in the morning, came to the MP station to pick them up, Riley thought.

"You're going to need help transporting them," he remarked to the other MP, a young corporal named Cheryl. He didn't transport prisoners himself, not with Jasper in the Jeep.

"I'll call for someone."

Riley reached inside the car while they waited, taking the keys from the ignition. The floorboards were littered with beer cans, and there was a strong odor of alcohol through the open window. Not one of the four was old enough to drink legally, and not one of them was smart enough to do it sensibly.

But he'd been older and more responsible than all of them when Liza had gotten married, and he had made a hell of an effort to drown his sorrows in a sea of booze. He had drunk to numb the pain, but by the time he had reached a state of near-unconsciousness, he had been numb to everything *ex-*

cept the pain. He had never known a person could hurt so badly and survive.

But he had survived.

And here he was getting involved with Liza again.

A third MP arrived. He took two of the trainees with him, and Cheryl placed the other two in her car. Riley gave the young soldier's car keys to her. She would turn them in to the desk sergeant, who would hand them over to the drill instructor. He would ensure that the kid didn't drive again until he was stone-cold sober.

After securing the car, Riley walked back to the Jeep, climbed inside and turned off the blue lights. Slowly he drove out of the lot and back onto the street. Back out on patrol.

He wished Liza's sister hadn't interrupted them this afternoon. He could have gone the rest of his life without seeing any of her relatives, but especially her father, because Garrett hated him so much, and her sister, because Gretchen reminded him...

He had met Gretchen only once, the night of his first date with Liza. The only time he had gone to her house. Mrs. Johnson's reaction had been disapproval—typical, he supposed, of any mother meeting her daughter's long-haired, leather-clad biker boyfriend for the first time. Garrett's reaction had been the same, ten times over. Ten times stronger. Ten times more vicious. And Gretchen...an awkward, giggly sixteen-year-old, she had loudly whispered, "Ooh, he's cute," before being banished from the room by her father.

The only other contact he'd ever had with her had been by phone. "Liza doesn't want to talk to you, Riley," she'd said with a seriousness that hadn't fit his image of the carefree teenager. "She—she doesn't want to see you anymore."

He had been stunned, too stunned to speak or even breathe. He hadn't believed her, and he had envisioned all sorts of wild scenes in which Liza's father had somehow forced her to break up with him. "I want to talk to her," he had coaxed. "Just for a minute, Gretchen. Just let me talk to her." If he could get Liza on the phone, he was sure he could make everything all right. He could convince her that whatever her father had told her was wrong. He could remind her that she'd said she loved him, and he could tell her that he loved her. He had never said those words to her, but they were true. He did love her, and if he could just get the chance to tell her that—

Then he had heard Gretchen exclaim, "I won't say that!" And in the background had been Liza's voice, his sweet, loving Liza, saying, "Tell him it's over. I don't want to see him again. Tell him to quit bothering me. Tell him to leave me alone."

He had hung up the phone and walked away. The next day he had found out about the wedding, and the next ten days had passed in an alcoholic blur. Joining the Army had probably saved his life.

Fourteen years had passed, but little had changed. He was fourteen years older and supposedly fourteen years wiser, but what was he doing? Falling for Liza again. But this time he wasn't going to give her the power to destroy him. If anyone was going to play the role of user in this relationship, it would be him. He would take what he wanted, whatever she offered, and when it was over he would walk away unharmed.

That was his plan.

Now if he could only stick to it.

"Riley won't be here again today," T.J. announced as Liza pulled into the MP station parking lot. "I don't like the guy who's taking his place so much."

"What?" She gave him a look of feigned horror. "You mean you've actually developed a fondness for that *cop?*"

Her son gave her a pained look, the kind she had once given her own mother whenever Rosalind had done or said something totally uncool. "Riley's not really such a bad guy."

She felt a sense of relief mixed with both satisfaction and pride. If she was going to continue seeing Riley, eventually she would have to tell T.J. She had wondered last night what his response would be. Anger? Jealousy? Rejection or acceptance? He had told her outright when they were still in Dallas that he wasn't putting up with any men other than his father, and she had told him with more than a little annoyance that *she* wasn't in the mood to put up with *any* man.

But T.J. liked Riley. "Not really such a bad guy" was, from her son, a high compliment for any adult who wasn't related to him. He used it sparingly, so far bestowing it only on his favorite teacher, the man who had coached last spring's soccer team and the neighbor down the street, who had helped him work on his bicycle.

And now on Riley.

"I'm glad you like him," she remarked casually. "I'd like to invite him over to dinner sometime, okay?"

There was nothing casual in the way T.J. looked at her. "Why?"

"Riley and I were friends long before you were born, kiddo."

"Friends, huh?" He shrugged expressively. "Okay. See you later."

She waved goodbye, then returned home. It wasn't long before Riley arrived, this time driving the beat-up truck instead of the sleek, shiny, trip-into-the-past cycle. She had to admit that she was a little disappointed. It was a lovely afternoon for a ride.

He wore his usual attire—faded jeans, a tight T-shirt and boots. In fourteen years that much hadn't changed, she thought with a bittersweet smile. Other things were still the same, too. He was still the most gorgeous man she had ever seen. He was still the only man who could arouse her by simply existing.

And he was still the only man she had ever truly loved.

He joined her on the porch, leaning against the railing, which he seemed to prefer over a chair. It meant that she had to look up at him, but that was okay. He was incredibly nice to look at.

"Do you spend all your free time outside?"

She folded the newspaper she'd been reading and set it on the floor. "Most of it. Actually, today I was waiting for you."

"I'm a little early."

"That's okay." She shifted position, then modestly tugged at her shorts. Most Sunday mornings she and T.J. went to church with her parents, but this morning she had skipped the services, slept in late, then lazed around the house. Regrettably, that had gotten easier to do since she'd told her parents that Riley was back in Augusta. Her father questioned her even in church, and how could she possibly lie there?

"Have a nice visit with your sister?"

It was a simple question, one she wouldn't have given a second thought to coming from anyone else, but from Riley it surprised her. In the past, because of her family's disapproval, they had always been off-limits as a topic of conversation, and she had rarely thought to ask about his. She knew that he was the oldest of six kids, that he had two brothers and three sisters. She even knew that he was extraordinarily close to the oldest girl, but she didn't know her name. She didn't know any of their names. She didn't know anything at all about them.

"It was all right," she replied. "Gretchen's nice. I think you would like her."

A faint look of skepticism crossed his face. He was entitled to dislike any and all Johnsons, Liza thought sadly. He had never been treated fairly by any of them—most especially her. "For the record," she said, her voice quiet, "Gretchen was on your side back then. She refused to be in my wedding because of the way I treated you. She was only sixteen, but she had more courage than I did."

He didn't say anything to that. What *could* he say?

She forced a smile and stood up. "Have you had lunch?"

Riley shook his head.

"Would you like me to fix you something, or would you rather go out?"

"Let's go out."

Her smile felt more natural this time. She had hoped he would choose that. It had been too long, years too long, since they had gone out together. "Let me change—"

"You look fine. Just get some shoes."

The goofy smile spread. As compliments went, it wasn't much, but it meant more to Liza than the most effusive praise another man might have offered. "I'll just be a minute."

It took her closer to five minutes to choose a pair of shoes, brush her hair back and fasten it with combs, and freshen the makeup she had put on earlier. At nineteen she might not have minded being seen by Riley without artificial enhancement, but at nineteen her skin had been soft and smooth, young and unlined. She was thirty-three now, and the last three of those years had caused more than their share of aging. There were fine lines at the corners of her eyes—laugh lines, they were called, but hers had been caused mostly by tears. She had cried a lot of tears...and there would surely be more in the future. But she wouldn't let herself think about that. She was living for the present. For today. For this afternoon.

With Riley.

They chose a Chinese restaurant a few miles away. After they filled their plates from the buffet, Liza said, "T.J.'s not thrilled with your replacement for this weekend. He's decided that you're not really such a bad guy, after all."

Riley gave her a dry look. "Is that supposed to be a compliment?"

"Come on. You can remember what you were like when you were his age. You wouldn't have been caught dead saying something nice about a cop, especially one who was overseeing your punishment."

"If I'd done what he did when I was his age, I wouldn't have had any punishment to oversee. My father would have just killed me and gotten it over with."

Liza sliced a nugget of fried pork in half, then dipped it in sweet-and-sour sauce. Choosing her words carefully, she asked, "Are you implying that I'm too lenient with T.J.?"

He replied just as carefully. "I'm not blaming you for his trouble, if that's what you're asking. He's a smart kid. He knew what they were doing was wrong, and he chose to do it, anyway. It wasn't your fault."

"Our families have all kinds of theories on why he did it. Because I'm irresponsible. Because I divorced his father. Because I moved him away from Dallas. Because I work and can't be there when he gets home in the afternoons."

"It wasn't your fault," Riley repeated.

"It's hard not to take pride in your child's accomplishments . . . or to accept responsibility for his failures." She sighed softly. "You'll see when you have kids of your . . ." She let the sentence trail off uncompleted. Riley a father. How often in their months together had she dreamed of having children with him? Their first would be a boy, she had decided, because most men secretly wanted their first child to be a son. And then they would have more sons and some daughters, too, until they had at least an even half dozen, like his parents.

But those had been only dreams. She had married Keith instead, and all she had now was T.J. And Riley had no children at all.

Riley knew what she was thinking—about the babies they should have had together. The family that he had naively assumed they would have. He had never given any real thought to how they would have supported a family. His salary certainly hadn't been enough, and she had still been in school, two years away from earning her degree. All he had ever considered was his desire for children, his love for Liza and her supposed love for him.

He wondered if he would ever have children. He doubted it. If he hadn't found a woman he could love in the past fourteen years, what were the chances of it happening in the future?

Very good, whispered a sly voice as he looked across the table at Liza.

No way, he insisted. He could like her. He could enjoy her company. He could—and already did—desire her. But he couldn't trust her. He couldn't let her hurt him again. He couldn't love her again because he couldn't bear to lose her again.

"You must have some nieces and nephews." Her voice was a little husky, the way it sounded when she felt awkward or shy. The way it had sounded when they made love.

Shaking away that thought, Riley concentrated on her question. "Yeah, I do. Robbie's got two kids, Steven and Mark have three each and Brenda has one."

"What's your other sister's name?"

"Marcy. She's the baby. She's getting married next spring."

The look on Liza's face had grown distant and sad. "I never knew much about your family."

"You never asked." When they had first started dating he had occasionally talked about his family, but it hadn't taken long to realize that Liza wasn't interested. She had never wanted to meet any of them, had never shown any curiosity about them. He had figured the time would come when she would ask to meet her future in-laws, and he had waited patiently, but it never had. Later he had decided that her reluctance must have had something to do with her refusal to discuss her own family, to introduce him to her friends or to meet his.

Because she had been ashamed of him. Ashamed of her relationship with him.

"No, I never did ask," Liza agreed. "I don't know why. Maybe I thought that my family had caused enough trouble already. We didn't need to bring yours into it." She smiled a little. "And I liked not having to share our time with anyone, not having to share *you* with anyone. We had so little time together, and I wanted it all to ourselves. I guess I was selfish."

That didn't sound like shame, Riley thought guiltily. In fact, it sounded exactly the way *he* had felt. He wouldn't have minded sharing a few hours of their time with his family or spending an occasional evening with his friends, but their best times together had definitely been when they were completely alone.

"Did they even know about me?"

He wished she would ask another question, any other question, because instinctively he knew his answer would hurt her. She might have lied to her parents about seeing him, and she might have sneaked around behind their backs to do so, but she had never denied his existence.

A brief reprieve came in the form of two soldiers entering the dining room. "Hey, Sergeant," one of them greeted him.

Riley stood as the men approached. He shook hands with them, talked for a few minutes, then said goodbye, and all the while his mind was on Liza's question and how he could avoid answering it.

Finally he looked down at her. She had pushed her plate away ten minutes ago, she had finished her tea, and her hands were clasped primly in front of her. "Ready to go?"

When she nodded he took the ticket from the table, then followed her to the register. She remained silent until they were outside, crossing the parking lot to his truck. Then she quietly, flatly said, "You never told your family, did you?"

He answered quietly, too, and just as flatly. "No. Only Robbie knew."

"I see."

His hand on her arm, he stopped her when she would have climbed into the truck. As soon as she turned to face him, he released her. "What is it you see, Liza?"

"That it wasn't important enough for you to tell them. That *I* wasn't important enough."

He swore softly. "Come on, Liza, you know me better than that."

"What am I supposed to think? I was the only woman you saw for months, and you never even bothered to mention my name to your family, to the family you lived with, that you saw every day. Do you have a better way to explain it?"

Turning away from her, he rested his arms on the side of the truck bed. "If I had told my parents that I was seeing Garrett Johnson's little girl, they would have died. They both would have known what I was too involved to see—that it couldn't last. That it couldn't bring anything but heartache."

"You could have told them you were seeing plain old Liza Johnson," she said softly. "That name wouldn't have meant anything to them."

"No, it wouldn't have. Then they would have said, 'Bring her to Sunday dinner so the family can meet her.' And I would have had to say, 'Sorry, but I can't. She prefers to pretend that I don't have a family. That's how she forgets that I don't have any money, any background, or any class.'"

"Maybe that was what *you* thought, Riley," she whispered. "But it never mattered to me."

After a moment he looked down at her. "Never? Not even when you chose to marry Davis?" He paused, but he didn't expect an answer, and she didn't offer one. "Tell me you didn't compare the two of us, Liza, and find me lacking. Tell me you would have been as quick to marry him if I'd lived on the Hill, too, if my family had had as much money, if I had had as much class."

She started to speak, then shook her head in dismay and turned away. Before Riley could make a move, though, she swung around again. "Do you want to know why I made Gretchen tell you that I didn't want to see you again? Did you ever wonder why I didn't tell you myself, why I didn't look in your eyes and tell you I was going to marry Keith?"

Did he ever wonder...? That was one of the questions that had haunted him the past fourteen years, and she had to know it.

He wanted to lie and say it didn't matter. That he didn't care. That it wouldn't have changed things. But it did matter, and even after fourteen years he did care. And maybe it would have changed things. Maybe if she'd shown that single small courtesy, he could have dealt with everything else and gotten on with his life. Maybe he wouldn't still be so angry and hurt fourteen years later.

She didn't make him ask. She simply offered the answer. "Because I would have asked you to run away with me. I would have pleaded with you to take me away to someplace, anyplace, where my parents couldn't have found us. I would have begged you to marry me."

In the stillness that followed, her gaze held his. The rich brown of her eyes had become liquid and shadowy, but that couldn't hide the sincerity there. She was telling the truth. He had cautioned himself against believing anything she said, against trusting anything she told him, but this was the truth. He knew it as surely as he knew what his answer would have been back then if she had found the courage to come to him. *Yes.* Yes, he would have run away with her. Yes, he would have left his family behind to take Liza somewhere safe. Yes, he would have married her. He would have treasured her. He would have loved her.

Forever.

She waited a moment, but when he said nothing she turned away. She climbed into the truck, closed the door and rolled the window down, then waited patiently. After another moment he joined her.

As he pulled onto the street he offered to turn the air-conditioning on, but she simply shook her head. In spite of the silver combs that held her hair back, the wind was blowing it around her face, weaving it into fine tangles that he knew from experience would fall free if he combed his fingers through them. Maybe he should offer her the rubber band in his pocket, the thick band covered with glittery crimson that he had removed from her hair at the lake.

But he didn't.

"Where are we going?" she asked after a couple of miles.

"Nowhere special. Do you need to go home?"

"Not until it's time to pick up T.J."

"How about the Riverwalk? Have you been there?"

She shook her head.

The riverside park was a nice place to spend a warm afternoon, public but usually not too crowded, and usually with something going on to provide a distraction if necessary. After Liza's last bombshell, he needed a distraction—maybe a whole lot of them, Riley thought with a grim smile.

They found a parking space in the dirt lot and walked the length of the park along the top of the levee before choosing to sit on a weathered bench in a shady waterfront spot. "This is nice," Liza remarked, watching the river flow for a moment before stealing a look at Riley. He looked solemn. Dark. Intense.

That intensity just below the surface had always drawn her. Because of it he had been quick to anger and slow—painfully slow this time—to forgive. He cared so deeply about things, and when he got hurt, he hurt so much more deeply. In the first few years of her marriage she hadn't realized just how much more. When she had allowed herself to think of him at all, she had imagined him happy and healthy and completely over her. She had never imagined that fourteen years later he would still feel the pain of her betrayal so strongly.

She wished he trusted her. It wasn't easy knowing he weighed everything she did now against everything she had done in the past. It was uncomfortable knowing he didn't believe everything she said the way he once had. In a sense, she thought, he regarded her much the same way he would regard someone he had arrested: warily. With uncertainty. Without trust.

"How did T.J. make friends with a kid who lives on post?" Riley asked.

It took Liza a moment to mentally shift gears to the night T.J. had been arrested. "Bryan used to live down the street. When his family got the chance to move into base housing a few months ago, they took it."

"How is he doing with the rest of his sentence—the restitution?"

She smiled wryly. "It's going very slowly. Between school and his hours out on post, he doesn't have a lot of time to do extra chores at home. I told him he had to earn all the money himself, that he couldn't use any of his savings for it, so he made a deal with Daddy that would pay him seven bucks an hour.''

''That's not much less than I make.''

''Me, too. So I told him I didn't approve. Now he can only work for Gretchen or me. I know she'll be fair. She'll make him earn it.''

''He misses his father,'' Riley stated.

Liza shifted her gaze downward so he couldn't read anything in her eyes. ''Yes, he does, but I can't do anything about that.''

''Why can't he visit him for a weekend? Surely Davis can afford the airfare. T.J. could leave Friday evening and come back Sunday evening. It's not long, but it's better than nothing.''

''Haven't you forgotten?'' she asked with a smile that felt strained. ''The Army has a prior claim on his weekends.''

''They'll make an exception for something like this.''

''He's too young to travel by himself.'' She knew the stiffness that had spread through her body at the mention of Keith had reached her voice, but she tried to ignore it. She tried to sound as natural as any divorced woman would when discussing her ex-husband, because she didn't want to rouse Riley's suspicions, but she was afraid she had failed. When he continued questioning her, she knew she had.

''Kids younger than T.J. travel alone all the time. That's why the airlines have employees to take care of them between flights and make sure they get on the right planes. Why not T.J.?''

''Someone would have to go with him. I can't, and weekends are generally busy for Alexander and Margaret.''

''He's a bright kid. He doesn't need a baby-sitter.''

He did with his father, Liza silently disagreed. Once Keith had been discharged from his second stay at the rehab clinic, they had tried weekend visits, as dictated by their custody agreement. For the first month everything had been all right. Then, on one visit, Keith had left T.J., then only nine years old, alone both days, returning to the house late in the evening in a less-than-respectable condition. The next weekend had been one endless party with Keith's friends, people she didn't know, people she had never heard him mention before. People she didn't want around her son.

The following weekend had been the last straw. She had dropped T.J. off at his father's house on Saturday morning, and he had called her at 3:00 a.m. Sunday, scared and crying. He had been alone since noon with no food to eat and nothing for company but the television. She had taken him home and, first thing Monday morning, had gone to her attorney. She had never found out where Keith had gone or when he'd come home, but he hadn't bothered calling her until Tuesday evening to make sure that their son was with her and not simply missing.

"You don't want him to see his father, do you?"

There was a hint of disappointment in his voice that almost made Liza smile. Riley might not like Keith, but he thought that any man, even a Davis, deserved a relationship with his son. Well, he was wrong. "Not without proper supervision."

"Are you afraid Davis will run off with the kid? Has he threatened to do that?"

"No." She sighed heavily. "Oh, Riley, please. . . . If you can trust me on anything, let it be this. Trust me to do the best I can for my son. I love T.J. more than anything in the world, and when it's okay for him to see his father, believe me, no one will be happier than me."

He wasn't satisfied—she saw that when she risked a look—but he let the subject drop. He watched the traffic on the river—fishing boats, an occasional pontoon boat, a couple of jet skiers—for a few minutes before he spoke again. "Why is T.J. an only child? You always said you wanted a half dozen."

She looked at him, meeting his gaze openly. "I wanted a half-dozen children with you, not Keith."

His face grew warm with a blush, his dark skin turning a rich, coppery shade. He ignored it, though, and asked another difficult question. "Were you happy with him?"

With her answer about children, she had left herself open to that line of questioning, so she had no one but herself to blame. But she hated having to come up with a satisfactory answer, one that was truthful—considering how he distrusted her, how could she ever tell him anything less than the truth?—and fair and painless.

She sighed again. "Once I accepted that I was going to marry Keith, I was determined to be a good wife and to be happy with him. I pretended that marrying him was what I wanted, not what my father needed. I...I pretended that I had never known you, that you had never been a part of my life. I was very careful, especially while we lived here in Augusta, never to think about you, never to wonder what you were doing. After we moved to Dallas it became easier, and finally I quit having to pretend. I really was a good wife. I really did care for Keith. I really was happy." For a while, she silently added.

"And you loved him." Riley made the statement without emotion. Hadn't she admitted as much at her house last week? *I guess in a way I did love him.* Those had been her exact words, but he wanted to hear them again. He wanted to hear her say, yes, Riley, I loved him—not you, but *him.*

But she didn't.

"Keith was my husband. For many years he was my best friend. We lived together. We slept together. We were raising a child together. I loved him the only way I could—as my best friend. As the father of my son. But it wasn't the way a woman should love her husband. Not as a lover. Not as the most important man in her life. Not as the missing part of her soul. And he knew that. He used to pretend, too. For a while."

He waited, wondering if she might finally tell him the reasons behind their divorce, but she didn't say anything more for a long time. When she did speak, it was in a lighter voice on a lighter subject.

"I want some lemonade. There's a stand down by the park entrance. Do you want some?"

"Sure." She was already walking away by the time he got to his feet, but he didn't hurry to catch up with her. He enjoyed watching the gentle sway of her hips too much. By the time he reached her she had already ordered two drinks and was watching the vendor mix water, sugar and ice with fresh-squeezed lemon juice.

When she started to open her purse, Riley shook his head and pulled a handful of wadded bills from his pocket. A penny and a fabric-covered elastic band fell to the ground. Shiny copper and bright, shimmery crimson, they created a brilliant contrast against the drab sidewalk.

Liza bent to pick up the objects for him. There was no doubt that she recognized the band as her own. She held it for a moment, fingering the fabric, but when he extended his hand, she laid it, along with the penny, in his palm. "Thank you," he said, returning them to his pocket.

They walked through the park one more time before heading back to his truck. It was after four o'clock, time to take her home so she could pick up T.J. Time for him to go back to the company and take a nap before starting tonight's shift. If he was lucky, sleep was all that would occupy him. No dreams, no memories, no desire.

But when was the last time he'd been so lucky? his sly inner voice asked.

The answer came quickly and more clearly than he wanted: the night he'd arrested T.J. Davis.

"Would you like to have supper with us this evening?" Liza asked on the way home.

"What about T.J.?"

"I explained to him that you and I were friends a long time ago. He doesn't mind."

"Just friends?" He gave the word a wry twist. Friendship wasn't exactly what came to mind when he remembered their past. Gentle passion, heated need, sweet loving, hopes and dreams and pain—those were the things he remembered about Liza.

"He's eleven years old," she pointed out. "He doesn't need to know the truth. So what about dinner?"

"Not tonight. I've got to get some sleep before work."

"I'm sorry. I forgot you had to work all last night. Maybe sometime this week?"

It would be so simple to say yes, so simple and easy and true. Yes, he would like to see her this week. Yes, he would like to spend an entire evening with her and even with T.J. But it was even simpler, and much, much safer, to turn down her invitation. Because he wanted to say yes, instead he said no. He pulled into her driveway, shifted into Park, then turned and looked at her. "I don't think so."

Her gaze dropped away from his, but not quickly enough to hide her disappointment. Not quickly enough to keep him from feeling like a bastard. "Okay." She opened the door and slid to the ground, then looked at him again. This time, in spite of the slightly wounded look, there was gratitude in her dark eyes. "Thank you, Riley."

For a moment he sat there, watching her cross the lawn, climb the steps and unlock the door. Even after the door had blocked her from sight he still sat there with the engine idling, fighting the urge to follow her inside and tell her that he had lied, that he was sorry, that he would like to have dinner with her. Anything to erase that look from her eyes.

But the only thing he did was reverse out of the driveway and head back to the fort. To his quiet, empty room at the company. To the place where he spent far too much time alone. Away from the place he really wanted to be.

What had she thanked him for? he wondered as he pulled onto the expressway. For taking her to lunch? Probably. But had there been more than simple gratitude for a simple date in her eyes?

He didn't want to think about it. He didn't want to believe she might be grateful that he wasn't still so angry with her, that he wasn't keeping his distance. He didn't want to believe that she was thankful to have him back in her life. Believing those things would mean believing she wanted some sort of relationship with him. It would mean believing she still cared for him. And if she did care, that would mean acknowledging that he was going to hurt her.

His features settled into a familiar frown. Maybe he was reading too much into one brief look. He was definitely thinking too much. His brain, weary from too little sleep, wanted nothing more than to shut down for a few hours. Sleep was what he needed right now.

A lifetime of sleep.

"I don't suppose I could call in sick today."

Kneeling beside her flower bed, Liza looked up at T.J., who was leaning comfortably over the porch railing and watching her work. Her son was a lazy child, much preferring to stand overhead and supervise rather than get down on his knees and help. But that was all right. He would do his share of work this afternoon. "Not unless you collapse in a feverish, babbling heap sometime before one o'clock."

Taking her at her word, T.J. straightened, grabbed his chest and dramatically sank to the floor, his head back, his eyes rolled up and his mouth open. After a moment's stillness he twisted his head slightly to see if she was watching. Seeing that she was, he quickly resumed his motionless, sightless posture again.

"Not bad," Liza said dryly. "But not good enough."

He rolled onto his stomach and pressed his face right up against the wooden spindles. "Oh, please, Mom, let me cut just today. I'll work extra hard tomorrow, I swear I will. It's too hot to work today. I want to go swimming over at Grandpa Davis's. Grandma said I could. She said I could spend the night if it's okay with you. Is it okay?"

"When did you talk to Grandma?"

"A little while ago. She said they're going to call Dad later today and if you'll bring me over, I can talk to him. And she said I could go swimming, since it's so hot today."

"You go call her back and tell her that I'll bring you over after you finish work."

"Oh, Mom . . ."

"Oh, T.J. . . . ." she mimicked. "Go on and call her."

He made a move, then suddenly froze. With a look of mock horror on his face, he cried, "Oh, no, Mom, I'm stuck! My face is caught between the bars! See?" He made a great show of trying with all his might to free himself, then suddenly collapsed. "I guess I can't go to work, after all. I'll just have to stay here and make sure you do a good job with those flowers. Maybe in a few days without food or water I'll lose enough weight to get free, and then I'll have the rest of the week to recuperate from my ordeal before I go back to work."

"Or I could go borrow the neighbor's power saw and cut you free," Liza said with a laugh. "I bet you wouldn't lose more than an ear or two and maybe a little hair."

T.J. popped free and rose to his knees, resting his chin on the porch railing. "Do I really have to go, Mom? It's so hot today."

"You really have to. Now go on and call your grandmother." She got to her feet as he disappeared inside the house. He wasn't exaggerating about the temperature, she thought, wiping her forehead on her sleeve. Last week had been cool, in the sixties. Now, according to the weatherman, they were due for a few days in the eighties and maybe even into the low nineties. They called this weather unseasonably warm in the forecasts, but she couldn't remember a fall and winter in Augusta that hadn't followed the same pattern: a frustrating switch from cool to warm, from hot to cold. She could remember seasons when she'd been wearing shorts one week and awakened to an ice storm the next.

Turning, she studied the flats of pansies she'd spread out in the shade of the live oak. Ideally, they should have been planted a month ago, but even at this date they would still bloom beautifully all winter long. She had picked up the flowers at a nearby nursery early this morning and spent the past few hours getting the beds ready—uprooting dead plants, raking pine bark, loosening the soil and working in peat moss to enrich it. Now all she had to do was plant the dozens of flowers and mulch the bed with the nuggets of bark, and she would be more or less finished until spring.

She was halfway through the first flat when the truck behind her interrupted her concentration. Sitting back, she wiped her face once more, then watched as Riley got out. Down inside she was more than happy to see him, but it didn't show on her face. She had been too disappointed when he had refused to join her and T.J. for dinner to give in so easily to the pleasure she automatically felt at seeing him.

He followed the winding path to the bottom step, where he leaned against the railing. Solemnly watching him, Liza drew off one gardening glove, tucked a strand of hair behind her ear, then slipped the glove on again. "Slide those flowers over here, would you?" she asked casually, as if she hadn't been at all hurt by the way their afternoon had ended Sunday.

He picked up the plastic flat and carried it to her, setting it down again beside her.

"What brings you out this way?" Without waiting for his answer, she chose a six-pack of delicate lavender-hued flowers, grasped one plant firmly by the stem and tugged it free. In a moment it was joined in the soil by the remaining five plants, then she started on a pack of white blooms.

"I was out, so I thought I'd give T.J. a ride to work."

"You're a little early, aren't you? He doesn't have to be there for another couple of hours."

"I know. In the meantime I thought I'd ask his mother if she—if they would have lunch with me."

Finally Liza paused in her work to look at him. Why the change of heart? she wondered. Why did he come seeking her out one minute, when the next it seemed that he couldn't get away quickly enough?

Then, looking away again, she smiled. What did his reasons for coming here matter? He was here. That was what counted. "Let me finish planting some of these, then I'll wash up and we can go." Balancing herself on one hand, she leaned across the wide bed and dug a series of holes. She was planting the flowers in wavy rows that stretched from front to back, alternating lavender and white blossoms with deep purple. Right now they looked a little sparse, she acknowledged, but in a few weeks they would start filling in until they formed a pastel mound that stretched all the way to the end of the house.

Feeling awkward just standing there, Riley crouched down and watched her. She worked methodically, digging the holes slightly larger than the tangled root systems of the plants, holding the stems straight, mounding the soil, tamping it down. He liked watching her move, seeing the muscles in her back tighten beneath the damp white T-shirt she wore, studying her body, all soft curves and long lines, when she stretched across the flower bed. She was sweaty, dirt was smudged across her cheek and her hair was damp and wispy in its ponytail, but she looked more beautiful, more real, than he could ever remember.

It wasn't long before she moved out of reach of the flat. Instead of sliding it over to her, he picked up one of the packs and began gently removing the plants, laying each one in her outstretched hand. "When I was a kid," he remarked, "we all used to help my mother plant flowers—daffodils and marigolds and daisies. Other than mowing my dad's grass a few times this summer, I haven't done any yard work since then."

"Living in the barracks, you haven't had a yard to work in," Liza pointed out.

"I haven't always lived in the barracks. Once we rented—" Realizing what he was about to say, he got to his feet and collected another bunch of flowers from beneath the tree. He wasn't going to get off that easily, though.

"Rented what?" Liza prompted.

"A house." The words sounded sharp, almost unfriendly, but he couldn't help it. He just wished he had kept his mouth shut.

"Who is 'we'?" she asked.

"Another MP and me."

"And being typical men, a pretty yard came at the bottom of your list of priorities."

He sifted bits of loose soil through his fingers after she accepted the next plant, and he said nothing. His silence must have seemed guilty to Liza, though—it certainly felt that way to him—because she stopped her work and faced him. Even though he couldn't meet her gaze, he felt it, steady and measuring. He felt it, too, when she looked away again, when she began once more methodically planting the flowers he'd handed her.

"Even in the nineties, when I think of cops I think of men," she said conversationally. "But there are female MPs, too, aren't there?"

He still said nothing.

"Were you lovers?"

Now it was his turn to look and hers to evade. What he could see of her face was blank, revealing nothing, but she couldn't control her voice, as well. He'd heard the stiffness that had turned a simple question into an accusation. He had recognized the jealousy behind it. Interesting that she could be jealous of a woman he hadn't seen in eleven years, of a woman he had used, much as he had used the others, to get over *her*.

"Yes," he replied flatly. "We were." Then, his voice soft with anger, he went on. "You're the one who ended it between us, Liza. You're the one who married someone else. I was free to sleep wherever I wanted, to live with whoever I wanted."

"I know," she whispered. After a long, still moment, she sat back on her knees and tilted her face up to the sky. "I wish..."

Her sentence trailed off unfinished, but he didn't prod her, because he suspected he knew exactly what she wished. He had wished a lifetime of wishes himself. That things had turned out differently. That Keith Davis had never been a part of Liza's life. That she had stood up to her parents. That she had come to him and asked him to take her away, to marry her and protect her from her father. That what they had shared had lasted forever.

But the facts were cold and hard: she *hadn't* stood up to her parents. She *hadn't* come to him and asked him to take her away. Davis *had* been a part of her life—her husband, her best friend, the father of her son. More important roles than Riley had ever filled. And what they had shared hadn't lasted even a year, much less forever.

And no amount of wishing could change it. Any of it.

That was the coldest, hardest fact of all.

Chapter 8

"There. I'll finish the others later this afternoon when it's not quite so hot." Liza stood, slipped off her gloves, then bent from the waist in a lazy stretch. When she stood again, her cheeks were red and the short tendrils of hair that framed her face were sticking to her damp skin. "Let me clean up a bit and get T.J., and we can go to lunch. Want to come in?"

Riley shook his head. "I'll wait out here." He watched her go inside, then sat on one of the steps. It seemed he did a lot of that—watching her walk away. One day in the future—a few weeks, maybe a few months, if he was lucky— he would watch her for the last time. He would go back to living without her. Even though seeing her was hell, not seeing her, he knew, would be ten times worse.

Behind him the screen door slammed, then T.J. sat down one step up. "Mom says we're going to lunch."

"Any suggestions where to go?"

"Dressed like this?" the boy said, tugging at his worn work clothes. "Someplace where I won't see anyone I know. I look like an escapee from a prison work farm."

"Aren't you a little young to be worried about fashion?"

"Grandma Davis says you can never be too young to take pride in your appearance," T.J. announced snootily. Then he rolled his eyes. "Of course, she says that when she's trying to make me wear slacks and dress shirts and ties. I hate ties." Before Riley could comment either way he abruptly changed the subject. "Do we have to work today? Can't you, like, call it on account of the weather?"

Riley gave him an admonishing look. "It's not a game, T.J., it's punishment."

"Like I forgot," the boy muttered.

"However..." He waited until the kid's attention was on him again. "They've cut the schedule back to two hours today. You'll be done at three."

T.J. brightened up. "Because of the weather? Man, I hope it stays hot for a long time."

"I don't know why." The call to notify him of the change had come just as he was leaving the company to come here, and he hadn't bothered to ask questions. All he had wanted at that moment was to see Liza again. To find out if she was angry with him over last weekend. To soothe that insistent ache deep inside that came from being away from her.

"When I get back today Mom's taking me over to spend the night at Grandma's. We're going to call my dad, then go swimming. They've got a big pool, and it's heated, and in the winter they've got this big sort of tent over it so you don't get cold. It's neat. I used to be on a swim team in Dallas, before Mom and Dad...you know."

Little after his first mention of his father registered with Riley. Frowning, he asked, "Why do you go over to your grandparents' house to call your father? Why can't you do it from here?"

T.J. shrugged carelessly. "Because that's the way we've done it ever since we moved. Mom and Dad don't hardly ever talk to each other, but Grandma and Grandpa call him pretty often, and if he's not feeling too bad, I can talk to him then."

"Is he sick?"

"Yeah, since before Mom and me moved out. He's been in the hospital a couple of times. Sometimes he seems okay, but sometimes he acts weird and—" Suddenly he looked at Riley and clamped his mouth shut on his next words. After a moment he went on, a gleam of defiance in his eyes— Liza's eyes—and in his voice. "But he's going to be all right. Grandpa says so. And when he's better he's going to come here so we can all live together again. As a family. Just the three of us."

Liza came out then. The distraction she provided couldn't have been better timed if she had planned it, Riley thought. He didn't feel like responding to an eleven-year-old's challenge, especially when his thoughts were preoccupied with the new information the boy had given him.

So Davis had been sick and in and out of the hospital for two years. Interesting that Liza had never mentioned that. Had his illness played a part in their divorce? Had it made him realize that life was too precious to spend with a woman who didn't truly love him, a woman who had married him for his family's money and nothing else?

"Where are we going?" Liza asked, stepping around T.J. and passing Riley to reach the bottom of the steps. She was still wearing shorts, giving Riley a too-close look at her long legs, but she had changed shirts, braided her hair and added a bit of makeup. As he looked at her he wondered again about her divorce. What had caused it? Who had been responsible? And most baffling of all, how had Davis coped without her? Life with Liza, any kind of life, had to be better than living without her.

In response to her question, T.J. named a nearby fast-food restaurant. Realizing that the boy was waiting for his agreement, Riley nodded and got to his feet.

The restaurant was crowded, but they found a table for two along one wall. T.J. opted to sit at the central island on a stool so tall that his feet dangled above the floor. "He's already starting to reach the age where he doesn't want to be seen in public with his mother," Liza remarked with a sigh.

"I don't remember ever feeling that way about my parents."

"You didn't need to feel that way about your parents." Riley took his lunch from the tray, then slid the rest across the table. "I was the one you didn't want to be seen with."

She spread a napkin for her fries, then unwrapped her hamburger before looking at him. "That's not true, Riley. We went out all the time."

"To places where you didn't know anyone. Places where your friends never went. Places where you never had to introduce or explain me to anyone."

"I never met any of your friends, either."

"You never asked."

"You never asked to meet mine." She smiled tautly. "In fact, what you were mostly interested in doing when we went out was best done without an audience."

He opened his mouth to deny her assertion, then closed it again without a word. She was right. What he had wanted most was to be with her, not her friends. He had wanted to talk to her, touch her, make love with her. He had wanted to live in a world where no one else existed, where nothing could come between them. To some extent they had created that world. They had had their own lives, which included family and friends and work for him, school for her, but had excluded each other. Then they'd had their private lives, which had excluded everyone and everything else.

Rather than admit that she was right, though, he changed the subject. "T.J. said he's going to his grandparents' when we're finished today."

She nodded.

"After you take him there, I'd like to talk to you."

"About what?" she asked, but he merely shook his head. A crowded restaurant with T.J. ten feet away wasn't the place for the questions he wanted to ask her, for the answers he had to have.

Liza didn't push. Maybe she was shameless, she thought without a trace of shame, but she would agree to almost anything in order to spend time with Riley. "Why don't you bring him home?'' she suggested. ''We'll drop him off at his grandparents' and then talk.''

Although he nodded, she suspected from the look on his face that his agreement was reluctantly given. It wasn't the first or last parts of her suggestion—bringing T.J. home and talking to her—that bothered him, she knew, but the middle part, going with her to the Davis house, made him uncomfortable. Many people were intimidated by Alexander Davis, and Riley had better reason than most to want to keep his distance. Fourteen years ago he had interfered with Alexander and Garrett's plans for their children. More recently he had arrested Alexander's only grandson.

And he was definitely a barrier to Alexander's hopes that one day Keith and Liza might get together again. Once, she had settled for friendship. She had settled for affection.

Now she knew she could never *settle* again. She could never give anything less than love. She could never accept anything less in return.

Seeing Riley again had convinced her of that.

Liza was waiting when Riley and T.J. returned from the fort. Carrying a small overnight bag in one hand and her purse in the other, she joined them in the truck. As she gave Riley directions to the Davises' house, he offered her a protesting look over the top of T.J.'s head. She simply smiled and ignored it. He was the one who had brought up the fact this afternoon that he'd never met anyone in her life fourteen years ago. Now he could see what he had missed.

T.J. chattered about the work they'd done this afternoon—painting, a chore Liza could have guessed at from the splatters on their clothes and arms. Occasionally he interrupted himself to tell Riley to turn right here, then left there, at last directing him into a broad circular driveway that led to the front of a Greek-Revival-style house that truly deserved the label of mansion. Even Liza, who had grown up only a few blocks away, was always impressed by the sheer beauty of the place.

She climbed out of the truck, stepped aside to let T.J. pass, then asked, "Want to come in and meet T.J.'s grandparents?"

He simply scowled at her.

By the time she'd turned away from the pickup, Margaret, awaiting their arrival, had already opened the door. She gave her grandson a hug in spite of his grimy appearance, then greeted Liza with a coolly elegant smile. "T.J., your grandfather is on the phone with your father right now. Why don't you run on into the study so you can talk?"

After T.J. gave her a kiss, then disappeared down the broad hall, Liza asked, "How is Keith?"

"It's one of his better days." Margaret glanced at the truck, then back at Liza. "How are you, dear?"

"I'm fine."

Unable to suppress her curiosity any longer, the older woman lifted one hand in a polite gesture. "Is that...?"

"Yes, that's Riley."

"I can see why you're attracted to him. He's very handsome."

Liza glanced at him over her shoulder. Even from here his frown was clearly visible. Maybe she should have let him wait at her house while she brought T.J. here. If he truly believed that she had once been ashamed of him, being this close to Keith's parents must play on his insecurities—insecurities that *she* had created. Insecurities that had lasted far longer than their relationship.

"Yes," she agreed, turning back to Margaret. "He is handsome."

"Are you seeing him again?"

"I'm trying," she replied with a wry smile. "But it's not easy. I have a lot to apologize for."

Margaret's sigh was uncharacteristically sad. "We all do, dear. Alexander manipulated your father, your father manipulated you.... I wonder sometimes how differently our lives would have turned out if we had let you and Keith make your own decisions. If we hadn't pushed you. You probably would have married your soldier, and you would have been happy, and your parents would have gotten more than one grandchild from you. And Keith . . . Maybe if he hadn't felt such pressure to succeed, to live up to the Davis name, he wouldn't have been so vulnerable. If he'd been allowed to live his own life, to do what he wanted where and when and with whomever he wanted, maybe he wouldn't have sought that kind of escape.''

Before Liza could think of anything appropriate to say, Margaret forced a pleasant smile. ''How old are you now, Liza?''

''Thirty-three.''

''Old enough to know your own mind. Old enough to know that someone special comes along only once—usually. Old enough to tell your father that you don't need his approval to fall in love or to get married or to be happy.'' She smiled and changed the subject again. ''Will we see you in church tomorrow?''

Liza nodded.

''You can get T.J. then. Enjoy your evening, dear.''

As the door closed behind her, Liza made her way to the truck. After she had fastened her seat belt, Riley drove away, waiting until they were several blocks from the Davis home before he spoke. ''Is anything wrong?''

''No. Why do you ask?''

''You both looked so serious. Did she . . . ?'' His fingers flexed around the steering wheel, and he scowled as he forced the question out. ''Did she say something about me?''

He meant, was she angry about seeing Liza with him, with that punk she had very nearly chosen over Keith, with that cop who'd had the audacity to arrest her grandson, Liza realized. He'd gotten nothing but hostility from her family; now he expected it from Keith's. ''As a matter of fact, she did.'' She turned to look at him. ''She said that you're a very handsome man.''

A tinge of color crept into his face and down his neck.

''Margaret is nice,'' she continued. ''So is my mother. It's the men in the family who are unbearable.''

A few weeks ago, she suspected, he would have had a response to that last statement, but today he said nothing. For that small gift, she was grateful.

When they got back to her house, he noticed the dozens of pansies still in their plastic pots underneath the live oak. "You haven't finished."

"I thought I would plant them while we talked."

"I'll help."

She started to point out that he'd already spent the hottest part of the day in physical labor. Instead she accepted his offer with a shrug. Leaving her purse on the porch, she put on her gardening gloves, settled on her knees and picked up the trowel. "What was it you wanted to talk about?"

Riley didn't reply. He had thought it would be easy to ask his questions, to demand her answers. *What happened to your marriage? Why did he leave you? How could he give you up? Is he sick? What's wrong with him? Why can't his son talk to him at home? What are you hiding?*

But the words wouldn't come. He didn't want to see her stiffen as she usually did when he asked too-intimate questions. He didn't want to watch the soft and calm and trusting look in her eyes turn wary and haunted. He didn't want her to draw away from him.

"Later," he said at last, his tone too sharp.

Surprisingly, she accepted that short, inadequate answer and went back to work. They talked a little—some about T.J., but mostly about unimportant things, the kind of small talk he could have exchanged with any stranger on the street. They had never made small talk before, he thought with a grimace. From the very first time they'd met, their conversations had been comfortable, easy, intimate. They had never discussed anything as meaningless as the weather.

"I'm going to get something to drink," Liza announced after commenting with a sigh on the heat. "Would you like something? I have iced tea, lemonade and soda."

"Tea, please."

She left her gloves on the sun-warmed soil and went inside. Moving into the giant oak's shade, Riley settled on the yellowed grass, then pulled his T-shirt off and wiped his face. The shirt was worn, faded blue and liberally splattered with white paint. There was a tear in the shoulder seam, and the corner of the pocket hung limply, ripped free of its stitching.

The rest of his clothes weren't in much better shape. His jeans were nearly white from too many washings, and the denim across one knee had been reduced to fuzzy strings. Along with his disreputably old tennis shoes, they, too, were splattered with paint. He would have made a hell of an impression if he had accepted Liza's offer to meet her former in-laws, he thought with a scowl. They would have taken one look at him and had one of the servants escort him off their property.

Not that it mattered. As long as Liza didn't judge him unsuitable, as long as *she* didn't send him away, he couldn't care less what anyone else thought of him. She was the one who mattered.

She brought two glasses and a pitcher of iced tea outside. After settling on the ground in front of him she filled both glasses, sealed the lid on the pitcher, then offered him a glass . . . and froze in midmotion.

Too late Riley remembered the scars. There was the small one, high on his chest, jagged and round and puckered. That was the entry wound from the bullet. Underneath it was the smoother, flatter, neater scar from the surgeon's incision. It started near his breastbone and looped around, following the curve of his ribs, to the middle of his back. He had lived with the scars for ten years, and he could forget them for months at a time, until someone reminded him. Until someone saw them for the first time and was sympathetic, repulsed or morbidly curious.

"Oh, Riley," she whispered. Setting the glass down in front of him, she touched the longest scar, laying her palm flat over it. Her fingers were cool from the glass and at the same time hot, making him shiver, spreading warmth through him. It was an innocent touch, yet the images it brought to mind were wicked.

His first impulse was to push her hand away, to deny himself the pleasure *she* had denied him for fourteen years. His second was to trap her hand in place with his own, to enjoy her touch as long as he could.

Before he could act on either, she lifted her hand, then with one fingertip traced the line of the scar until it vanished from sight. "What happened?"

"I got shot."

Shock turned to dismay. "I didn't realize . . ."

He smiled thinly. She hadn't equated being a military police officer with being a *real* cop. She had assumed that working as a cop on a military base with primarily military people somehow meant less risk, less danger. It was an assumption his mother had made, and his sisters.

It was wrong.

"What happened?" she asked, her voice returning to normal. "Who did this to you?"

He told her in quiet, unemotional tones about the burglary he had interrupted ten years ago. About the men who had both been in jail before and hadn't wanted to go again. About the surgery and the long, painful recovery and the days that remained blank in his mind.

But he didn't tell her about the MP who had found him following the shooting and his report of the only thing Riley had said before losing consciousness: *Tell Liza . . .* He didn't tell her about the doctor coming to his room after the surgery and asking who Liza was. He didn't tell her that he'd dreamed of her when he had thought he was dying, that when he had realized he would live, that he would live without her, he had *wanted* to die.

"It must have been awful," she said quietly when he was finished. "They almost killed you."

Slowly he shook his head. "You, Liza . . . *you* almost killed me. They just tried to finish the job."

Looking away ashamedly, she moved to get up, but Riley countered the movement, rising quickly to his knees, blocking her way. "Don't walk away from me, Liza," he demanded—pleaded—in a husky voice. "Not this time. Please."

When she looked up at him, he saw the tears in her eyes. Were they tears of shame for what she'd done so long ago? he wondered. Of regret for what he'd suffered? Or of sorrow for what they'd lost?

It didn't matter. Leaning forward, he touched his mouth to the drop on her cheek, tasting its salty flavor. Her eyes fluttered shut, and he placed his next kiss, gentle and brief, on her eyelid. The third landed on her forehead, the fourth once more on her cheek.

Something inside him—years of hunger, a lifetime of longing—urged him to hurry, to kiss her, really kiss her, now, to seek that small intimacy he remembered too well. But something stronger held him back: the desire to prolong the moment, to savor each small contact, to delay the pleasure he sought until he couldn't wait any longer.

Gentle. He had always treated her so gently, Liza dazedly recalled. Even when passion had knotted his muscles and made him weak, he had always been gentle. Like so much else, that hadn't changed. His kisses were gently tormenting, his hands on her arms tenderly trapping her. She wanted to tell him that he didn't need to hold her, that she would never walk away again. But more than that assurance, she wanted his kiss. She wanted his mouth on hers. She wanted to taste his need. She wanted . . . Lord, more than she could stand.

He murmured her name, and she turned blindly toward the sound, seeking his mouth, brushing her lips against his, opening her mouth to his tongue, beckoning him inside. When he accepted her invitation with a slow, leisurely foray, she trembled. When slow gave way to insistent, when leisure turned to hunger, she moaned.

It was a tiny sound, soft and helpless, that Riley felt more clearly than he heard it. In fourteen years he had never forgotten the sounds of their lovemaking—her uneven breathing, her desperate pleas, her satisfied moans. Even the sounds had aroused him, the soft, breathless proof that she had wanted him as much as he'd needed her.

He felt her hands on his chest, tentative touches that seared his skin and made his muscles clench. She could create such feelings with no more than a touch. Breath-stealing hunger. Soul-deep need. Pleasure and pain, anguish and joy. And love. Dear God, how he had loved her.

How easily he could love her again.

He withdrew from her slowly, every part of him protesting the loss. But he continued to hold her, his hands on her arms, as he sat back and looked at her.

If she didn't open her eyes, Liza thought crazily, she couldn't see that he had pulled away. She couldn't see that he regretted kissing her, touching her, even knowing that she existed. She could pretend that he was preparing to kiss her again and again, until they had made up for fourteen long years apart.

But finally she did open her eyes, and found him watching her. There were countless emotions in his eyes—bewilderment, sadness, arousal, tenderness—but regret wasn't one of them. He wasn't sorry he had kissed her. Relieved, she smiled, a helpless gesture that started with a tremble and grew until it filled her. It grew even more when he smiled, too, the sweet, charming, loving smile she hadn't seen since their last night together at the lake. So long ago.

"If I'd known I would get a smile from you, I would have asked you to take your shirt off weeks ago," she murmured.

"You always were anxious to get my clothes off." He slid his hands down her arms until his fingers were clasped around hers. After a moment he gave up even that touch. Liza missed it dearly.

He shifted until he was sitting again, Indian-style. The position did nothing to hide his arousal. One brief glance warmed her cheeks and made her force her gaze higher, over the flat expanse of his stomach and the smooth muscles of his chest to his face. As she sank onto the grass, she said very softly, "I've missed you, Riley."

He gave her a long, steady, unrevealing look, and she wondered despairingly if his defenses were already back in place. Then, after a moment, he spoke with the same softness and the same certainty. "I've missed you, too."

After their break they went back to work and finished the gardening chores in little more than an hour. Liza studied their work with an approving smile, then slipped off her gloves for the last time and faced Riley. "Would you like to do something this evening?"

He could think of dozens of things he would like to do. Such as kissing her again. Touching her. Holding her. Undressing her and discovering every minute change giving birth and growing up had made in her body.

Most of all he would like to make love to her. With her. Over and over until he was too weak to even think about desire. And then he would like to sleep beside her—something they had never done—and when he was rested he would like to do it all again.

Failing that, he would like to spend a few more hours in her company.

"Sure," he replied, shaking out his shirt and pulling it on again.

"Would you like to go out...or stay in?"

Staying in evoked such pleasurable images—fixing dinner together, eating and cleaning up, talking or being quiet, sharing the sofa and watching a movie, or doing nothing at all but sharing the time. They had never done any of those things, had never had any place to go but out. They had never had such privacy and the possibilities it allowed.

"Let's stay here," he suggested. "We can get something for dinner and maybe rent a movie."

"Okay. But I have to clean up first."

"So do I. I'll be back around seven or seven-thirty." She looked so appealing, standing there all grimy and flushed from a hot afternoon's work, that he didn't want to leave, not even for the hour or two it would take to go home, shower and come back.

But of course he did leave, and he did it without fanfare, without a kiss, with nothing but a light touch of her hair and a soft "See you."

Back in his room at the company, he showered and shaved. He was in the process of dressing in clean jeans and a new black T-shirt when the phone rang. Had Liza changed her mind? he wondered as he sprawled across the bed to reach the receiver.

The voice at the other end was soft, feminine and sexy. Before he'd heard more than the greeting he knew it wasn't Liza. "Hey, Colette."

"I tried to catch you after work today, but you left too quickly," the social worker said. "I wanted to see if you'd like to come over this evening."

"Sorry, but I'm on my way out."

"You have a date?"

"Yeah, sort of." A date, he thought with a wry grin. With Liza. After all these years. He never would have believed it.

"With *her?*"

His grin disappearing, he rolled onto his back and studied the ceiling. "What do you need, Colette?"

"You *are* seeing her, aren't you? You're going out with her. With the mother of one of the kids you're supervising in the work-service program." She gave a soft little laugh. "I won't deny that I'm jealous, Riley. I've been hoping for something more between you and me for a long time. But I'm concerned, too—professionally. Don't you think that what you're doing might be perceived as unethical?"

"Have I been easier on T.J. because of his mother? Have I been harder on him? Can anyone honestly say that I treat him any differently than I treat Jamal and Trevor?"

"As far as I can tell, no. But—"

"Then what's the problem?"

Colette sighed. "She's not good for you, Riley. Do you know who she is, who her father is, who her ex-in-laws are?"

"Yes, I do."

"And you think you can fit into their world?"

"I don't know. But I know that she can fit into mine." At least, for a while, he added silently. "Look, Colette, I appreciate your concern, but—"

"She's going to break your heart."

Maybe.

Or maybe she would put it back together again.

"I've got to go, Colette," he said, rising from the bed. "I'll see you tomorrow." After hanging up, he tucked his shirt into his jeans and fastened his belt, then combed his hair and checked his wallet to be sure he had money. Before sliding it into his pocket, though, he opened it again and drew out the folded newspaper announcement.

For the first time in years he read it all the way through, from the date, time and location of the wedding ceremony to the biographical information—where Liza was attending college, her major, the names of her grandparents and, in the next paragraph, similar information about Davis. They had both been honor students, had come from the same background, had grown up in the same neighborhood, had shared so much in common. On the surface, no two people could have been better suited to each other.

Yet their marriage had failed.

He thought without conceit that things would have been different if *he* had somehow been able to take Davis's place, if *he* had been standing beside Liza on those church steps so long ago. Maybe he had been a punk—he had definitely grown up poor—but he had shared something with Liza far more important than background, breeding or class: love. With love, all the other differences between them wouldn't have mattered.

How would it feel, he wondered, to celebrate a wedding anniversary with Liza? To raise a family with her? To know that she would always be there with him?

Instead of returning the paper to his wallet, its home for fourteen years, he slid it into a drawer that held a dozen pairs of olive drab socks. Grabbing his keys and his worn leather jacket, he left his room and headed back to town.

* * *

"What was it you wanted to talk to me about earlier?" Liza's voice cut quietly through the still night air. She had waited all evening for Riley to initiate the conversation. He had seemed so serious when he'd requested the talk at lunch, but he hadn't brought up anything, not through dinner, not through the movie they'd watched, not through the quiet moments following the movie.

Now he was ready to return to the barracks. She had followed him outside onto the porch before asking her question. If this discussion was a serious one, she reasoned, it would be easier to conduct in the dark, in the cool, quiet night.

His back was to her, his hands resting on the dew-damp railing. After a moment he spoke. "Keith."

Sighing, she joined him at the railing. No night would ever be dark enough to make her comfortable with this subject with this man. But he had a right to know. Before he got any further involved with her, he deserved to know everything.

"What happened to your marriage, Liza? What's wrong now?"

She sighed again, heavily enough to make her shudder. "I told you that Keith found something he wanted more than T.J. and me."

He glanced at her. She couldn't see his face, but she could feel the weight of his gaze. "Another woman."

He said it so matter-of-factly, as if he found it perfectly understandable that Keith should choose another woman, any woman, over her. If she'd cared at all about her marriage, her feelings would have been hurt. But she didn't care. "No, not another woman."

"Another man?" There was disbelief in his voice this time, and it made her smile.

"I didn't say some*one*, Riley. I said some*thing*."

"I don't understand."

She gripped the rail tighter. "God, this is hard. I haven't told anyone but our parents and Gretchen. The funny thing is that you're a cop. You could find out for yourself if you wanted. The Dallas Police Department would probably tell you far more than they ever told me."

He turned to face her then, and incredulity and surprise were in his voice. "Are you saying that Davis was in trouble with the law? Was he arrested?"

"Like father, like son," she replied with a flippancy she didn't feel.

"Is he in jail?"

"No. Davises don't go to jail. He knew someone who knew someone who knew someone. . . ."

"What were the charges?"

Her fingertips were starting to ache, but she couldn't release her hold on the railing. She couldn't let go and face Riley and tell him these things that just might make him walk out of her life, for good this time. "Possession with intent to distribute. Only he didn't. He intended to keep it all for himself."

For a long time Riley was silent. She wished she knew what he was thinking, what he was feeling, whether he was judging. Just when she was certain that he must have gone past thinking about Keith's weakness to focusing on his criminal activities, to considering whether he wanted to be associated with the ex-wife of a crook, he broke his silence. "Intent to distribute what?" he asked evenly.

"Cocaine. Today's drug of choice."

After another long moment he asked, "How did it happen?"

Grateful that he sounded so normal, so unaccusing, she shrugged. "I don't know. He worked hard. He wasn't particularly unhappy at home. He had his own friends, his own activities. I didn't suspect a thing until I found out we were practically broke. We were being threatened by everyone we owed money to, and the bank was going to foreclose on the house."

"So these hospitals he's been in—they're drug treatment centers, aren't they?"

Finally she loosened her grip and faced him. Even this close, she couldn't make out his expression. "How did you know that?"

"T.J. mentioned it. He doesn't know, does he?"

"No," Liza whispered, hugging herself tightly. "He's just a little boy. How can I tell him that his father is addicted to cocaine, that he loves some white powder more than he ever loved us?" A sigh shivered through her. "We just tell him that Keith is sick. That that's why T.J. can't call him whenever he wants. That that's why he can't visit him alone."

"That's what caused the divorce, isn't it?" Riley made a soft sound of dismay. "I'd been wondering how any man in his right mind could give you up. You left him, didn't you? You divorced him."

"I gave him a chance," she replied, willing him to believe her. "I didn't just run out on him. He went through the rehab clinic the first time, and he got straightened out. He had another chance. But he lied to me. He started using again. He started stealing from me. We couldn't pay our bills without his parents' help because he kept taking and taking. That car—" She gestured toward it in the dark. "You probably think I bought it with my divorce settlement, but you're wrong. After we were divorced Keith took my car, forged my signature on the title and sold it to get money to buy more drugs. Alexander was afraid that I might have him arrested, so he bought me that car instead."

"And that's why Keith sold T.J.'s dog."

Even though he probably couldn't see, she nodded.

For a long time he said nothing. Liza waited, listening to the sounds of traffic on the nearby expressway, to the wail of an ambulance siren somewhere in the distance, to the faint rumble of a plane overhead. But louder than all those other noises was the sound of her heart, thumping irregularly in her chest.

When he finally spoke, his words surprised her. "I'm sorry."

"For what?"

"The things I said. The things I thought."

"You were entitled."

He came a step closer. "It must have been hard for you."

"Yes." She swallowed hard as she came to the most difficult part. "If it makes a difference to you...I understand."

Earlier, Riley acknowledged, she had expected him to somehow blame her. *I gave him a chance,* she'd said defensively, pleadingly. *I didn't just run out on him.* Now she was offering *him* a chance—a chance to end this relationship right here. A chance to condemn her for Davis's weakness. A chance to add to the load of guilt she already carried.

Had Davis's family somehow blamed her? Had they wondered what she had done to drive him to such extremes? Did she blame herself? If she had realized what was happening sooner, if their marriage had been stronger, if he'd been happier at home... She could torment herself forever with ifs.

She was waiting for his response, for him to say yes, it made a difference to him, and no, he didn't want to see her anymore. He moved closer, and she backed away until she had trapped herself in the corner. And still he came closer, until it was impossible to move any more. Until she was all he could feel along the entire length of his body.

He slid his fingers into her hair and tilted her head back. He wished he could see her eyes, could see them go soft and smoky, but it was too dark. But he could feel her lips part for his kiss. He could hear her breath catch. He could feel the muscles in her body tighten.

He kissed her lazily, as if he hadn't waited forever to do it. He teased her with his tongue, with his fingers, with his body. He captured her hands and brought them to his chest, pressing one against his pounding heart, and then he placed his own hand over her heart. Over her breast, soft and full. Even through the fabric of her blouse he felt her nipple grow hard, and he heard her soft groan of pleasure.

Breaking off the kiss, he brushed his mouth across her ear, making her shiver, then left a damp trail along her jaw.

When he kissed her again she was all soft and yielding and hot, welcoming his tongue, responding to his body.

After a moment she twisted free of his kiss and whispered, "Come inside with me, Riley. Don't go."

Don't go. Stay. Make love. If he hadn't already been impossibly hard, her husky invitation would have made him so. Spend the night. In a bed. With Liza. Fourteen years ago that would have been his idea of heaven. Now she had offered it to him, but he couldn't accept. He wanted more. He wanted...

God help him, he didn't know *what* he wanted. Assurances. Promises. Guarantees. He wanted control...but when had he ever made love to Liza without losing control?

He wanted to trust her. He wanted to forgive her. He wanted to know that this was right, that he wouldn't hurt her, that, if there was a God in heaven, she wouldn't hurt him again.

He wanted to know that he could survive her a second time.

"I have to go," he muttered, half hoping she would stop him, that she would kiss him and change his mind. But when he backed away from her she remained where she was. In his mind he knew how she must look—the way she had always looked when they'd made love, with her hair mussed, her eyes hazy, her mouth full, her breasts swollen—and the image almost made him groan. It almost made him stay.

He'd reached the bottom of the steps when she murmured his name. Slowly he turned back to her.

"Be careful."

He smiled bleakly. He was trying so damned hard to be careful, but it might all be for nothing.

He just might get hurt anyway.

Chapter 9

Fort Gordon was a large post, much of it wooded and sparsely developed. All the offices, barracks and quarters were centrally located, with the warehouses, riding stables and kennels on the outer fringe. Much of the rest was devoted to training areas. It was that area Riley decided to patrol after dinner on Thursday. The main post was quiet, and the areas out around Mirror Lake and Gordon Lakes Golf Course were often worth a drive by.

In the back of the Cherokee, Jasper was restless. He made a complete circle around the vehicle, lay down and thumped his tail for a moment, then got up and walked around again. Riley could sympathize with the dog. *He* was restless, too. He didn't want to be working tonight. He didn't want to be cooped up for hours inside the Cherokee.

He wanted to be with Liza.

By the time he'd fallen asleep sometime Sunday morning he had cursed himself a thousand times for not accepting her invitation to spend the night. Of course, he wouldn't have gotten much more sleep if he had stayed at her house, but being aroused with Liza had to be a hell of a lot more satisfying than being aroused alone.

He'd hardly seen her since Saturday night. When she had dropped off T.J. Sunday afternoon he'd been too busy with Jamal's parents to speak to her, and when she had come back a few hours later, her sister, Gretchen, had been with her. Since then he'd been working evenings. By the time she got off, he was already at work, and by the time he got off, she was already asleep.

He slowed for the stop sign ahead, then brought the Cherokee to a halt as the radio operator called one of the canine officers under Riley's supervision. There was a moment's silence, followed by the deep, excited bark of a dog. The sound brought Jasper, growling softly, to an alert stance directly behind Riley. None of the dogs could be trusted with the others—on the rare occasions when two of them had gotten together, a fight had ensued—and Jasper harbored a particular dislike for this one. The mere sound of her barking made him bristle.

"K-9 Jackie, put your partner on the radio," the radio operator requested, as if a dog on the radio wasn't unusual, and an instant later Jackie's handler responded.

He and Jasper weren't the only ones who were bored tonight, Riley thought as he turned onto yet another deserted road.

He would have missed the car pulled off the road into the edge of the woods if Jasper hadn't barked. Slowly he backed up until the Cherokee was blocking the dirt trail. He called in on the radio, then got out and lowered the back door, snapping Jasper's leash onto his collar.

There could be any number of reasons for the car's presence out here. These woods were a popular spot for hunters—the fort even had its own game wardens—but hunting at night often meant spotlighting deer, and that was illegal. Then again, the car could have broken down out here. Or it could have been stolen and abandoned here.

Or, he saw with a grin as he came up beside it, the occupants could have the simplest and probably oldest reason in the world to wander off into the woods. Hadn't he and Liza put in their share of back-seat time when they were younger? Of course, they also had been lucky enough never to get caught. The only lucky thing for these young soldiers tonight was that they'd gotten caught while they were both still clothed.

More or less.

To be young and in love—in lust—and with no place to go, Riley thought with a grin when he had completed the call and was back on the road. Some of these young trainees seemed to think they would die without sex, and some of them were pretty brazen about satisfying the urge. But you could want until it hurt and still survive. He was proof of that.

Of course, he was also old enough—just barely—to be those kids' father. He was supposed to be more mature. He was supposed to exercise more restraint. He was supposed to be more cautious. Yet walking away from Liza on Saturday night had been almost more than he could bear.

After a while he returned to the main post and drove aimlessly before stopping at a pay phone near the PX. He didn't remember consciously making a mental note of Liza's phone number when he'd read the investigator's reports following T.J.'s arrest, but the information had stuck with him. On the third ring the answering machine picked up, but almost immediately it cut off again when T.J. answered. "This is Riley, T.J. Can I speak to your mother?"

"She's got company," the boy replied, his voice dark with belligerence.

When they were alone or with the other boys, Riley thought with a scowl, T.J. was good-natured, friendly and talkative. The minute Liza came into the picture, though, his defenses went up and his attitude turned sour. Maybe it was a normal response for a child of divorce, particularly a boy—a boy who wanted his parents back together. Still, Riley couldn't help feeling annoyed by the kid's changeable moods. "This will only take a minute," he said patiently. "Could you call her?"

Without another word T.J. dropped the phone with a clatter. An instant later Riley heard him yell, "Mom!" as if she were somewhere in the next county instead of the next room.

It was only a moment before Liza came on the line. Her voice was soft and sweet as always, although a bit impersonal until she realized it was him. Then it turned warm. Welcoming.

"T.J. said you have company, so I won't keep you."

She laughed. "Gretchen's here. She's family, not company. Are you working?"

"Yeah, I've been on evenings all week. Listen, you want to go out Saturday?"

"Out?"

His scowl grew fiercer, keeping pace with the desire that had begun curling through him at the first sound of her voice. "Dinner? Maybe a movie?"

"Or maybe dancing, instead? I haven't danced in so long."

Neither had he, and he had always enjoyed it, especially with Liza, but he wasn't enthusiastic about the prospect now. There was something entirely too intimate about dancing, about dimly lit rooms and soft, slow music and holding her close. Still, he agreed. Pushed by whatever self-tormenting tendencies had lately surfaced in him, he said yes. "Okay, dancing, then. I'll pick you up at seven."

When Liza hung up she was smiling secretively. Her pleasure slowly diminished, though, when she realized that T.J. was sitting at the top of the stairs, watching her with undisguised antagonism. She moved to the bottom of the steps and looked up at him, her gaze steady. "When did you take up eavesdropping?"

"When did you take up dating *cops?*"

"My dates are none of your business," she said sternly, then relented. "Besides, I've told you before that Riley and I are old friends."

"Old friends don't go out dancing. Old friends don't hang around the way he does."

She climbed halfway up the stairs, then sat down sideways, leaning against the wall. "Maybe, maybe not. But Riley and I were friends... and more. We dated before I married your father."

"Grandpa Johnson says he's a troublemaker."

"Grandpa Johnson doesn't know what he's talking about. He never knew Riley. He never talked to him or learned anything about him. But you do know him, T.J." She tried a cajoling smile. "I bet somewhere down inside you even like him."

"Not as your boyfriend!" he exclaimed. "He doesn't belong here! My dad's going to get better soon, and he's going to come back, and we're all going to live together again! I know he is. I *know* it!" He jumped to his feet and headed to his room, but Liza called his name sharply.

"*T.J.*" As he slowly turned, she also stood. "I hope your dad does get better. I pray that he does. But it's not going to change things between us. We'll still be divorced. Even if he does come back to Augusta, I'm never going to live with him again. We'll never be a regular family again."

"It's because of *him,* isn't it?" he cried. "Because of that dumb cop." He paused to catch his breath. "You're wrong. I don't like him at all. I hate him!" After another brief pause he finished in a deadly quiet voice, "And I don't like you much, either."

He stomped down the hall to his room, then slammed the door so hard that Liza felt the vibrations. Part of her wanted to go after him, to calm him, to tell him...

She sighed wearily. The only thing she could tell him that would make him feel better was that she wouldn't see Riley again. That she would go back to Keith. That she would sacrifice the rest of her life and her happiness for his childish demands.

And she couldn't do that. Not even for T.J.

"He'll get over it," Gretchen said from below.

Ruefully, Liza smiled down at her. "I hope so."

"He's never made any secret of the fact that he wants you and Keith together again."

"And I've never made any secret of the fact that it isn't going to happen."

"But all the times you told him that, you were alone. You'd never gone out on a date. You'd never shown any real interest in another man. There were no prospects to take Keith's place in your life. In spite of what you said, T.J. could still hope." Gretchen shrugged. "Now he can't."

Liza went downstairs and followed her sister back into the kitchen. "The funny thing is that he likes Riley. He likes spending time with him. He likes having his attention."

"Liking him as a man is one thing. Liking him as a prospective stepfather is something else altogether." Gretchen sat at the kitchen table and refilled her coffee cup from the pot in the middle. "He feels threatened, Liza. The one thing he wants most in the world is for you and Keith to remarry so that he can have a real family again. You and I both know there's no chance of that because of everything that's happened. But in T.J.'s mind, the only thing standing in the way of his dream is Riley. If he can get rid of Riley, he can save his father's place for him."

Liza filled her own cup, then breathed deeply. The coffee was still hot, and the aromas of chocolate, cinnamon and cloves drifted on the steam. "Maybe I should have been honest with him in the beginning. Maybe I should have told him that Riley and I were more than friends."

"The only thing that would have accomplished is making T.J. hostile from the beginning. At least this way he got a chance to know the guy. That ought to work in Riley's— and your—favor...eventually." Gretchen settled back more comfortably. "So...how is it going? Will we hear wedding bells in the near future?"

The question filled Liza with a bittersweet ache. Marrying Riley. What could be more perfect, more right, than marrying the only man she had ever loved way down in her soul?

But he hadn't given her any hint that his future included her. He hadn't even wanted to make love to her last Saturday night, even though he'd made no effort to hide his arousal. Even though she had offered herself shamelessly. Even though she hadn't asked for anything from him in return. No promises. No declarations. No vows.

She tried to smile cheerily for her sister but knew it was a dismal failure. "Dinner and dancing do not a marriage proposal make," she replied airily.

"If you do marry him, this time I'll be your maid of honor."

"That's matron of honor."

"I'm too young to be a matron. Better yet, I could give the bride away. Daddy wouldn't do it, not to that particular groom, and T.J. certainly wouldn't."

Liza frowned at her. "Don't you think talk of marriage is a little premature? We haven't even—"

Before she could finish, Gretchen laughed wickedly. "No wonder you're grouchy. Let's see, that must be his decision. I know you. It's been at least two years since you've even let a man touch you, and you always did have a special thing for Riley."

Groaning softly, Liza hid her face in her hands. "We haven't even had a real date," she said through her fingers, carefully pronouncing each word. "And I'm not grouchy."

"Maybe frustrated is a better word. Abstaining from sex for months on end can do that to you."

Uncovering her face, she warned, "Gretchen—"

Instantly her sister became serious. "Do you still love him?"

Liza stared at her, her eyes suddenly misty. That was a question she avoided asking herself. It was one thing to talk about loving Riley fourteen years ago. That was easy. He had been her first serious boyfriend, her first lover. She was *supposed* to love him.

But things were different now, and there was nothing easy about it. There were problems and complications—her son, their past, her foolish mistakes, his bitterness. No matter how much he seemed to enjoy her company, no matter how sweetly he kissed her, he might not ever truly forgive her for what she'd done. He might not ever completely trust her again.

He might not ever be able to love her again.

Accepting her silence as an answer in itself, Gretchen impulsively squeezed her hand. "Things will work out, Liza. Don't worry about T.J. Sooner or later he'll have to accept that you and Keith are finished, and he'll come around. He'll warm up to Riley again."

Liza smiled glumly. "I wish I shared your confidence," she murmured.

"Oh, and Saturday night...?" Gretchen laughed that wicked laugh again. "T.J.'s spending the night with us."

Saturday was cloudy and cool, the way a November weekend should be. It was the eighth week of the experimental program, and Riley's group had come full circle: they had been assigned to the stables again. The boys were waiting for him at the picnic table outside the MP station, Jamal and Trevor sharing a bench and T.J. sprawled across the top.

As Riley approached, Jamal and Trevor began laughing, childish giggles that they tried to contain but couldn't, and when he got closer he understood why. Behind them, his hands cupped to his mouth, T.J. was doing a very creditable imitation of a pig's snort.

Pig. He hadn't been called that in a long time. These kids were so young that he was half-surprised they even understood the insult.

He stopped in front of them and briefly looked at each one, his expression unamused. Trevor immediately stopped laughing, and Jamal offered a chastened apology. T.J. merely looked back. There was no friendliness in his dark eyes. There was nothing there but arrogance.

"We're going to the stables," Riley said flatly. "Come on."

They grumbled and fussed but accompanied him to the waiting van. To his surprise, T.J. fell in step alongside him. "So you're taking my mom out tonight."

Riley didn't reply.

"She and Dad used to go out all the time in Dallas."

Still he said nothing.

"They went to the country club a lot and to nice restaurants. You know, the kind of places where she'd get all dressed up and wear her diamonds and have her hair done." His smile was malicious for an eleven-year-old. "No, you probably don't know, do you? You've probably never been in that kind of place. Grandpa Johnson says you were poor."

He emphasized the last word as if nothing could possibly be worse than poverty, a little something he had probably learned from his grandfather, Riley thought. Stopping beside the van, he waited pointedly for the boy to get inside. T.J. looked up at him before he did so. "Where are *you* taking her?" he asked.

Riley slid the door shut behind him with more force than necessary, then stood motionless a moment, his eyes shut, his jaw clenched tightly. If he wanted reminders that he and Liza came from different worlds, he could provide them himself from his memories. He could just look at her and see the breeding he lacked. He could ask Colette to once again point out the disparities between them.

But he didn't need to hear them from an angry little boy.

Finally he climbed into the front seat beside the driver. He listened halfheartedly to the conversation between the three boys in back, but mostly he thought about Liza.

He didn't doubt what T.J. had said for one minute. Appearances were important to people like Keith Davis. When things had been good between him and Liza, undoubtedly he had shown her off every chance he'd gotten. After all, she was a beautiful woman, well suited to country clubs, fancy restaurants and diamonds.

But, he reminded himself, she was equally suited to fast food, jeans and a ponytail. If she required all the trappings of wealth to be happy, she never would have gotten involved with him fourteen years ago. Hell, she never would have gotten involved with him now. As much as he liked his job, he was still just a soldier living on a soldier's income. He would never be rich, but he could pay his bills. He could help out his family when they needed it, and he had a little money saved. He could even take care of a family of his own—not lavishly, but he could provide the necessities and an occasional luxury.

When he realized what he was doing, he grinned wryly. As he had reminded himself a few nights ago, he was thirty-six years old—definitely old enough to be a father. Supposedly mature enough not to let an eleven-year-old kid get under his skin. Hopefully intelligent enough not to let that kid play on his insecurities.

Once they arrived at the stables they went right to work. Riley had hoped that T.J.'s attitude would improve, but every time he spoke to the boy he received a flippant, disrespectful reply or none at all. To make matters worse, the kid had decided that he didn't want to work today, forcing Riley to prod him on a regular basis.

The only bright spot in the entire afternoon was the arrival of the gray van that signaled the end of their workday...and the start of the countdown until his date with Liza. A few more hours and they would be together. Alone.

And alone with Liza had quickly, too quickly, become his favorite way to be.

Dark and romantic.

Those had been Liza's only requirements when she had asked Gretchen to recommend a place to go dancing, and her sister had very definitely come through. The club was quiet, the drinks cold, the floor uncrowded, and the music was wonderfully slow.

They had been dancing a long time, long enough for her high heels to pinch her toes, but she didn't care. She was in Riley's arms, and that was all that mattered.

"How did you find this place?" he murmured in her ear.

"It's a favorite of Gretchen's."

"She has good taste."

"Hmm. She likes *you.*"

After another moment he asked, "What time are you supposed to pick up T.J. tonight?"

She lifted her head from his shoulder and, for the first time since they'd walked onto the dance floor, missed a step and landed instead on his foot. "Sorry," she mumbled with a blush.

"Let me rephrase that question. *Are* you supposed to pick up T.J. tonight?"

Withdrawing from his embrace, Liza met his gaze. It had seemed such a good idea when Gretchen had offered to keep T.J. overnight. But after the rejection Riley had dealt her last Saturday night, when her son had been at his grandparents' for the night, she was embarrassed to admit that T.J. was gone again tonight. It seemed so orchestrated, so obvious.

"No," she finally replied. "He's spending the night there."

Riley didn't say anything. He simply looked at her.

"Gretchen just decided..." She took a shaky breath. "I didn't know how late... This doesn't mean I expect you to..."

He stopped her with a kiss, sweet and gentle, that made her mind shut down so that all she could do was feel—and, oh, heavens, how she felt! Did he know what he was doing to her? she wondered helplessly. Did he know that if he let go of her, she would probably float right to the floor? Did he know that if he stopped kissing her, she would die?

He did stop, and she didn't die. But she felt ridiculously lost and achingly lonely... until he spoke. "Let's go home, Liza."

They were the sweetest words he could have offered.

They left the dance floor and were on their way to the door when a woman called Riley's name. Automatically Liza turned to look at her even as he went to meet her. She was about Liza's height, dark haired, dark eyed and pretty. An old lover? she wondered with a twinge of jealousy.

Then she heard him speak the woman's name, and jealousy turned to interest, which gave way to a small, dull ache deep inside. *Robbie*. The woman was his sister, the one he was so close to.

The one he showed no intention of introducing her to.

She stood there, a few yards away, aware from Robbie's frequent glances that they were talking about her, aware, too, that she wouldn't be welcomed by Riley if she walked those few feet across the lobby to join them.

He didn't want his sister to meet her. That knowledge hurt. It hurt like hell.

As Riley watched, Liza moved from the spot where he'd left her to a more distant one near the door. She'd had a strange look on her face before she turned away. Envy? Did she think Robbie was someone he'd dated?

"Why don't you introduce us?" his sister asked, drawing his attention back to her.

"Not tonight."

"Why not?"

Because Robbie was family, and Liza was... an affair. Robbie was permanent. She would always be a part of his life. Nothing could ever change that. And Liza? Sometime soon she would be gone from his life. Nothing could change that, either. Not even the love they would soon be making in her little white house. "Not tonight," he repeated with more than a touch of grimness.

"Are you ashamed of your little sister?"

He gave her a thoroughly brotherly look of exasperation.

"Are you ashamed of *her?*"

If he felt any shame at all, it was for himself. Because he was using Liza. Because he was taking so much from her and giving her so little in return. Because he was letting her believe they could share a future when all they could possibly share was heartache.

"Why don't you bring her to dinner at Mama's tomorrow?"

"Yeah, right. If I took a woman home, Mom would have us married and raising a family in no time."

"Isn't that what you want? Isn't that what you've always wanted with Liza?"

Dear God, yes. But it had never happened, and he couldn't let himself believe it ever would. He couldn't let himself hope. Living without her would be hard enough if he was honest and faced the facts. Living without her if he let himself want more . . . That would be unbearable.

"I've got to go. If I don't make it to Mom's tomorrow, tell her I'll stop by during the week."

"Riley—"

He walked away, ignoring her call. At the door he slipped his arm around Liza's shoulders and guided her outside. She seemed a little stiff at his side, and he remembered that funny look. "That was my sister, Robbie," he announced as they crossed the parking lot.

She drew away as they reached the car. In deference to her dress and heels, he had agreed to leave his truck in her driveway and take her car instead. It had been almost too enjoyable to drive—finely tuned, luxurious, responsive—but he was still satisfied with his beat-up old truck. He helped her into the car then circled around to the driver's side. He was fastening the seat belt when Liza finally responded to his remark about Robbie.

"I would have liked to meet her," she said in a wistfully soft voice.

He became still, staring for a moment at the keys in his hand. *Not my family,* he thought silently, fiercely. He couldn't share his family with her. He couldn't share any part of his life with her except these few hours. He couldn't live with memories of her in his room in the barracks, at his parents' house or with his family or his friends. He couldn't let her touch those aspects of his life or he would never get over her. He would never survive her.

But no matter how valid his reasons, it didn't make her sound any less hurt.

And it didn't make him feel any less a bastard.

They covered the few miles to her house in silence. Taking her keys from him, Liza unlocked the door and went inside, turning on a small lamp on the hall table before she removed her coat. Riley stopped at the threshold, leaning one shoulder against the jamb, and watched her. "You don't have to invite me in," he said quietly. When they had left the dance floor fifteen minutes ago, the way this evening would end had seemed inevitable. But seeing Robbie had changed that.

He had changed it.

Liza draped her coat across the banister, then faced him. She was smiling as if the evening hadn't turned sour. As if he hadn't, only a few minutes ago, deliberately shut her out. She returned to the door, grasped a handful of his coat and pulled him inside.

He closed the door with his foot, then reached blindly behind him to secure the lock. Then he put his arms around her, drawing her close, bending his head to brush a kiss across her temple. He was grateful that she hadn't changed her mind, that she hadn't taken him up on his offer and sent him home alone.

Grateful. That had a familiar—and bittersweet—ring to it, he thought. Fourteen years ago his gratitude to Liza had been second only to his love for her. He had been grateful for every evening she'd given him, every hour she had spent with him, every intimacy she had shared with him. He had known he didn't deserve her, had known that he never even should have met her, so he had been doubly thankful to have whatever she would give him.

And then he had turned greedy. He had wanted it all.

He was feeling more than a little greedy tonight.

Liza leaned back in his arms so she could see his face. "Would you like some coffee?"

He shook his head.

"Tea?"

Another no.

Her voice grew softer, huskier. "Want to catch the late movie on TV?"

For the last time he shook his head. "I want to make love to you," he murmured. He watched the desire steal into her face, softening, shadowing, and he thought for one uneasy moment that he was too damn close to wanting more. He was too damn close to loving her—not the way he had before, blindly, passionately, heatedly, but the way a man loved a woman. Seriously. Intensely. Endlessly. If he thought about it, he would worry. He would be frightened. And so he pushed the thought from his mind and concentrated on Liza, soft and yielding in his arms.

She smiled. It was sweet and innocent, yet it made him think of sinful pleasure and pure satisfaction. "What a coincidence," she whispered. "That was going to be my next offer." Pulling away, she started up the stairs.

For a moment, bemused, Riley simply watched, then he prodded himself to follow. By the time he reached the top of the stairs she was already in her room. The door was open, a pale wedge of light shining into the hall. He approached it slowly, stopping once more in the doorway.

If he had ever allowed himself to place Liza in a bedroom in his mind, he supposed he would have imagined someplace elegant yet feminine, with satin, lace and ruffles. Someplace where he would feel totally out of place. Someplace he couldn't belong. But there was no elegance in this room. No satin, lace or ruffles. The furniture was cherry, the pieces big and solid. The colors were forest green and crimson, the patterns bold, the lines clean. It was a room he could live in.

She waited for him near the foot of the bed, looking nervous and suddenly shy. The brashness that had brought her this far, he suspected, had disappeared, leaving her unsure of how to proceed. He would bet she had never seduced any man but him, and at twenty-two he hadn't required much effort. At twenty-two all it had taken was a simple kiss, a gentle touch, sometimes no more than a knowing look, and he had been ready. He had always been ready for her.

"Take your hair down." His voice was sharp edged and raw, like everything inside him. Like his nerves. Like his heart. Like his soul.

Obediently she removed the combs, dropping them on the nearby dresser. Then she found all the little pins that held her hair off her neck, drawing each one out until it fell free. She shook her head, leaving her hair tangled and tousled and untamed. That was the way he had always liked it, as if she'd just gotten out of bed—although they'd never shared a bed. There had been grass and sand and cramped back seats, but never a bed.

Until tonight.

He didn't move from the doorway, even though his fingers ached to bury themselves in her hair, even though his entire body ached to bury itself within hers. He wanted to draw this out, to experience the pleasure and the pain and the longing to the fullest, so that the satisfaction would also be full. "Your shoes. . . ."

Bracing herself on the dresser, she removed first one, then the other, tossing them aside. They were fragile-looking shoes, all narrow straps with impossibly high heels that made her long legs seem even longer, leaner, sexier. He had never fantasized about women's clothing before, but those heels could conjure up a wicked thought or two.

She stood there motionless, palms pressed together, awaiting his next command, and he gave it hoarsely. "Now the dress."

It was blue, royal blue, and had a deep neck and buttoned down the front and was fastened with a wide black belt at the waist. She removed the belt first and dropped it on the dresser. It slithered off onto the floor. Next she began undoing the buttons, bending, her hair swinging forward, to reach the last few. When she straightened, the dress slipped from one shoulder, and she pushed it off, holding it by the collar, letting it puddle on the floor near the belt.

No fancy lingerie for this single working mother, Riley thought with a smile. No teddies or camisoles or those provocative lace-edged panties. Just a slip the color of cream and a lace-edged bra to match. Simple. Practical. And sexy as hell.

He had waited long enough, he decided.

He had waited too long.

Slowly he moved into the room, closing the distance between them, walking in a nerve-quiveringly close circle around her. "Why are you embarrassed?" he murmured in her ear from behind when he saw the blush that colored her face.

"I'm not nineteen anymore."

"So?"

"I'm not . . ." She shrugged helplessly. "I'm not the girl you used to know."

Still behind her, he laid his hands on her shoulders and felt her shiver. He slid them along her spine to the two small hooks that fastened her bra and eased them open. "You were a pretty girl, Liza," he whispered, touching his mouth to her shoulder in an open kiss. "But you're a beautiful woman." He kissed her again, this time a little lower.

Slowly, bit by bit, he pushed the straps off her shoulders and followed them down with his fingers. Her skin was so soft, so warm and smooth. Just touching her, even innocently, had always aroused him, and there was nothing innocent about the way he was touching her now.

His hands cupping her breasts, he moved closer until nothing, not even his fears, could come between them. Undoubtedly he would pay later for feeling this good now, but he didn't care. He would pay forever if it meant holding her like this. If it meant being inside her once again. If it meant loving her once more.

"Oh, Liza . . ." Her name came in a taut groan. "So beautiful. . . ."

He made her feel beautiful, she thought dreamily. The way he was touching her, the way he was kissing her, the way he wanted her . . . He made her feel special. Precious. Dear.

His hands were creating such incredible need in her breasts. His caresses made her nipples hard, made them ache for more intimate attention, for the sweet pain of his kisses. She ached elsewhere, everywhere, for his attention. For his caresses. For his body. For his love.

"Riley..." She couldn't find her voice, could manage only a whisper, a whimper, of need.

He turned her in his arms and kissed her, an insistent, hungry thrusting of his tongue, and her knees went weak. She clung to him, kissing him, silently pleading with him for something to make this ache go away, something to fill this emptiness inside, for something, anything, everything.

Then he moved his kisses lower, along her throat, across her breast to her nipple, and she cried out, arching her back, pressing even closer, harder, until she trembled, until she thought she would die. She did plead then, asking, demanding, begging, for more.

Riley found her hands around his neck and guided them to the front of his shirt, closing her fingers around the top button. He had wanted to impress her tonight, so he'd traded his usual jeans and T-shirt for dark trousers and a white dress shirt. The T-shirt would have been so much simpler to get off, he thought, suppressing a groan as she fumbled with the first button, then the second, then the third.

Halfway down she lost interest in the buttons and slid her fingers inside, caressing his chest, leaving fiery little trails across his skin that made him suck in his breath, that made his muscles go taut and his blood pump hotter. He managed the last buttons himself and discarded the shirt while she amused herself with kisses and hungry little bites. She paid particular attention to the thin line of his scar until it neared his nipple.

This time he couldn't hold back the groan. He couldn't even try. All he could do was thread his fingers into her hair and endure—enjoy—the hot, wet, quivery jolts delivered by each slow stroke of her tongue across his nipple. Each touch sent lightning through his body until his legs felt rubbery and his hands trembled, until he knew he could take very little more before he exploded.

"Liza . . ." His voice was thick and sounded strangled.

Ignoring him, she continued the sweet torture of her kisses, while at the same time her hands moved to his belt.

The earlier clumsiness that had made unbuttoning his shirt an ordeal had disappeared; her fingers worked nimbly to unfasten the buckle, then the snap and the zipper. She slid one hand inside his trousers, wrapping her fingers gently around him, and Riley swore.

"No more," he said harshly, carefully removing her hand, then forcing her away with one hand while tugging at his trousers with the other. "No more waiting."

An instant later the rest of her clothing had joined his on the floor, and he was lowering her onto the bed, supporting her weight, finding his place within her even as they moved. By the time they were settled, she gloved him, tight and hot and, oh, so familiar. He had never forgotten this feeling, this sensation, this rightness. It was a part of his soul, a part of his very being.

She was a part of his soul.

She shifted underneath him, her breasts rubbing his chest, her muscles clenching around him—such simple actions to send such pleasurable torment through him. Everywhere she touched him he burned with need, with desire and spirit-deep longing. He wanted until his body throbbed with it; he hungered until his muscles quivered uncontrollably.

"Please, Riley," she whispered, moving again. Then, in a small, weak, helpless voice, she repeated his last words. "No more. No more waiting. *Now.*"

Damn straight, no more waiting. Hadn't he already waited a lifetime for this?

He moved against her, stretching her, withdrawing, then thrusting deep, powerfully deep, again. With his kisses and his hands and his long, steady strokes inside her, he drew her along with him, building her need to match his, feeding her desire, making her burn for him, making her burn *with* him. And when she stiffened and shuddered, when the muscles deep inside her belly convulsed around him, when her breath came in tiny little gasps and all she could do was cling to him, he joined her. He filled her.

He gave her a part of himself.

He gave her a part of his future.

He gave her all of his soul.

After more than two years of sleeping alone, sharing a bed with a man wasn't the romantic pleasure Liza had expected, especially with a man who took his half out of the middle. A man who had somehow managed to kick all the covers but the sheet she was clutching off the other side of the bed. A man who was sleeping soundly without knowing that she was crowded, shivering and wide-awake.

Then she rolled over and looked at him in the early-morning light, and her petty complaints were forgotten. This wasn't just any man—it was Riley. The man who had made love to her so sweetly last night. The man who had taught her everything she knew about love and loving.

The man *she* had taught all about betrayal and hurt.

She moved closer to him, pillowing her head on his shoulder, and even in his sleep he made room for her. He wrapped his arm around her, drawing her against his chest, patting her soothingly. He was warm, and in a few minutes his body heat had chased the chill from her skin. He made her feel comfortable, safe and protected.

He made her feel loved.

Even though he didn't love her.

Even though he probably never would.

But that was all right, she consoled herself. He had never promised her anything, and she wouldn't ask. She would just take whatever he wanted to give, and when that was gone, when *he* was gone, she would go on. She would be all right. She would get over him.

Nonsense, her evil little voice taunted.

When she lost him again, she would die. She would have to, because her heart would be broken.

Tears began filling her eyes, and Riley hated tears. They made her grateful for the ring of the phone on the bedside table, even though she knew that at this hour on a Sunday morning it could only be family calling. T.J. wanting some favor or other? Gretchen calling to see how last night had gone? Her mother wanting to know if she would be in church?

She turned away from Riley again and picked up the phone on the second ring. Her hello came out deep and throaty; if it was Gretchen, she thought with an exasperated frown, she would have the answer she wanted right there.

It wasn't Gretchen. No such luck. No, it was Alexander on the phone, and his tone was friendlier than Liza had heard in a long time. That meant he wanted something, and it didn't take long to find out what.

"Keith's doctor thinks it would be a good idea if he saw T.J. He's really trying hard, Liza, and he's doing much better. And, of course, the boy would be supervised. Margaret and I wouldn't go off and leave him alone with Keith. We would make sure he was taken care of."

She sat up in bed, leaning against the headboard, tucking the sheet beneath her arms. Her former father-in-law wasn't asking much of her—just that she send T.J., her child, her little boy, a thousand miles away to visit his father, his father who couldn't be trusted to even remember that he had a child when the need for the drugs began clawing at him.

But if Keith's condition had improved, didn't he have a right to see T.J.? And hadn't Alexander just promised that he and his wife would stay right there with them? And hadn't she sworn to Riley just a few weeks ago that when it was all right for T.J. to visit Keith, no one would be happier than she would be?

"Have you discussed this with Keith?"

"He called last night and asked if we would talk to you."

"When do you want to go?"

"Wednesday."

"This Wednesday? You want me to take him out of school—?" She checked her mental calendar. "You want to go for Thanksgiving," she said flatly.

"Yes. We would be back on Sunday."

Thanksgiving without T.J. She had never spent a holiday apart from him. "I don't know, Alexander," she said with a sigh. "I don't know if it's a good idea. I don't know what to do about his work that weekend. Let me think about it, and I'll let you know this evening."

He didn't argue with her or demand that she agree right away. He simply said that they would wait to hear from her, then hung up. Such docile behavior from a man so used to getting his own way meant it was important to him.

When she replaced the receiver she realized that Riley was awake and had heard most, if not all, of the conversation. He was looking at her, his dark eyes sleepy and measuring. "I know," she muttered. "You think T.J. ought to be allowed to see Keith."

"If Keith is all right. If they're supervised."

"But Thanksgiving!"

He raised himself up on his elbow. "You've got the rest of your family here, Liza. Who does he have?"

The rest of her family, she thought bleakly. But not him. Even though they'd made love only hours ago, even though he was lying naked beside her, she surely didn't have him. He would spend Thanksgiving with the people who were important to him—*his* family. People he wouldn't introduce her to even if they accidentally ran into them in some public place.

"What about work?" she asked glumly. "Can he get excused from that?"

"Just tell the major today that he's going out of town for the holidays."

She rested her head against the headboard and stared at the ceiling. "I've never spent a holiday away from T.J."

"How many holidays has his father spent without him since the divorce?"

Looking down, she scowled at him. "Why are you taking Keith's side? You don't even like him."

"I don't even know him," he reminded her. "But I know how I would feel if I had a son and I couldn't see him. Let him go, Liza. You owe it to both of them."

He was right. It didn't make her like the idea any better, but, damn it, he was right.

He must have seen from her expression that she was giving in, that he was winning this argument, because he slowly smiled and began pulling her down into the bed. "Now that that's settled," he murmured, shifting onto his back, drawing her into place above him, "I've got another small problem here...."

She let him guide her hand between their bodies until she was intimately touching him. Had he awakened aroused, she wondered, and merely waited until their discussion was finished to do anything about it? Or had he gotten aroused that quickly, that powerfully? she marveled. "It doesn't feel so small to me," she said innocently as she stroked him. "And it's getting bigger all the time."

"Liza..." His threatening tone ended in a groan as she took him inside her, using the easy rocking of her hips to coax him deeper and deeper. "Oh, baby..."

Her smile was secretive and sweet. Riley was here, they were making love, and he had called her baby. All those years ago, when he had made love to her, when he had loved her, he had always called her baby.

Maybe the future wasn't so hopeless, after all.

Chapter 10

As soon as she got home from work Wednesday evening, Liza handed a suitcase over to Alexander, then wrapped her arms around T.J. "You mind your grandparents," she said, hugging him close. "Have a good time with your father."

He squirmed in her embrace, and soon enough—too soon—she let him go. "I'll be good. I'll do everything I'm told." He grinned excitedly. "And I'll have a great time."

He hadn't even realized that he was going to miss Thanksgiving with her, Liza thought with a good dose of self-pity. He was too thrilled about returning to Dallas, about seeing his old home and some of his old friends and especially about seeing his father. She hadn't realized just how much he had missed Keith.

But Riley had. He had tried to tell her that day at River-walk and again last Sunday.

In spite of T.J.'s impatience she hugged him again, then kissed his forehead. "I love you, kiddo."

"We'd better get going. I love you, Mom." He and Alexander went outside, but Margaret hung back a moment.

"Thank you for letting him go with us. I know it's not easy for you, under the circumstances."

Liza smiled bittersweetly. "Have a good time, Margaret. And give my best to Keith."

"I will. And I'll have T.J. call you when we get to Dallas and again tomorrow evening."

"Thanks." She stood in the doorway and watched them leave, then, shivering from the chill air, she went back inside. Four days without her child. Lord, she was going to miss him.

Then her newly awakened womanly nature took over from her motherly side. Four days without T.J. Four days off work because of the holiday. It sounded like a vacation to her. A time to have fun. And the fun would start when Riley picked her up in little more than half an hour for dinner and a movie. Instead of moping around down here, she needed to get upstairs and take a quick shower, to get dressed and make her bed . . . just in case he wanted to mess it up a little later tonight.

She was halfway up the stairs when the phone rang. She hurried into the bedroom and caught it just as the answering machine came on. When the machine clicked off again, she heard Riley's voice. "Did T.J. get off okay?"

"They just left for the airport."

"Are you all right?"

"It's only four days. I'll survive."

"Of course you will. Listen, I'm going to be a little late tonight. I have to run by my mom's first, but I should be there in an hour or so."

Slowly she sat on the edge of the bed, twisting the phone cord around her finger. "Why don't we do that on our way to dinner?" she suggested, her voice steady but her hands shaking, her heart thudding. "I don't mind."

For a moment there was dead silence on the line, then he cautiously went on as if she hadn't spoken. "It won't take very long. Be thinking about where you want to go when I get there."

"Okay." The word was little more than a whisper, all she could squeeze through the bands that constricted her throat. Without even saying goodbye she hung up.

Riley listened to the hum until the connection dropped and the dial tone returned. Swearing, he hung up, rose from the bed and kicked the nearest object. The chair crashed to the floor, taking a stack of magazines and an armload of clean clothes with it.

He should have lied to her. He should have told her that he'd had to work late, that he had to run an errand, that he needed to go to the bank or get gas or any of a dozen other things. Any excuse would have been better than the truth.

But even hurting Liza had to be better than taking her to his parents' house. If he had given in on that, she would have wanted to go inside and meet them, and his mother would have welcomed her. Hell, formalities aside, she would have declared Liza a member of the damn family.

And it wouldn't have been just his parents. Marcy would probably be there, too, and her fiancé—the guy practically lived at the Cooper house these days—and probably even a few of the others. No matter that they were all grown-up, that they all had families and homes of their own; Mom and Dad's was still the place to go.

But, damn it, she'd sounded as if she was about to cry.

He straightened the chair, then picked up the magazines and his laundry. He might as well leave the place in some sort of order. If Liza didn't have enough sense to kick him out—and he hoped she didn't—he wasn't coming back here tonight.

It didn't take him long to run his errand, to spend a few minutes with his parents and give his sister the loan she had asked for. His mother had already started cooking for tomorrow's dinner, and she asked him to stay for a while, bribing him with a slice of warm pecan pie. Any other time he would have enjoyed spending a few hours with them, but Liza was waiting for him tonight.

Wouldn't that—Liza waiting at home for him—be something to look forward to for the next fifty or sixty years?

He was exactly an hour late when he pulled into her driveway. He wondered if she was still hurt, or if the pain had turned to anger. Would he have to start the evening with an apology, or would she act as if nothing had happened?

He had reached the top of the steps before he realized that she was sitting in the rocker there, wearing a down jacket, a pretty yellow quilt spread over her legs to ward off the cold. After a moment's hesitation he crouched in front of her, bracing his hands on the wooden arms. "Hey."

In the dim light he wasn't sure, but he thought he saw a faint smile touch her lips. "Hi."

"Why are you out here freezing?"

"It's too quiet in the house. And I like cold, dark nights. Besides, it's warm under here. Want to join me?" She lifted a corner of the quilt, and after a moment he accepted her invitation. It was a cozy fit in the rocker, with him seated in the chair, Liza cradled in his lap and the thick quilt covering them both.

But cozy was the best way to be with Liza.

For a while they didn't talk. Occasionally he set the chair to rocking, but mostly he just enjoyed the feel of her body against his, the softness of her hair beneath his cheek and the slow, steady sound of her breathing keeping time with his. He enjoyed it too damn much.

"You already miss T.J., don't you?" he asked to distract himself.

"Yes."

"This is something he needed."

"I know."

"He'll be all right."

"Probably." She sighed softly. "He was so excited about going. I had never realized that he missed Keith so much. I guess because I never missed him, I didn't think T.J. really would."

"Never?" he echoed, brushing her hair back from her ear so that his breath made her shiver. "You never missed Keith when you moved out? You never wished you could go back to him?"

"Never. By the time our marriage ended I had lost whatever good feelings I'd ever had for him. And because of you, they had never been much to start with."

"You really wouldn't go back to him?"

"No." Liza nestled closer, resting her head on his shoulder. Simply being held like this went a long way toward soothing her hurt feelings, but she wanted more. She wanted him to make love to her the way he had Saturday night. She wanted him to make her feel special again. She wanted him to give her reason to hope again.

"Are you sure? Not even if his father offered to give you everything you could ever want? Not even if your father pressured you to?" He paused. "Not even if T.J. asked you to?"

"Alexander can't give me the things I want most—pride, self-respect, integrity and happiness." *Or you,* she silently added. God help her, she wanted *him*. "As for my father, the kind of influence he had over me is only good for a one-time shot. He used it to get me to marry Keith the first time. He could never convince me to try it again. And T.J...." She sighed heavily. "He's old enough to learn that you can't always have what you want. It might be making him unhappy right now, but eventually he'll have to accept it. He'll have to understand that I won't sacrifice the rest of my life to make him happy."

She shifted against him, rubbing him in intimate places in a thoroughly innocent manner—or so she told herself. "What about you, Riley? Are you ever going to settle down? Or will you spend the rest of your life moving every few years and leaving a string of broken hearts behind?"

"I've never broken anyone's heart."

He'd avoided answering the question about settling down, she noticed, and in a way she was glad. She would prefer to wonder about their future to hearing hard, cold evidence that they didn't have one. "Not even your lady MP's?"

"She was just using me for sex," he said with a grin. "I've gotten pretty good at that sex stuff in the last few years."

"Oh, honey, you were always good at that," she said under her breath, but of course he heard her.

"You aren't bad yourself, sweetheart," he said with a chuckle.

"I had a good teacher." When he grinned immodestly, she offered him an innocent smile. "Remind me to tell you about him someday."

"Tell me about him now," he demanded playfully. "Tell me what he did to you. Touch me where he touched you. Show me how he kissed you. Tell me how he made you feel."

Her pleasure in the teasing drained away as she raised one palm to cup his cheek. "I loved him," she whispered. "Oh, God, Riley, I loved you so much...."

He pressed her cheek against the cool leather of his jacket, then slid his arms around her, holding her close. "I loved you, too," he replied, his voice gruff, almost harsh.

"You never said..."

"But you knew it."

"Yes," she whispered. She had known it, and she had married Keith anyway. Fourteen years ago she had turned her back on the only man she had ever loved, and in the process she had broken her own heart. Now chances were good that it would happen again, only Riley would be the one to leave. He would be the one to want something else, something more than she could give. But the end result would be the same.

Her heart would be broken.

"Hey, Liza." Awkwardly he tilted her face up. "Don't be sad."

"I can't help it. Things could have been so different. They should have been. I wasted all those years...."

"They weren't wasted. You have T.J. and that's something no other man in the world could have given you."

Of course, she knew that—hadn't she pointed it out to Gretchen a few weeks ago?—but the knowledge did little to diminish her regrets. She wouldn't give up her son for anything in the world, but, oh, how she wished he were Riley's instead of Keith's. How she wished she'd made the right choice so long ago. How she wished she could make things right now.

But she couldn't. Not without Riley's help. Not unless *he* wanted them set right. Not unless he found the generosity to trust her and the strength to love her again. It was in her favor that he was a generous and strong man.

But was he that generous? That strong?

She didn't know, and not knowing made her shiver.

Mistaking uncertainty for cold, Riley tucked the quilt closer around them. "Do you want to go inside?"

Maybe she couldn't have everything. Maybe she couldn't have a future with Riley, or his love or his trust or his children. But she could have this evening. She could make the most of what he was willing to give her.

"Inside?" She slid her hand lower until she cupped the swelling that tightened his jeans. "To bed?"

"Maybe later."

Gently she stroked him through the denim. "Later?" she echoed weakly. "What do you want to do until then?"

"This." He bent his head and brushed his mouth across hers, then slowly slid his tongue inside. It was a lazy, sensual kiss that made her shivery hot and greedy, shamelessly greedy, for more.

After a moment he broke away, and for a long time he simply looked at her. What could he see in the pale light? she wondered. That she was aroused? That she was flushed and suddenly achy? Probably.

Could he see, she wondered, that she loved him?

He kissed her again, and then again, and while his mouth worked its magic, underneath the quilt his hand was performing a little magic of its own. It had found its way inside her jacket and underneath her sweater, his cold fingers making her shiver as they slid across her stomach to her breast.

"We always made love in the dark," he murmured, his lips brushing hers. "Did you ever realize that? I touched every inch of your body with my hands and my mouth, but the only time I ever saw you was by moonlight. My greatest fantasy then was to make love to you in bright sunlight so that I could see you, all of you.''

As he gently pinched her nipple, Liza clenched her jaw on a groan. Maybe she was overly sensitive. Maybe it was because she'd been alone for so long, or maybe it was all because of Riley, but these little caresses, these simple little touches, made her quake. They made her breath catch and the muscles in her stomach clench. They made the heat of desire, of passion and heartache and longing, pool between her thighs.

They made her easy.

But when it came to Riley she had never wanted to resist. She had never played hard to get. She had been easy, because she had been in love. Fourteen years later everything else in her life had changed, but not that. Those two things would never change.

''Liza? Let's go inside.'' His words were a thick whisper, a raspy mix of need and arousal. ''Let's go to bed.''

She captured his hand when he would have removed it from her breast, and she pressed it hard, feeling the exquisite sensations of his callused palm against her nipple. ''I thought you wanted to wait until later?''

''If that's what you want.''

But he kissed her once more, a kiss designed to arouse her beyond bearing, and he continued to torment her with his feathery light caresses until she whimpered. With more strength than she had believed she possessed, she forced his hand away and freed her mouth. ''All right,'' she surrendered, her voice unsteady and breathless. ''You win. Take me to bed.''

Riley laughed and, still holding her in his arms, scooted to the edge of the chair. ''*I* win?'' he repeated. ''I suppose you're just going to endure my lovemaking in silence?''

''I'll be brave,'' she teased, clutching his shoulder as he stood and carried her to the door.

There he set her down, opened the door and ushered her inside, where he drew her hard against the full length of his body. "You've never made love to me in silence," he taunted. "You make the most erotic little sounds. You moan and pant and say, 'Oh, please, Riley.'" He cradled her bottom in his hands and drew her closer still, until his hardness pressed, rigid and unrelenting, into her belly. "And I do, don't I, Liza?" he whispered. "I do please you, don't I?"

She cupped his face in both hands and solemnly, intensely, met his gaze. "More than anything in the world," she replied. "Riley, I—"

Abruptly he kissed her, cutting off her words. Only one other time in his life had he been afraid of the words a woman might say. That was the day he had called to find out why Liza had been avoiding him, the day that he'd heard her instruct her sister in what to tell him.

Now he was afraid again. Afraid that she might have said, "Riley, I love you." Afraid that he would have said, "*I* love *you*, Liza."

Afraid that he would have said, "I want to stay with you. I can't live without you."

He was afraid as hell that he would have said, "I want to marry you."

And so he kissed away her words, kissed away her desire to speak, her desire for anything but him.

They made it upstairs to her bedroom, barely. Just inside the door Liza dragged his T-shirt over his head and dropped it to the floor even as she began a trail of kisses that extended across his shoulder to his arm, where they suddenly stopped. When he felt the tentative touch of her fingertip on his upper arm, he knew what had caught her attention. Looking down, he saw that she was smiling.

"You have a tattoo," she said, her voice full of wonder and surprise as she traced the set of pistols that adorned his arm. "How did I not notice it before?"

He remembered the times she had seen him without a shirt—in the yard, when her attention had been riveted on the scars on his chest, and in this room the night they had made love. "You were concentrating on something else," he pointed out. Then, with more than a little strain in his voice, he reminded her, "I have something else that needs your attention now, too."

"Gretchen will be happy to hear that. She always said that all you needed to be perfectly wicked was a tattoo."

Taking her chin in a gentle grip, he forced her to look up at him. "You want perfectly wicked, baby, I'll be perfectly wicked—*now*. I'll make you wild. I'll make you writhe." He paused, and the tension and need disappeared from his voice to be replaced with boredom. "Or you can stand here and admire the artwork."

She backed away, but her seductive smile and sinuous movements invited him to follow. "I like the way you say that," she murmured. "*Writhe.* You give it extra syllables."

"I've seen you do it," he reminded her. "You give it something extra, too, honey."

In only a few more steps she reached the bed. For a moment she simply stood there, then she gave him a look that was both seductive and shy, enticing and wistful. "Undress me, Riley. Make love to me."

He had to swallow hard over the tightness in his throat. She had made that same request in that same husky, unsure voice the first time they'd made love. She hadn't been completely innocent—they had kissed and petted; he had suckled her breasts, and she had touched him so intimately that he had experienced true pain when she'd stopped—but she had been a virgin.

Then, that night at the lake, they had settled on the beach for their usual petting, and she had looked at him, her dark eyes big and frightened, and she had very softly said, "Undress me, Riley. Make love to me."

And he had. He had made love to her as gently as he'd known how.

That night he had realized that somehow, somewhere along the way, he had fallen in love with her.

And tonight it had happened again.

"Riley?"

He took the last few steps that brought him to stand in front of her. "Why me, Liza?" he asked hoarsely, then suddenly stopped her with his fingers across her lips. "No. I know better than to question a gift."

Moving his hand, he kissed her briefly, then slid his hands across her sweater, from her shoulders across her breasts to her stomach. Grasping the hem in both hands, he slowly drew it up and over her head. She was naked underneath it, naked and aroused, her breasts swollen, her nipples hard and incredibly responsive to his slightest touch.

Her breasts weren't large—he could cover them with his hands—but they were delicately shaped and beautiful. Once he had fantasized about seeing his child at her breast. Now his fantasies involved only the two of them. Only him and Liza.

Without releasing her, he shifted until he was seated on the bed and she was standing between his thighs. He stroked her breasts and listened to her breathing grow more rapid. When he took one rosy-hued nipple into his mouth, she gasped, and he felt the tension rocket through her body. She was rigid, her fingers clutching his arms for support, the muscles in her legs trembling.

When her quaking increased, he turned his attention back to her clothing. Soon her legs would refuse to support her and she would collapse against him. Better that she be undressed when it happened.

He could do so much more with her that way.

He drew his fingers across her stomach, and her skin rippled. Her jeans provided only a minor obstacle. He unfastened the row of metal buttons with ease, then began inching the material over her hips.

Only a few nights ago he had thought her lingerie was practical, but there was nothing practical about the panties she wore now. Little more than ribbons and strips of lace, they were immodest and revealing and infinitely erotic. Too bad, he thought regretfully as he slid his fingertips underneath them, that they had to go with the jeans. Simply looking at her in those and nothing else would probably provide all the stimulation he needed to reach a shattering climax.

He needed only two fingers to guide the bits of lace down. That left the other fingers free to explore, to stroke through down-soft curls, to probe moist heat and to make her groan so deeply that her muscles deep inside clenched around his finger.

Pressing a kiss to her hip, he bent to finish removing the last of her clothing. When he sat back to leisurely look his fill, though, he realized that she wasn't naked, not completely. Around her neck she wore a gold chain, and dangling from that chain was the diamond that he remembered so well. He reached up, wrapping his fingers around the stone, then used it to gently pull her to him for a kiss, a hungry mating, a sudden urgent thrusting of his tongue. At the same time he fumbled with his jeans, popping the snap, yanking the zipper down, taking time only to free himself before lifting her into place and thrusting hard to fill her in one long stroke.

Her eyes closed, Liza remained motionless, letting him do all the work. It was different, making love to her this way, sitting face-to-face, her breasts rubbing sensuously against his chest while the coarse denim of his jeans scraped her thighs. Then she wrapped her arms around his neck and took control, compelling him to become motionless while *she* moved. She loved him slow and easy, teasing, playing, feeding his hunger mercilessly while offering no satisfaction.

He didn't mind, though. The satisfaction would come in time, and with an intensity that just might destroy him. Then he would want it all again—the pleasure, the pain, the raw need, the torment, the completion. He would want it just this way, with just this woman, until he died.

Every time she took him inside her, Liza thought, biting her lower lip, his flesh rubbed hers in the most exquisite way. It generated such heat that it spread to the rest of her body until her skin was slick with it, until her hair clung damply wherever it touched. It was sweet and intense and wild, and

it made her want more. It made her increase the tempo of
her thrusts, made them harder and faster, and she was re-
warded with increased pleasure, increased heat. Her heart
was pounding, her breath coming in ragged gasps, and
dimly, from somewhere, she heard soft cries, whimpers,
pleas. *You make the most erotic little sounds,* Riley had said,
and she knew these were coming from her.

The need built until it was unbearable. It burned until it
consumed her, until she cried, a harsh, sharp-edged en-
treaty. She heard Riley's own groan and felt his hot liquid
release fill her, and she welcomed her own release, welcomed the shudders and the uncontrollable tightening and
the powerful sensations.

He held her tighter, supporting her when her own body
could no longer manage, stroking her, murmuring softly to
her. There, in the safety of his arms, the shudders still grip-
ping her, she remembered her cry, remembered the only
thing in her mind in the midst of such sensation.

Riley.

"Writhe." Stretched out across the bed, Liza said the
word with obvious relish, mimicking the added length his
accent, to say nothing of his desire, had added to it earlier.
"My, my, I do like that word."

Riley finished removing the rest of his clothes, then joined
her on the bed, rolling onto his side to face her. With a grin
he indulged in a little mimicry of his own. "My, my, I do like
the way you bring it to such vivid life."

She slid so that her hair, damp and tangled, hung over the
side of the bed. She was still naked, her breasts were still
swollen, and the curls between her thighs were still damp
with his fluid and her own. She looked wanton.

Shameless.

And well loved.

He did love her, but he wasn't sure how well. He wasn't
sure he would bring her anything more than a little sexual
fulfillment and a whole lot of heartache. Wouldn't that be
ironic, if the first heart he ever broke belonged to the woman

who had broken his so many years ago? All this time he had thought the damage she'd done was irreparable, but apparently not. He had simply needed not any woman but *her* to put it back together again.

Maybe they had a future, after all. Maybe, if she loved him enough . . .

But she had claimed to love him fourteen years ago. He had believed her, had trusted her, and what had it gotten him? How could he trust her now? Knowing what it would cost him, how could he take that risk again?

And speaking of risks . . . "Are you taking birth control pills?"

She rolled her head to the side and gave him a slow, amused smile. "Aren't you a little late in asking?"

He wasn't amused. *Yes*. That was all he wanted to hear her say.

"I've been divorced for more than two years," she said patiently. "I didn't have sex with my husband for several months before that. No, I'm not taking the Pill. I had no reason to."

She read him too well, Riley thought grimly. He looked away almost immediately, but that instant was enough for her to see his dismay. She sat up, got her robe from the foot of the bed and slipped it on, belting it securely.

"I take care of my son and myself, Riley," she said quietly. "I have for a long time. If I have another child, I can take care of him, too. You don't have to worry. I wouldn't expect anything at all from you."

It was a nice speech, he thought with a scowl, but she knew damned well that a pregnancy would change everything. Whether he loved or trusted her would be immaterial. He would have to marry her. His conscience would demand it.

Staring up at the ceiling, he said stiffly, "You don't seem to be concerned about the possibility."

"It's not likely at this time of the month," she replied just as stiffly.

"I'm glad that doesn't worry you," he lied. "You're probably not much concerned about disease, either, but just for the record, I've been tested and I'm clean."

She stood, but paused beside the bed. "Just for the record, so am I."

He started to ask why she had been concerned enough to have the necessary tests, but then he remembered: her ex-husband, the drug addict. She would have been a fool not to be tested, and he had been a fool to make love to her, knowing about Keith, without asking. But he had trusted her to...

He had trusted her.

He had trusted *Liza.*

Without thinking he rose from the bed and blocked her way when she would have left the room. "I'm sorry."

She refused to look at him, instead focusing her gaze on his chest. "I know you have no reason to believe me," she said haltingly, "but I would never try to trap you into marrying me. I've been through one marriage without love, and I won't ever get caught in another one. *Never,* Riley."

In her first marriage she hadn't loved Davis. Whose love, he wondered bleakly, did she think would be missing in a second one? His?

Or hers?

Was she saying that she didn't love him? That she couldn't?

He didn't have the courage to ask.

"Are you hungry?" she asked suddenly.

That was quite a change in topics, from marriage and love to food. But he *was* hungry, he realized. He had been when he'd arrived here, and their activity since then had only fueled it. "I still owe you dinner."

"You don't owe me anything, Riley."

"Hey, it's a figure of speech, okay?" Touching her shoulder, he smiled tentatively. "Lighten up, would you?"

"That's hard to do, Riley, when I never know what's going to make you pull away. Maybe I should have sent you away Saturday night, but to be honest, birth control and safe sex were the last things on my mind. Unsophisticated, I admit, but after all, I've only been with two men in my life. Maybe when I've had more experience I'll be more careful.''

She tried to move around him, but he sidestepped, blocking her again. ''More experience?'' he repeated, his eyes narrowing dangerously. ''What are you planning to do, Liza? If you think you're going to make up for fourteen years of marriage, fidelity and celibacy by using other men, you're crazy.''

''So it's okay for you to sleep around, but not me.''

''I don't sleep around.'' He denied it guiltily, because for far too long he had done just that. In his first few years away from Augusta he'd had more meaningless encounters than she could imagine. ''You've got someone to make love with—me. You don't need anyone else.''

Her expression slowly shifted from anger to a curious sadness. ''You're not going to be around for long. Eventually you'll get orders and go somewhere else. I'm going to stay here. I'm going to fall in love again, and I'm going to get married again. To do that I have to meet men. I'll want to sleep with some of them. Thanks to you, I'll be more careful when I do.'' She pushed past him, then stopped in the doorway. ''Get your jeans on and come downstairs. I'll fix something for dinner.'' Then she was gone.

He wasn't a violent man. His hands clenched in fists and his breathing tightly controlled, Riley kept reminding himself of that. Kicking the chair in his room earlier this evening had been out of character for him. Fortunately, it had also been harmless. But now he had the urge to hit something, anything, an urge so strong that he trembled with it. But he couldn't put his fist through the wall, and the furniture in here was so sturdy that the best he could hope for was a broken hand.

But if she really thought that he would let her turn to other men, she was crazy. She was a fool. She was . . .

Probably right, he admitted, his anger suddenly draining away. Who was he to tell her no? What right did he have to interfere with her future? He was just having an affair with her. That was all he'd wanted, wasn't it? All he could let himself have? An affair. Pleasant company and outstanding sex. The freedom to walk away whenever he wanted without so much as a twinge of regret. No strings. No ties.

No rights.

No damn rights at all.

She had the right to go out with every man in town, and she could sleep with every one of them, too. Even if it killed *him*.

Get your jeans on and come downstairs, she'd told him. At least she hadn't told him to get dressed and go. At least she hadn't suggested that he get the hell out so she could put her new experience to work on someone else.

He was on his way downstairs when the phone rang. "Will you get that?" Liza called from the kitchen. Leaning over the polished banister, he picked it up.

After his greeting there was a moment's silence, then T.J. sullenly asked, "What are *you* doing there?"

He ignored the question and evenly said, "Hold on and I'll get your mother."

"You shouldn't be there," the boy muttered before Riley set the phone down.

He went into the kitchen, where Liza was cooking a frozen chunk of ground beef. "It's T.J."

She handed the fork to him, then went into the hall, leaving the door open behind her. He could hear her end of the conversation all too clearly. *How was your flight?... We're having dinner. Are you glad to be in Dallas again?... Yes, it is late for dinner. How is your father?... No, that's okay. I don't need to talk to him, sweetheart. T.J.? T.J.?... Hello, Keith.*

Riley scowled at the meat in the skillet. She had sounded so positive out on the porch about never wanting to get together again with Davis, but he couldn't help but be jealous that she was even talking to him. Even though she sounded guarded and cool. Even though she might as well have been speaking to a stranger.

Nothing could change the fact that for twelve years she had been married to the man. She'd had a child with him. She had spent more than a third of her life with him.

And nothing could change the fact that Riley was jealous. He was jealous as hell. He was so jealous that he felt sick with it.

She ended the call and returned to the kitchen. Sometime since leaving the bedroom she had brushed her hair. Now it was sleek and smooth and pulled back in a ponytail. Instead of sexy and wanton, she looked wholesome. Innocent.

Either way, she was still beautiful.

Liza didn't take over the job of browning the meat from him. Instead she began removing items from the refrigerator—onions, cheese, sour cream. From the pantry she took a tomato, a box of taco shells and a bottle of salsa, then began grating the cheese.

"How's T.J.?"

"Thrilled to be with his father." She picked up a single shred of cheese and nibbled it. "Furious that you're with his mother."

"Typical Johnson family response."

"Hmm. At least my family knows about you and has a response. Your family doesn't even know I exist."

He didn't speak.

"What was your reason for not telling them before?" She pretended to consider it. "Oh, yes, because they might have wanted to meet me. And if they had, they would have told you that you were making a mistake, that I was no good for you. Is that still your excuse? Are you still concerned about what they think? Are you still afraid that you're making a mistake in seeing me?"

He turned from the stove to face her. "When did my family become so important to you? You never cared about them before. In all those months we were together you never asked about them, not once. You never bothered to learn Robbie's name—my sister, my best friend. You never wanted to know where they lived or what they did or what they were like. Why do they matter now?''

She considered the truth: because she was in love with him. She wanted to know that he cared enough about her to let her meet them. She wanted to be a part of them. She didn't want to be shut out of that part of his life.

She didn't want to think that he didn't consider her worthy of meeting his family.

She didn't want to believe that he was ashamed of her.

He was waiting for an answer, but she didn't have one to give him. She couldn't tell the truth, and she wouldn't tell a lie.

Finishing with the meat, he stiffly asked for a colander, and she had to brush against him to get it. She was turning away again when he caught her shoulders. "I don't want to fight with you, Liza," he said, the intensity in his voice visible in his eyes. "We don't have much time together as it is, and when T.J. comes home he's going to make things even tougher. Please, let's enjoy what we've got."

"What do you want to do, Riley? Draw up a list of subjects that are off-limits? My use of birth control, or lack thereof. Your family—"

"Your men."

She let her head fall forward to rest on his chest. "I don't have any men."

Gently he tilted her chin up. "You have me."

But for how long? she wanted to ask. How long would he continue to want her? How long until he left her alone?

"There have been more than a few women in the past who have found that idea appealing," he said dryly. "You look like it's cause for sorrow."

There had been more than a few women in his past, she thought bleakly, and there would be still more in his future. And what did her future hold? Growing old alone? Because in spite of what she'd told him upstairs, she couldn't imagine getting married again. She couldn't imagine loving any man but Riley.

"Oh, Liza." His sigh was soft and tugged at her heart. "What will it take to make you smile again?"

"I'm sure you'll think of something," she said softly, then slipped away to set the table.

They were seated across from each other, halfway through their meal, when she said, "Tell me about the tattoo."

He glanced down at it, then shrugged. "You can probably figure it out yourself."

She gave it a moment's thought. "You hadn't been in the Army very long when one night you got drunk, as young soldiers tend to do, and the next morning you woke up with that on your arm."

He acknowledged the accuracy of her guess with a sheepish nod.

"Why the crossed pistols?"

"It's the insignia for the MP Corps. Actually, I wanted a heart and a flower, but I wasn't *that* drunk."

"A heart and a flower?" she echoed, finally giving him the smile he'd asked for. "Isn't that a little bit sentimental for a big, macho military cop?"

"A broken heart," he clarified quietly. "And a peach-colored rose."

Liza stared at him. As a rule she preferred to forget the details of her wedding day, but some things couldn't be forgotten. The bouquet her mother had insisted on was one of them. Costing a small fortune—such a waste for so brief a service—it had been made up of dozens of delicately shaded roses. Roses of softest peach. "How did you know?" she whispered.

"I was there. Across the street from the church." Using a small wedge of shell, he concentrated on gathering every bit of filling that had fallen from his tacos into a neat pile in the center of the plate. "I had seen the wedding announcement in the paper. I wanted to know that you had gone through with it. I wanted to see that you really had married him. I wanted proof that it was over for us. And I got it." He looked up at her then. "I saw you come out of the church with Davis. His arm was around you, and you were holding all those roses, and you looked so damn beautiful."

Would it have changed anything, she wondered numbly, if she had known he was there? Probably not. Most likely she would have gone through with the ceremony and the reception as planned.

Then she remembered a moment before the service had started. Her hair had been fixed and her makeup applied, and her mother and Margaret had been waiting to help her into the beaded white satin gown they had chosen for her. She had stood there in a strapless bra and a long white slip, in silk stockings and white heels, looking at that gown, and she had been gripped by a desperate urge to flee. She hadn't, of course. She hadn't had the courage. She hadn't had any place to run. But if she had known that Riley was outside, if she had known that he was waiting across the street . . maybe she would have found the courage.

"Well . . ." She had to clear away the huskiness from her voice. "I like that better than hearts and flowers. Did it hurt?"

"I don't remember."

"Were you really that drunk?"

His smile was crooked and bittersweet. "For a time back then I got really good at getting really drunk."

"But not anymore," she whispered, her tone hopeful.

"No. Not anymore."

She felt a little shiver of relief tinged with sadness. "Being in the Army has certainly left its mark on you."

"The tattoo is my fault. The scars—" he touched the one on his chest "—are just part of the job."

"Have you been happy?"

"With the job? Yeah. Joining up was the right choice for me, even though I made it for the wrong reasons. I wasn't interested in serving my country or getting job training or earning money for college. I just wanted to run away, to get as far away from Augusta and you as I could. But I like it. I like the people I've met and the places I've been. I like the work I do."

She didn't ask the question that should naturally follow. He'd been happy with his career choice, so how about his personal life? Had he been happy there, too? Or had he carried so much bitterness and resentment, thanks to her, that he'd never been able to find anything else?

She didn't want to know the answer.

She didn't want to feel any more guilt.

She didn't want to experience any more sorrow.

She just wanted to enjoy what was left of the evening. She wanted to look at him until every feature, every line, every expression was burned into her memory. She wanted to talk to him about anything or nothing. She wanted to listen to the deep, even, quiet tones of his voice. She wanted to touch him everywhere, innocently and not so innocently.

More than all of that, she wanted to make love with him again.

And more even than that, more than anything in the world . . .

She wanted to love him.

Chapter 11

T.J. and his grandparents got back from Dallas early Sunday evening, coming straight from the airport to Liza's house. Although he'd spent the past night and all of that day with Liza, except for a few hours at his volunteer job on post, Riley had cravenly suggested that he should leave before they arrived. And Liza hadn't insisted that he stay. She hadn't even asked him to, actually. She had simply looked at him with that soft, sad little look that he'd seen too often lately and said, "I wish you wouldn't go."

So that was how he found himself, shortly after seven, standing in the broad hallway with Liza, T.J., and Alexander and Margaret Davis.

The older couple were polite. Mrs. Davis was even warm. She offered her hand, called him Riley in her cultured Southern drawl and said what a pleasure it was to meet him. He had expected hostility because he was seeing their former daughter-in-law. Resentment because he had arrested their grandson. Aloofness because of who they were and who he wasn't. Snobbery.

But if the Davises surprised him, T.J. didn't. Clutching a small gift bag in both hands, he turned to Liza, so angry that there were tears in his eyes. "Why is he here?" he demanded.

Riley felt the heat building in his face as Liza spoke her son's name, her tone an impatient warning.

He went on before she could say more. "Why don't you make him go away? I hate him! He's just a dumb cop! He'll never be important like my dad! He'll never be as good as my dad!"

Just a dumb cop. It was an angry insult from an angry little boy, but it stung more than Riley wanted to admit. He had suspected that the more involved he became with Liza, the more his relationship with T.J. would suffer, but that didn't make such animosity easier to accept. It seemed that he had just learned to like the kid, to enjoy his company and care about him, and now T.J. had turned on him.

Now, when things were getting too damned serious with Liza. Now, when he needed the boy's support and friendship more than ever.

"Grandpa, make him leave," T.J. pleaded. "Make him go away and leave us alone. You can do it. You're always talking about how powerful you are, and he's nobody. Make him go away!"

"T.J.," Liza admonished.

At the same time Alexander said sharply, "That's enough, young man."

Seeing that not even his grandfather would support him, the boy shoved past Riley, hitting him hard, and raced up the stairs. At the top he leaned over the railing, raised the paper bag over his head, then hurled it to the floor. "Here's your stupid present!" he cried. He didn't wait to see it land but ran down the hall to his room, slamming the door behind him.

The bag sailed past Liza and missed Riley by only a few inches, landing at his feet with the curiously delicate tinkle of shattering glass. For a moment that was the only sound, then Margaret's gasp broke the silence.

He stared at the bag, listening only dimly to the conversation around him. There were apologies from everyone except the one who had misbehaved, he thought with a bleak smile. There was shock, followed by dismay and assurances that the child would calm down, that he was simply wound up from the trip, excited about seeing his father again and agitated about leaving him.

Finally the Davises left. Riley heard Liza close the door behind them, then slowly approach him. She slid her arms around his waist from behind and pressed a kiss to his arm. "How did you know?" she asked softly.

He turned so that he was facing her and clasped his hands together at the small of her back. "Know what?"

"That he would be such a brat when he came home. The other night you said that when he came home he was going to make things even tougher for us. How did you know?"

"Common sense. He wants you and Keith back together. He went to see his father for the first time in months. He got to live with him again, even though it was only for a few days. You think he didn't spend those few days convincing himself that someday it would be like that again permanently? That someday Keith would get better and come here and live in this house with you and him?" He shrugged. "And then he came home. His father was still in Dallas, and *I* was here. With you."

She cupped her hand to his cheek. Either her fingers were unusually cool or his face was still flushed from T.J.'s outburst. He suspected it was the latter. "I'm sorry," she murmured. "The last thing you need is a snotty kid treating you that way."

"Why are you apologizing? You didn't do anything wrong."

"He's my son. He knows better. He should behave better."

"He's a little kid whose world has been turned upside down in the last few years. He'll accept that you're not getting together with Keith again, but it will take time. Dreams die hard." He should know. Not even fourteen years of anger, hatred and resentment had been able to destroy his dreams of Liza, and he was a hell of a lot older and a hell of a lot more capable than T.J.

With a sigh she pulled away and picked up the brightly colored bag from the floor. Sinking down on the step, she poured a pile of fragile glass shards into her palm. There was a rainbow of translucent colors in the narrow strings and graceful curves. "Blown glass," she murmured, but there was no way to identify what the object had been. The largest intact piece was no bigger than her thumbnail.

Sighing again, she returned the glass to the bag, then got up. "Are hot dogs okay for dinner?"

"Maybe I'd better go on home."

"And send him the message that all he has to do is throw a tantrum and you'll go away?" She shook her head. "You agreed to stay for dinner before he got here. Don't let him change things, Riley. I'll get it started."

"Do you object if I talk to him?"

When she hesitated he thought she might say yes. She might think she didn't know what to say to T.J. She might think he didn't have the right to interfere. She might believe he would only make matters worse. But after a moment she smiled and shrugged. "You must be a sucker for abuse."

"Maybe I'm a sucker for an unhappy kid with eyes like his mother's."

She made a sweeping gesture toward the stairs. "He's all yours."

If only that were true, Riley thought with a touch of regret. If T.J. were his, they wouldn't be having this problem. If T.J. were his . . .

He climbed the stairs slowly. He really didn't know what to say to the kid, and there was a better-than-even chance that he might make matters worse. But he wanted to try.

There were three bedrooms upstairs. T.J.'s was across and down the hall from Liza's. At the door he stopped and knocked. Sniffling sounds came from inside, but there was no invitation to come in. After a moment Riley opened the door and stepped inside.

"Go away." T.J. was lying on his stomach across the bed, his face half-buried in his pillow, his voice muffled. He was staring at a framed picture, a large formally posed family portrait. It was about four years old, Riley guessed, judging from T.J.'s size. Keith sat in the center, and T.J. stood beside him, his hand resting on his father's shoulder. Liza was standing behind T.J., touching both of them. They looked like the perfect family, but even then they had been falling apart. Only the kid hadn't known it.

"Nice picture."

T.J. whirled around to scowl at him. "Get out."

"I want to talk to you."

"I don't want to hear it. I don't have to listen to you."

Riley moved a coat and a stuffed animal from the chair at the foot of the bed and sat down. "So don't. But I'm going to talk anyway." He paused, then said, "You hurt your mother tonight."

T.J. simply stared harder at the portrait.

"I know you're angry, T.J., and I understand why. I also understand that it doesn't have anything to do with me, not really."

"I hate you!"

"No, you don't. You hate that I'm dating your mother. You hate the idea that she might like another man more than your father. You hate the idea that someday she might marry another man and never be with your father again. But you don't hate *me.*"

Forgetting that he wasn't intending to listen, T.J. rolled onto his side. "I do hate you. You don't belong here. You're just a—a greedy, worthless troublemaker trying to get your hands on something you don't deserve."

Words of wisdom, Riley thought grimly. Probably from Grandpa Johnson. The day after Liza had finally told her parents about T.J.'s arrest, the kid had repeated a few of Garrett's comments to him at work. Apparently the old man had had more to say. Didn't he ever stop to think before he spoke? Didn't he realize the harm he could do talking like that in front of a vulnerable, impressionable child?

"You want your mom and dad to get married again, don't you?"

"They're going to! Just as soon as my dad is well again."

"Do you really believe that?" he asked evenly. "Has she told you that? Has he told you that?"

"I *know* it," he muttered fiercely. "I *know!*"

"Listen, T.J., if your mom really wants to marry your dad again, I can't stop her. I'm not standing in her way. All she has to do is tell me, and I'll leave. I'll never come back." Hadn't they already been through that once before? Hadn't she chosen Keith over him, and hadn't he gone away for fourteen long years?

"So leave."

Riley shook his head. "She has to be the one to tell me. Not you. Look, I want to make a deal with you. You don't like me coming around here, you don't like me spending time with your mother—that's fine. You can resent me all you want. But don't take it out on her. Don't be hateful to her. Don't yell at her and throw things and hurt her. She's your mother, and you have no right ever behaving that way with her."

T.J. sat up and leaned toward him, resting his arms on his thighs. "I have a better idea. Why don't you get lost? We were fine without you. We were happier without you. I wish she'd never met you."

Riley didn't doubt that T.J. had been happier without him. He'd had his dreams of putting his family back together and no one to make him question whether it would ever really happen. So what if Liza had never given him any reason to believe that she still loved or wanted his father? At least she had never given him any reason to believe that she might love another man. There had never been any threat to his fantasies.

Until *he* had come along.

"There are some things, T.J., that wishing can't change," he said quietly. "I'm sorry that you're unhappy. I'm sorry

No Retreat

that you can't live with both your mom and your dad. I'm sorry that you can't see him more often and do things with him the way you used to. And I'm sorry that you don't want to be friends with me anymore. But take it easy on your mother. None of this is her fault. You can't blame her. You can't cause trouble for her." He stood and walked to the door. "Your mom's fixing hot dogs for dinner. Do you want to come down and eat with us?"

T.J. glowered at the floor without saying a word.

"If you change your mind..." Letting the offer trail away, Riley left the room. As he was pulling the door shut he heard T.J.'s anguished whisper.

"This is *my* house. *You* don't belong here."

Instead of going straight to the kitchen Riley went into Liza's room. He stood there for a moment in the dark. He knew the room as well as his own. He'd spent more time here in the past week than he had in his own room. He felt more comfortable here. More at home. In spite of T.J.'s words, he did belong here. He could spend the rest of his assigned time at Fort Gordon here.

He could spend the rest of his life with Liza.

But at what cost to T.J.?

Where was she supposed to draw the line? Was it okay to date a man her kid hated but not to make love with him? Was it okay to make love but not to get married? Because T.J. was a child, was he denied a say in who shared their lives? Was his opinion of Riley any less valid, any less important, simply because he was only eleven years old?

"I thought I might find you here." Liza slipped into the room, closing the door behind her. "Did he throw anything at you?"

"No."

"That's a good sign." After a moment she sought his hand in the darkness and twined her fingers with his. "I never knew he had such a temper."

"He never had any need for it until now. You'd be surprised at what people are capable of when they feel threatened."

"I feel sorry for him." She laughed softly. "I feel selfish. Isn't that ridiculous? If you or I had ever acted that way, the last thing our parents would have felt was selfish. Did they do a better job of raising us than I'm doing with him?"

"Things were different then. When you were T.J.'s age, did you know anyone whose parents were divorced? Did you know anyone with Keith's problem?"

"Not personally." Liza wished for better light so that she could see his expression. "Thanks for talking to him."

"Not that it did any good."

She claimed his other hand and squeezed both tightly. "Don't get any dumb ideas in your head about being noble and dumping me for T.J.'s sake," she warned.

"Do you think I'd do that?" His tone was wry enough that she knew the thought must have crossed his mind.

"Do you think I'd let you?" She swallowed hard. "If you get tired of me, if you don't want to see me again, or if you decide that seeing me isn't worth putting up with T.J., that's different. But to let an eleven-year-old boy dictate who you can and cannot have a relationship with..."

Before she could finish, Riley kissed her. It wasn't an intimate kiss, meant to arouse, but a simple, comforting, reassuring touch of his mouth. When he raised his head he chuckled softly. "He was right about one thing. I *don't* deserve you. Now..." He kissed her again quickly before drawing her toward the door. "I don't think he'll be joining us for dinner, but if he does come out of his room and finds us in here in the dark with the door closed, there will be hell to pay. Let's go eat those hot dogs."

Liza lay on her side in bed, her head pillowed on her arm. It was after midnight and Riley was long since gone. He had left her with a kiss and an invitation for dinner Tuesday night, and a regret that he couldn't spend the night as he had the past four nights. Her bed felt lonely without him—spacious, she thought with a smile, without him to crowd her, but lonely. But with T.J. home they'd had no choice. Riley had been right. If her son even suspected how seriously they were involved, there *would* be hell to pay.

What was she going to do about T.J.? She didn't have many options. Give up Riley? Never. As long as he wanted her, she would be here. Go back to Keith? No way. That wasn't even within the realm of possibility. Continue seeing Riley without caring how it affected her son? That wasn't very appealing, either. How long could a relationship endure such relentless hostility? How long before Riley decided that she wasn't worth the hassle?

A tap at the door interrupted her musings. "Come in," she called, turning onto her back.

The hall light was burning, outlining her son in the sweatpants that he wore for pajamas. "Can I come in?"

He looked so tall standing there. He was still thin, but he was finally starting to fill out. Her baby was growing up, Liza acknowledged with a lump in her throat, and it wasn't easy for her. Already she missed the sweet little boy who had liked nothing better than to cuddle with her while she read him stories of tigers and bears and cats who wore hats. She missed the adorable child who had accepted everything she said as God's truth, who had rarely thought to argue with her, and then only over silly things like bedtimes and broccoli.

Sitting up and propping a pillow behind her back, she patted the mattress beside her. "Come and sit down."

He shuffled across the room, tentatively seating himself on the edge of the bed. "I'm sorry about the present."

"What was it?"

"A blown-glass ornament for the Christmas tree. A reindeer with a wreath around his neck. I shouldn't have broken it."

"No," she agreed softly. "You shouldn't have."

"Dad gave me the money—" He stopped abruptly, then started over. "Grandpa gave Dad the money to give me to buy it."

"How was your visit with your dad?"

"It was okay. I saw Steven and Erin and Betsy. Travis has moved away, and Kerry's parents are divorced. Her dad lives in Houston now, and her mom's got a new husband."

Those were names she hadn't heard in a long while, Liza thought with a smile. The neighborhood kids had spent so much time at her house that she had sometimes wondered if all six were hers, instead of only one. "What about your father? Did you have fun with him?"

Slowly he edged toward her, all the while looking at the comforter instead of her. "Yeah, it was okay." He sat in silence for a moment, then asked, "Mom? Are you going to marry Riley?"

She sat motionless for a long time, then sighed. "He hasn't asked me to marry him, T.J."

"But if he did, would you?"

"Yes."

"I don't want you to. I don't want him for a father. He's a *cop,* Mom. He's in the Army. He's—he's awful. He's—"

"He's not your father. That's what you dislike most about him, isn't it?"

He stubbornly refused to answer her question. "I won't be nice to him. I won't like him."

She reached out to comb his hair down. "I can't make you like him, T.J.," she admitted. "But you will show him the respect he deserves. If that's asking too much, then you'll be spending a great deal of time in your room from now on."

"Why do you have to see him? We got along fine without him. Things were so much better without him."

The bewildered plea in his voice tugged at her heart. He was growing up, but not enough. He didn't understand that maybe he had been fine before Riley had entered their lives, but she hadn't. He probably didn't even realize that mothers could get lonely. He certainly didn't understand what it was like to love someone the way she loved Riley. In his childish innocence he truly believed that she could simply stop seeing Riley and everything would go back to the way it had been before. He probably even believed that if he wished hard enough and long enough, he could make it happen.

But he was wrong.

"Riley is a very important part of my life, T.J.," she said quietly, firmly. "He has been for a very long time. You and he are the two most special people in my life. That's not going to change. No matter how badly you behave, no matter how bratty you are, I'm always going to love you. *Always.* And no matter whether Riley's here or a million miles away, I'll always love him, too. I wish for my sake, and for yours, that you would try to be friends with him again. He can be a very good friend, and you can use one. But if you—"

T.J. jumped to his feet. "You're lying!" he cried. "If you loved me, you would make him go away! If you loved me, you would go back to Dallas and live with my dad, or let him come here! If you loved me, you wouldn't try to make me be nice to some stupid jerk that everyone else hates!"

She felt suddenly, infinitely weary. "Go to bed, T.J."

"Mom—"

"Go to bed," she repeated sharply. "I'm not going to listen to anything else from you tonight." She turned onto her side, her back to him, and closed her eyes. Her breathing was deep and tightly controlled, almost obscuring the sound of T.J.'s leaving.

She needed Riley's arms around her. If he were here, she wouldn't ask him to make love to her—although, naturally, she wouldn't turn him down, either—but merely to hold her. To feel his body against hers, to feel his arms around her, to know that he was there and she was safe would release the tension that knotted her muscles, and would bring her peace.

But he wasn't here, so the best she could hope for was sleep. Deep, sound sleep. Dreamless sleep.

Unless they were sweet dreams.

Hopeful dreams.

Dreams of Riley.

* * *

Late Tuesday evening Riley drove to the kennels, traded his truck for one of the Cherokees and picked up Jasper, then returned to the MP Company to pick up his pistol at the armory. Strict regulations governed the use of the weapons. Each MP checked one out at the beginning of his shift and returned it at the end. Sometimes, he thought as he left the parking lot and headed out on patrol, it seemed as if strict regulations governed every part of his life.

Except his personal life.

Right now, after one of the most frustrating evenings in recent memory, he would have given almost anything for a few rules there. Any guidelines for dealing with a belligerent, resentful eleven-year-old boy would have been deeply appreciated.

Liza had given T.J. the option of staying home while they went to dinner, but the boy had insisted that he wanted to go. He had wanted, all right—had wanted to make the next two hours as miserable as possible for Riley. He had whined about Riley's choice of restaurant and argued with his mother over the meal he'd ordered, then had refused to eat. He had dominated the conversation, deliberately cutting Riley out every chance he got. He had fidgeted and fussed and pouted and been thoroughly offensive through the entire evening. Liza had gotten onto him more times than he could count, but it hadn't done any good. T.J. had been determined to ruin the evening for everyone, and he hadn't cared what it cost him in terms of punishment to come.

He hadn't even gotten a decent kiss for his efforts, Riley thought with a scowl. Liza had gone outside with him to say good-night, but T.J. had followed with the claim that there was a phone call for her *now*. Maybe there had been, or maybe the kid had lied. At this point there wasn't much Riley would put past him.

"Hey, Jasper, want to go to dinner with us next time?" he asked, glancing at the shepherd in the rearview mirror. That was the one sure way he could think of to control the kid—set him down and give Jasper the order to watch him.

But somehow he didn't think Liza would approve of using a trained police dog to hold her son at bay.

He was trying to be patient. Even though he wasn't used to some smart-mouthed kid insulting him every time he turned around. Even though he was already, after only two days, frustrated with the constraints T.J.'s presence put on his relationship with Liza. The boy objected to Riley even touching her; the simplest kiss would make him blow up, and anything more intimate was out of the question. They would just have to find some way to be alone . . . and soon.

But those were short-term problems. He could endure anything, even T.J.'s mouth, in small doses. He could get by without kissing her in front of her son, and she had enough willing baby-sitters that they ought to be able to manage a night or two alone this weekend.

But how long could the kid go on this way? How much hatred could such a scrawny little child hold inside? When would his attitude start wearing on Liza's patience, and on his own? How would it affect them in the long run? Those were the questions that concerned him.

"Gordon seven-zero, MP Control."

Reaching for the microphone, he radioed in with his location and status, then listened to the call. He was to provide backup to another MP who had stopped a carload of soldiers on Twenty-fifth Street. It was probably just a routine stop, but if Gordon one-nine, the uniformed patrol for that area of the post, felt the situation called for backup, that was his decision. Just as Riley trusted his own instincts on the job, he also trusted those of the officers he worked with. As the old saying went, better to be safe than sorry.

He was only a few minutes away. When he turned onto Twenty-fifth, he saw the patrol unit ahead, pulled to the side of the road behind another car. Its light bar was on, casting eerie blue shadows over the young men lined up on the grass. There had been six passengers in a car that was less than comfortable for four, and they were all soldiers, probably all trainees. Gordon one-nine was going down the line, collecting military IDs from them, as Riley slowed to a stop nearby.

He hadn't even turned the key off when the soldier at the far end of the line made a break for it. Jumping from the Cherokee, Riley opened the rear door, shouting as he did, "Military police! Halt! Stop, or I'll release my dog!"

Often enough that was all it took. The mere threat of being attacked by Jasper could stop most people in their tracks. But not this one.

"Take him, Jasper," he commanded. "Go get him, boy."

Jasper leaped to the ground and was off like a shot, quickly outdistancing Riley, who ran behind him as they crossed the parade grounds. On the other side were several signal battalion headquarters and, beyond that, trainee barracks. No doubt the kid thought if he could make it that far, he could hide and avoid punishment for whatever crime he might have committed. If he made it that far. If his friends kept their mouths shut and didn't identify him. If he could outrun the dog.

But no one could outrun the dog.

This kid must have a damned good reason for trying.

Jasper was steadily, rapidly, closing the distance between him and the suspect. When he was close enough he brought the soldier down, launching himself into the air, hitting the young man with his full weight of more than a hundred pounds and spinning him around before they hit the ground.

The kid was either desperate or frightened—probably both, Riley thought as he approached. Instead of becoming still, he tried to scoot away from the dog, all the while pleading, "Get him off! Call him off!" When Jasper nipped his hand while trying to find a good grip on his arm, the soldier gave a yelp of pain, then finally gave up his struggle.

When Riley reached them Jasper had the suspect's arm in his mouth, shaking his head back and forth like a dog playing with a new toy, only there was nothing playful about it. Now he was merely holding, but if the prisoner made any attempt to pull away or to escape, he would bite—and his bite was powerful.

"Out, Jasper," Riley commanded when he was standing over the soldier. "Watch him, boy."

The dog immediately released his prize and took up a position nearby, and Riley reached down to roll the suspect onto his stomach. His breath coming in shallow, winded gasps, he fastened handcuffs around the kid's wrists, then warned him, "Don't try to run again. He'll bite you if you move."

Blue lights flashed in the night as yet another MP drove across the parade grounds from Barnes Avenue. Backup for the backup, Riley thought dryly. Ordinarily, after handcuffing the suspect he would also search him. But with help only seconds away, this time, he thought, he would stand back, join Jasper in watching and catch his breath.

"Look what we have here," the MP said only seconds into the search, removing a small plastic bag from the young man's coat pocket.

Riley didn't need to move any closer to see the odd-shaped rocks the bag held, and he didn't need a better look to know that it was crack. Cocaine. What had Liza called it? Today's drug of choice. No wonder the kid had run.

That simplified matters for them, at least. Now the kid would be turned over to the duty agent for the drug suppression team at CID, the Army Criminal Investigation Division. Now it was their case.

"Nice evening for a little jog," the MP said once the soldier had been placed in the back seat of his car.

Riley was still breathing unevenly as he fastened Jasper's leash. He gave the other man a look of pure aggravation. "I'm too damned old to be chasing eighteen-year-old kids."

"That's why you have that beast. He catches 'em. All you have to do is lock 'em up. See you at the station."

Praising the dog for his work, Riley headed back to the Jeep. One thing he had to say for T.J.—the night he'd been arrested he must have been at least as frightened as that young man, but he'd had the sense not to agitate an already-excited dog. He'd shown a maturity and intelligence that that young man, nearly twice as old, couldn't match.

There was hope for the kid yet.

But did that hope extend to him and Liza? Was there a chance they could somehow fashion a future from their past? Could they create something between them that would last forever, that could withstand her family's disapproval and her son's hostility? Could they make it work this time?

With a little patience and a lot of love, they could. He truly believed that. Well, he had a lot of patience and even more love. But what about Liza? Her patience was wearing thin these days, and she'd never said a thing about love. She had never hinted that she wanted to be with him ten years, ten months or even ten days from now. She had never talked about their future, just her own. When she began dating again. When she took other lovers. When she got married again.

Not once had she given him any reason to believe that he was the man she wanted. The lover she wanted. The husband she wanted.

A month ago Riley had decided he would have an affair with Liza. Nothing more, nothing less. The thought had held little threat to him. He had indulged in casual relationships for the past fourteen years. He knew how to stay uninvolved. He knew how to walk away.

But in the past week and a half it had become painfully clear that an affair wasn't enough. He wanted more. He wanted it all: love, marriage, a family—everything. He'd gotten greedy.

And he remembered what had happened the last time he'd gotten greedy. He had lost her.

What if that happened again? What if all she wanted from him was an affair?

What would he do then?

Everyone had an opinion of what hell must be like. By five o'clock Saturday afternoon Riley knew what his own personal hell was: four hours with T.J. in a bad mood. Four

hours of unrelenting anger and bitterness. Four hours of
bragging about his father. Four hours of "When Dad comes
to live with us . . ."

And it wasn't over yet. He had told Liza he would bring
T.J. home after work. They were giving the child as little
time to clean up as was necessary, then taking him over to
his aunt's to spend the night. T.J. didn't know about that
yet. He didn't suspect that they were getting rid of him so
they could have a peaceful evening—and a passionate
night—together. When he found out, Riley expected another full-blown tantrum like last Sunday evening.

"Where are we going?"

Riley glanced across the truck at him. It was a simple
question and should have been inoffensive, but it was laced
with spite. "To the company. I need to shower and change
clothes."

"Well, take me home first. I don't want to wait around
for that."

"It won't hurt you to wait. You can watch television."

"Oh, wow, like that's such a big treat," he said scath-
ingly.

Gritting his teeth, Riley parked in the barracks lot, then
had to order T.J. out of the truck. Crossing the lot, he
stopped for a moment beside his motorcycle, bending to
check the rear tire.

"Is that yours?"

"Yeah." He gave T.J. a sidelong glance, seeing his interest, faint and almost hidden in the ferocity of his scowl.
"You like cycles?"

The interest faded. "Of course not. My dad says they're
stupid and dangerous. He says only a fool would ride one."

Riley stood and looked at the boy across the bike. "Your
mom likes them," he said softly. After a moment he turned
toward the door, and T.J. reluctantly followed him.

Unwilling to leave the kid alone long, Riley showered and
shaved in record time. He could hear the television blaring
in the next room. Maybe T.J. didn't consider it a treat, but
apparently he had decided that it was a way to pass the time.

Wearing fresh jeans and a towel around his neck, Riley returned to his room . . . and stopped short.

T.J. wasn't stretched out on the bed in front of the TV, as he'd expected. He was standing at the bureau, and the top drawer was open, the drawer where Riley kept his socks. Where, a few weeks ago, he'd left the newspaper announcement of Liza's engagement. The announcement that was in T.J.'s hands right now.

Startled by Riley's appearance, the boy dropped the paper and stepped back. Almost immediately, though, he regained his bravado. "Why do you have this?" he asked. "Did you know my mom then?" Then, slowly grinning, he made a damned good guess. "You wanted to marry her, didn't you? And she chose my dad over you. She didn't want you then, did she?"

Riley simply stared at him. "You looked through my belongings?"

"You weren't good enough for her then. You were poor. Grandpa says you were a punk. She wanted my dad instead of you."

Riley bent to pick up the paper where it had fallen and returned it to the drawer, then closed it quietly. "You had no right going through my stuff, T.J."

The boy shifted uncomfortably but tried to bluff it out. "Like it really matters?" he asked sarcastically. "Grandpa says—"

"I don't give a damn what your grandfather says!" Riley shouted, making the boy flinch. Then he drew a deep, calming breath, took a T-shirt from the next drawer down and pulled it on. He put on his shoes, got a jacket, his keys and wallet, then went to the door, opening it, silently waiting for T.J. to leave. His head down, the boy did so, leading the way outside to the truck.

They were off post and practically to the expressway before T.J. spoke. "Maybe I shouldn't have done that."

"Maybe?" This time it was Riley's turn to be cold and angry.

"I suppose you're going to tell Mom and make it look like I did something bad."

Riley didn't reply to that. He didn't say anything at all until they reached T.J.'s house. Sitting there in the driveway, he simply looked at the boy, then said, "I'm disappointed in you. I thought you were a better person than that."

For a moment T.J. looked as if he'd been punched. Then, fumbling with the handle, he jerked the door open. "Do you think I care what you think?" he demanded tearfully. "You don't matter! You aren't important, not to anybody!" He slammed the door, rocking the truck, then raced to the porch and disappeared inside the house.

Liza came out a few seconds later. She paused at the top of the stairs, then crossed the yard and climbed inside. "Hey."

He gave her a bleak smile. "Hey."

"Bad afternoon, huh?"

"You could make it better."

When he offered his hand she accepted it with a smile, letting him pull her across the seat and into his lap. The kiss she expected didn't come right away, so she kissed him, holding his face between her palms, nipping his lower lip, filling his mouth. It felt good to kiss him, she thought, closing her eyes so she could fully enjoy the sensation. It felt like pure pleasure.

Pulling away, she pressed her face to his shoulder. "Mmm, you smell good," she murmured.

"T.J.'s still spending the night with your sister, isn't he?"

The husky sound of his voice whispering above her ear made her shiver. "We can drop him off anytime. Are you staying?"

He pushed her back and gave her a long, dry look. "As if anything could make me leave." Brushing his fingers through her hair, he sighed. "Liza—"

"Mom!" T.J. shouted from the door. "Aunt Gretchen's on the phone!"

Reluctantly she moved away and slid out the door, where she waited until Riley joined her before returning to the house. Picking up the phone, she called to T.J. at the top of the stairs to get in the shower.

What had Riley been about to say? she wondered while she half listened to her sister chat. He had looked serious and sounded so solemn. So earnest.

Goodbye? Was that on his mind? She knew it had to come sometime, knew he wasn't interested in making a commitment to her. He had tried that once before, and look what she'd done in return. He had been deeply hurt, his pride wounded, his love betrayed. That wasn't something he would easily forgive. It was something he would never forget.

Besides, she knew Riley. If he'd wanted permanence with her, he would have told her by now, though maybe not in so many words. He would have talked about their future, would have made plans and shared dreams the way they had before. He would have introduced her to his sister Robbie. He wouldn't have ignored her hints to meet his family. He wouldn't have kept her so separate from the rest of his life.

Once she had asked him why he kept coming around, and he had answered with painful honesty. *Because I can't stay away.* Not because he wanted to see her. Not because he cared about her. But because he couldn't stop himself. Because he'd been drawn, unwillingly, by something stronger, something he couldn't control. But someday he would learn to control it. He would get his fill of her, and he would leave her.

Someday.

Finally she got off the phone with Gretchen. "Do you want to go out or have dinner here?" she asked Riley, who was leaning in the doorway, watching her. "I have spaghetti sauce left over from last night and a casserole in the freezer that won't take long to bake."

"Whatever you want."

Starting toward the kitchen, she gave him an inviting smile over her shoulder. "Whatever I want?" she repeated. "Hmm. I like a man who's easy to please."

Once the door was closed behind them he reached for her, but the clomping of T.J.'s sneakers on the stairs made him back off. With a sigh of regret she removed the casserole from the freezer and set it on the counter just as her son entered the room.

"What's for dinner?" he asked, disappearing briefly inside the refrigerator before coming out with a can of soda.

"Listen, kiddo, Gretchen's invited you to spend the night at her house."

"No, thanks." He smiled innocently. "I'll stay here with you."

Liza folded the foil over the baking dish a little tighter before trying again. "I already told her that we would bring you over as soon as you got out of the shower."

"I don't want to go, Mom."

She looked at him, leaning against the cabinets, then at Riley, who was standing near the window as if he weren't a part of this scene. Tuesday night he had done that, had sat quietly while she and T.J. fussed. He hadn't interfered or spoken a word that was less than patient and polite. He hadn't said much at all. On the one hand she was grateful that he was remaining on the sidelines, that he wasn't trying to force himself into a position of authority in T.J.'s life. Nothing would have alienated her son quicker.

But on the other, she could have used a little help, maybe a little moral support.

"I'm not asking, T.J.," she said quietly. "I'm telling you that you're going to spend tonight at Gretchen's."

The innocent smile disappeared and was replaced by the rebellious, angry-with-the-world look that she was becoming all too familiar with. "Why? So you can spend a little time with *him?* He talked you into this, didn't he?"

"No, he didn't. It was my—"

"Why do you give in to him? Why are you sending me away just so he can come to my house? Why don't you make *him* go away?" He set the soda on the counter so hard that the can fell over when he let go, and a stream of sticky dark cola spread over the counter and dripped onto the floor. "You want to get rid of me for some dumb cop? Fine! Send me to my father. I'll go live with my dad. At least he cares about me. He would never be so mean and hateful. He would never make me put up with someone like that. He would never treat me like I don't matter."

Something inside her, something that had kept her calm and balanced and anchored, snapped. Maybe it was frustration at the uncertainty of her future with Riley. Maybe it was anger at her eleven-year-old son's insistence that she let him run her life. Maybe it was the unfairness of listening to him put down the best man she'd ever known in favor of his father, a weak, spineless man if ever there was one. Whatever the reason, she'd heard enough. *Enough.*

"All right," she agreed, her voice unsteady, her tone dangerous. "I'll call your father tomorrow and make the arrangements."

T.J. simply stared at her, his mouth open, his eyes dark with dismay.

"If you want to live with your father, that's fine with me. He can take care of you for a while. He can treat you the way he treated you when we lived in Dallas. Do you remember that? Do you remember the times you went to spend the weekend with him and he hardly even noticed you were there? Remember that last weekend when he went off and left you alone in that big house for God knows how long? Remember calling me at three in the morning, hungry and scared and begging to come home?"

Finally Riley intervened. "Liza, that's enough."

"No, it's not enough!" she snapped with a glare in his direction. "All I've heard from him for days is my dad, my wonderful, perfect dad. Well, damn it, he's not wonderful, he's not perfect, and he just barely qualifies as a father!" Folding her arms across her chest to hide the trembling of her hands, she faced T.J. again. "Let's talk about your dad. Let's talk about why he and I are divorced, about why I will never live with him again no matter how badly you want it. Then let's talk about his illness. Let me tell you what's wrong with him and see if you still think—''

"Liza!"

In all the time she'd known him, even on the rare occasions when they had argued, Riley had never yelled at her, not once. Now the sharp commanding tone of his voice stopped her midsentence, and in the sudden silence that followed, she heard the echo of her words. *Let me tell you what's wrong with him....*

Oh, God.

She looked at T.J., trembling and on the verge of tears, then at Riley, who was watching her, not with anger, but concern. "Not now, Liza," he said softly. "Not like this." He came toward her, pausing for a moment beside T.J. "Go to your room for a while, will you?"

T.J. hesitated, but when Riley lightly touched his shoulder he nodded and crossed the room. At the door he stopped. "I'm sorry, Mom," he whispered plaintively. "Please don't make me go live with Dad. He's not much fun anymore, and I—I'd really rather stay here with you." Then he left, making his way quietly to his room.

Turning to face the corner, Liza squeezed her eyes shut, then let out a deep, weary, quavering sigh. She felt raw inside, raw and reckless and tender. It hurt right now—thinking, feeling, breathing. Everything hurt.

Then Riley came up behind her, wrapping his arms around her, and suddenly everything was all right. The pain was still there, but she would survive it. With him, she could survive anything.

Without him...

She couldn't think about living without him. Not now.

For a long time Riley simply held her. He didn't say anything. He didn't know what to say. That everything would work out? It would, eventually, but that didn't offer much consolation now. That T.J. would get over his anger and their relationship would be stronger than ever? That was something to look forward to a few months or a few years down the line, but it didn't provide much hope at the moment.

That *he* would be here to help her through the next few months, the next few years, the next fifty years? Yeah. And what if she said thanks, but no, thanks?

And what if she didn't?

Wasn't it time to say something, to tell her how he felt? In all the months they had been together before, he had never told her that he loved her. Maybe it wouldn't have mattered. Maybe she would have married Davis anyway. Maybe it wouldn't have made a damn bit of difference.

But maybe it would have.

And maybe it would now. Who knows? he thought with a humorless smile. Maybe she would just conveniently announce that she loved him, too, and put him out of this misery.

Wasn't it worth a try?

"Liza?" His voice was husky, too husky, but clearing his throat didn't help. Nothing would help but saying what he had to say.

When he didn't speak again right away, she covered his hand with hers and squeezed it gently. "What is it, Riley?"

"Instead of staying here this evening...could we go over to my mom's house?"

The instant the last word was out, he silently cursed himself. How cowardly could he get? He had intended to make a declaration of love, had opened his mouth to say three simple little words, and somehow those other words had come out. Was he really so afraid that he couldn't even say "I love you"? Was he really so insecure?

Maybe not, he thought an instant later. When she turned in his arms, she looked surprised. Happy. Downright delighted. "To your parents' house?" she whispered, her voice filled with wonder. "You want to take me to meet your parents?"

Riley realized then that maybe he *had* said exactly what he'd wanted. Introducing her to his family meant her presence in his life was complete. There would be no area that was off-limits to her. No safe place to run if he lost her.

Gently he brushed a tear from the corner of her eye. "All of them—my mom and dad, my brothers and sisters and in-laws and nieces and nephews. The whole gang."

"Why now?" she asked softly.

She was looking at him solemnly, steadily, understanding in her dark eyes. She knew, he realized. She knew what he was about to say, knew why it was now all right for her to meet his family, and her knowledge gave him courage. "Because I love you."

He had admitted last week on the porch that he had loved her fourteen years ago, but this was the first time he'd ever said those exact words, *I love you,* meaning right now, always and forever. Considering that, they had come pretty easily, he thought with a hint of relief. And he would get plenty of practice in the years to come. Someday they would be as natural as breathing. As natural as living.

As natural as loving Liza.

"I love you, too."

"Is it that easy for you?" he asked curiously, and she smiled her gentlest smile.

"Loving you has always been easy, Riley. It's living without you that's hard." Sliding her arms around his neck, she murmured, "I do love you, Riley."

Her mouth was only a breath away and he took it, kissing her tenderly, possessively, lovingly. After a moment, though, he ended the kiss, took her by the hand and led her to the phone in the hall.

"How are you going to introduce me to your parents?" she asked innocently as he dialed the number.

He paused, his finger poised over the last digit, and gave her a long, steady, measuring look. "As the woman I love," he said at last as he pressed the last button.

Then he drew her close and quietly, confidently amended that. "As the woman I'm going to marry."

Epilogue

Tearing a strip of tape from the dispenser on the table, Liza glanced up at the kitchen clock. It was a few minutes before three. Riley was working midnights and sleeping days this week, and he had asked her to wake him at three. That would give him time to eat a late lunch and open the gift she was wrapping before they had to leave for her parents' house.

Choosing a Father's Day gift for him hadn't been easy. She had wanted something practical; their budget these days didn't stretch to cover many luxuries, and Father's Day was a bigger burden than usual. There had been this gift for Riley, one for her father and one for Riley's father Bobby, a package sent to Dallas for Keith and a present from T.J. to Alexander. She had considered the usual choices for Riley and discarded all of them, when T.J. had finally suggested a cover for the motorcycle. Since they had no garage, the cycle had gotten waterlogged in the heavy spring rains. Practical, and not too expensive. She had been grateful to her son for the idea.

Holding the brightly colored paper in place, she stuck the last piece of tape on, then turned the package over and placed a big yellow bow right in the center. Next she sorted through the cards she'd bought: one for her father, one for Bobby, one for Alexander and, at the bottom of the stack, two for Riley. She had already signed hers; now she slid it into an envelope and folded the flap inside. Opening the second one, she picked up a pen, then glanced at T.J. "Do you want to sign this card for Riley?"

Seated across the table from her with his baby sister asleep in his arms, T.J. shook his head.

Liza was disappointed. She and Riley had been married for eighteen months; the ceremony had been only two weeks after T.J.'s threat to go and live with Keith. The first year hadn't been easy, especially when she'd gotten pregnant only a few months after the wedding. But in spite of his angry promises to the contrary, T.J. adored his baby sister, and lately he seemed to have warmed up to his stepfather. Riley had coached his soccer team this spring, and whenever his work schedule allowed, the two of them were regulars at Augusta's minor-league baseball games. T.J. even joked with him from time to time, and he hadn't thrown a tantrum in months. She had hoped . . .

Sighing softly, she signed five-month-old Alyssa's name to the card and put it in its pale green envelope. Rising from the table, she put away the wrapping paper, tape and scissors, then stopped beside T.J. "She needs a clean diaper," she said, stating the all-too-obvious.

Her son wrinkled his nose. "I was hoping that wasn't what I was smelling."

"Are you implying that anything else in my kitchen could smell so bad?" Liza mussed his hair, then held out her arms. "Give her to me. I've got to go up and wake Riley, anyway."

"That's okay. I'll change her."

She hid her surprise. T.J. was a wonderful brother, and Riley a wonderful father, but being typical males, they both usually managed to be someplace else when it was changing time.

Together they went upstairs to the nursery. Liza stood in the doorway for a moment, watching as T.J. laid the baby on the changing table. Her arms and legs twitched, and she gave a soft sigh, but she didn't wake up as he removed the messy diaper. In spite of his lack of experience with babies, T.J. was good with Alyssa. Although she was sure he wouldn't admit it, Liza knew that he'd learned from Riley. On more than one occasion she had caught him watching his stepfather and later mimicking his actions.

Knowing that Alyssa was in good hands, she went into her own room, closing the door behind her. Her husband was asleep, sprawled in the middle of the bed, as usual. Every night when he wasn't working he went to bed fully intending, he swore, to remain on his side of the bed, and every morning Liza awakened to find that only the strength of his arm around her waist had kept her from sliding off the edge.

She couldn't imagine any better way to sleep.

Slipping her heels off, she lay down beside him, resting her head on her hand, using her other hand to stroke his beard-roughened chin. He looked tired, she thought, and she wished she could let him sleep for a few more hours. But they were due at the Johnson house at four and at the Cooper house at seven, with a stop in between at the Davises'. Besides, it was his first Father's Day. He would never want to sleep through that.

But before she woke him she leaned forward and pressed a gentle kiss to his mouth. "I love you, Riley."

He smiled slowly, his eyes still closed, and turned his head for another kiss. "You're so much better than an alarm clock," he murmured, turning onto his side and drawing her near. "What time is it?"

"Three o'clock." She caught her breath as his hand moved unerringly to her breast, stroking tenderly through her clothing.

"What time do we have to be at your folks?"

"Four."

"Where are Alyssa and T.J.?"

"In her room. He's changing her diaper."

Still without opening his eyes, he kissed her chin, then began searching for the buttons that would open her blouse. In the process his fingers brushed across her diamond pendant, and he smiled drowsily. "You wear this a lot these days."

"For the same reason that I rarely wore it when I was with Keith. It reminds me of you." She guided his fingers to the top button, then sighed softly as he opened her blouse to her waist. His caresses on her breasts felt so exquisitely sweet that she couldn't bring herself to stop him, even though she knew she should. "We don't have time," she whispered.

"If I don't eat lunch . . ."

"But you haven't eaten since last night. You must be hungry."

"I'd rather make love to you."

She was weakening. Riley could see it when he finally opened his eyes. In another moment she would help him remove her clothing, and he would slide so easily inside her. He was ready, already hard and thick and—

"Mom!" T.J. called from the hall. "Alyssa spit up all over both of us."

She sighed regretfully. "Okay, hon."

Riley watched her button her blouse, then brush her fingers through her hair as she rose from the bed. He wasn't disappointed. There would be time for loving this evening, before he had to go to work. There would be plenty of time in the weeks, months and long, long years ahead.

She brought their daughter into the room, holding her away so that her own clothes wouldn't get soiled, and set her on the bed. Alyssa looked as sour as she smelled, Riley thought, leaning over to stroke her down-soft black hair. But when she saw him her dark eyes lit up, and she smiled and softly babbled.

Liza removed the frilly white dress Alyssa had worn to church and wadded it into a tight ball. "She doesn't light up like that for anyone else, not even when I pick her up at the baby-sitter's after work.''

''We're kindred spirits,'' he replied, then added with a grin, ''And I'm the only person she ever sees who has less hair than her.''

His wife gave him a stern look. Teasing about Alyssa's hair, or lack thereof, had started with T.J. the first time he'd ever seen her. ''She takes after Riley,'' the boy had said flatly in his mother's hospital room. ''No hair.'' The fact that he had exaggerated—his sister had hair; it was just thin—didn't make Liza appreciate the joke any more.

''It's growing in,'' he innocently assured her, then slyly added, ''Slowly.''

Liza went to put the dress in the hamper, and Riley picked up his daughter. ''Hey, baby,'' he murmured, settling her on his stomach. ''You're a chubby little thing, aren't you? Of course, you should have seen your mom just before you were born. She was—'' From the corner of his eye he saw Liza standing in the bathroom door, her arms crossed, listening, and he abruptly changed his next words. ''She was beautiful. Absolutely beautiful.''

Giving him a chastening look, she came across the room and took the baby from him. ''Get dressed. You have a gift to open, and we've got three sets of relatives waiting for us.''

When they left him alone he got up and headed for the closet. Because it was a special day, he bypassed his customary jeans and T-shirt and chose instead gray trousers and a white dress shirt. By the time he had shaved and dressed, the others were waiting in the kitchen.

His *family,* he amended, was waiting in the kitchen.

Balancing Alyssa on one knee, he ate his lunch, then opened his gift. He knew immediately that it had been T.J.'s suggestion; the last time they had tinkered with his motorcycle, Riley had mentioned that he needed a cover for it. Nice to know the kid did listen to him. After thanking them, he opened the cards, first Liza's, then the other. They were pretty and sentimental and contained messages of love, both in the printed verses and in Liza's handwritten note.

But neither one contained so much as a mention of T.J.

Why did he expect anything else? he berated himself as he gave first Alyssa, then her mother, a kiss. T.J. already had a father whom he loved very much. He'd never wanted a stepfather, and he had certainly never wanted *him*. It had taken them a long time to rebuild their friendship—a small miracle in itself. He ought to be grateful for that and not want more.

But he did.

He wanted his stepson's love, because he surely did love him.

"We'd better get going," Liza said as she tugged another frilly dress, this one pale pink, over Alyssa's head while the baby sat on Riley's lap.

"Can't she wear a T-shirt and shorts?" T.J. asked. "She looks like an Easter egg in that."

"She does not," Liza disagreed, then looked to Riley for support. "Does she?"

He looked from T.J. to his wife to his chubby little girl, then took the easy way—the safe way—out. "I have the right to remain silent, and I think I'll exercise it."

She took Alyssa from him and gave them a huffy look. "I can't believe the two of you are making fun of this sweet, angelic child on today of all days. We'll just go to Grandma and Grandpa's without them, won't we, sweetie?"

Riley started to stand, but stopped when T.J. pulled an envelope from his back pocket and casually tossed it on the table in front of him. Without a word the boy walked over to the refrigerator, ducking inside to find some snack to tide him over.

Sinking into his chair again, Riley picked up the envelope. It was yellow and had been folded in half to fit into the kid's pocket. His name was scrawled across the front, the ink smearing from the *R* all the way to the *y,* and the back was not only sealed, but taped. He slit it open, then glanced across the room at Liza before removing the card. She looked as surprised as he felt. She hadn't known that T.J.

had gotten him a card, which meant the boy had picked it out and paid for it himself.

The card was funny and made him smile, but his smile faded as he read the note at the bottom. T.J.'s writing was as bad as his own, but he had no problem making out the words that slanted from left to right. "I'm sorry I was such a brat," he'd written, "and I'm glad Mom married you and that we have Alyssa."

In tiny letters across the bottom, as if an afterthought, or something he didn't feel comfortable saying, he had added three little words. Words that Riley himself had once had difficulty saying. Words that pleased him as much now as hearing them from Liza for the first time had.

I love you.

T.J. straightened and closed the refrigerator door as Riley stood. He looked awkward and even a little embarrassed. If he made a big deal out of it, Riley knew the kid would be even more embarrassed, so he simply extended his hand. After a moment, T.J. shook hands with him.

"What the hell," Riley muttered, and he used his grip to pull the boy close, giving him a solid hug. "I love you, too."

Watching them from the door, Liza shifted Alyssa to her other hip, then surreptitiously wiped away a tear. Then, as if nothing unusual, nothing out of the ordinary—nothing *miraculous*—had happened, she said, "Come on, guys. We're going to be late. We've got family to visit."

He had always been greedy, Riley thought as he and T.J. followed her down the hall. He had wanted it all—Liza, love, marriage, a family, forever. He had wanted everything. And now he had it.

Dreams die hard, he had once told Liza.

But sometimes they came true.

* * * * *

For all those readers who've been looking for something a little bit different, a little bit spooky, let Silhouette Books take you on a journey to the dark side of love with

SILHOUETTE Shadows™

If you like your romance mixed with a hint of danger, a taste of something eerie and wild, you'll love Shadows. This new line will send a shiver down your spine and make your heart beat faster. It's full of romance and more—and some of your favorite authors will be featured right from the start. Look for our four launch titles wherever books are sold, because you won't want to miss a single one.

THE LAST CAVALIER—Heather Graham Pozzessere
WHO IS DEBORAH?—Elise Title
STRANGER IN THE MIST—Lee Karr
SWAMP SECRETS—Carla Cassidy

After that, look for two books every month, and prepare to tremble with fear—and passion.

SILHOUETTE SHADOWS, coming your way in March.

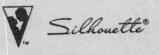

SHAD1

AMERICAN HERO

It seems readers can't get enough of these men—and we don't blame them! When Silhouette Intimate Moments' best authors go all-out to create irresistible men, it's no wonder women everywhere are falling in love. And look what—and who!—we have in store for you early in 1993.

January brings NO RETREAT (IM #469), by Marilyn Pappano. Here's a military man who brings a whole new meaning to macho!

In February, look for IN A STRANGER'S EYES (IM #475), by Doreen Roberts. Who is he—and why does she feel she knows him?

In March, it's FIREBRAND (IM #481), by Paula Detmer Riggs. The flames of passion have never burned this hot before!

And in April, look for COLD, COLD HEART (IM #487), by Ann Williams. It takes a mother in distress and a missing child to thaw this guy, but once he melts...!

AMERICAN HEROES. YOU WON'T WANT TO MISS A SINGLE ONE—ONLY FROM

Silhouette Books
is proud to present
our best authors,
their best books...
and the best in
your reading pleasure!

Throughout 1993, look for exciting books
by these top names in contemporary
romance:

CATHERINE COULTER—
Aftershocks in February

FERN MICHAELS—
Whisper My Name in March

DIANA PALMER—
Heather's Song in March

ELIZABETH LOWELL—
Love Song for a Raven in April

SANDRA BROWN
(previously published under
the pseudonym Erin St. Claire)—
Led Astray in April

LINDA HOWARD—
All That Glitters in May

When it comes to passion,
we wrote the book.

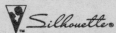

It takes a very special man to win

She's friend, wife, mother—she's you! And beside each Special Woman stands a wonderfully *special* man. It's a celebration of our heroines—and the men who become part of their lives.

Look for these exciting titles from Silhouette Special Edition:

January **BUILDING DREAMS** by Ginna Gray

February **HASTY WEDDING** by Debbie Macomber

March **THE AWAKENING** by Patricia Coughlin

April **FALLING FOR RACHEL** by Nora Roberts

Dont miss THAT SPECIAL WOMAN! each month—from your special authors.

AND

For the most special woman of all—you, our loyal reader—we have a wonderful gift: a beautiful journal to record all of your special moments. See this month's THAT SPECIAL WOMAN! title for details.

TSW1

**Silhouette Intimate Moments
is proud to present
Mary Anne Wilson's
SISTER, SISTER duet—
Two halves of a whole,
two parts of a soul**

In the mirror, Alicia and Alison Sullivan both had brilliant red hair and green eyes—but in personality and life-style, these identical twins were as different as night and day. Alison needed control, order and stability. Alicia, on the other hand, hated constraints, and the idea of settling down bored her.

Despite their differences, they had one thing in common—a need to be loved and cherished by a special man. And to fulfill their goals, these two sisters would do anything for each other—including switching places in a life-threatening situation.

Look for Alison and Jack's adventure in TWO FOR THE ROAD (IM #472, January 1993), and Alicia and Steven's story in TWO AGAINST THE WORLD (IM #489, April 1993)—and *enjoy!*

SISTERR